"Tall? Silver hair? Attitude?"

Jake grinned. "Yes."

"Watch out," Jerry warned. "That's Aurora Jones. She can emasculate you with one look. The woman makes my life miserable."

"You're, uh, involved?"

"God, no! There isn't a man in town who would take her on." He looked around the room, half expecting Aurora would pop out from behind a flower-covered post and badger him about her building permit again. "We have a professional relationship."

"I thought she was nice," his daughter said, glaring at him as if he'd just said Cinderella was a bitch.

"I suppose she can be," he offered. "When she wants to."

Les's grandfather leaned forward. "Did you see the grizzly bear inside the Dahl? Owen MacGregor's grandfather shot that bear and had it mounted for the Dahl. There are some people around here who think a grizzly would be easier to get along with than Aurora Jones."

D0589407

Dear Reader,

Last summer I went to Willing. Really, I did. Although the town of Willing is a fictional place, it's based on many small Montana towns I've visited over the years of road trips between north Idaho and New England. But in planning the Willing to Wed series, I needed a specific location for "my" town. Out came a map of Montana and there, in the center of Montana, was Winifred. I'd never been there, but I knew it was going to be perfect.

So in June my husband and I were as excited to drive to Winifred as we'd been to fly to London years ago. Our visit coincided with the onset of the town's 100th anniversary. Over a thousand people (in a town of 200) were expected to arrive for a weekend reunion and celebration.

Our impromptu stop in the only bar resulted in a warm welcome, town stories, introductions to one and all and an open invitation to return. Frank and John Carr could not have been more hospitable. I am now the proud owner of a Winifred T-shirt and I wear it proudly. Winifred, like Willing, had also faced its demise. But a former resident became the town's benefactor and invested in businesses, the school and projects that would attract new residents. Winifred is a special place. Ask anyone who lives there!

Physically the town was much different from my invented Willing. But the people were just as special and kind and welcoming as those in Meg's café. I can't wait to go back.

I hope you've enjoyed the Willing to Wed miniseries. I'd love to hear from you!

Kristine

KristineRolofson@hotmail.com
www.KristineRolofson.com

HARLEQUIN HEARTWARMING

USA TODAY Bestselling Author

Kristine Rolofson

The Husband Show

❧ Willing to Wed ❧

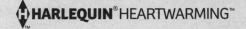

Recycling programs
for this product may
not exist in your area.

ISBN-13: 978-0-373-36671-2

THE HUSBAND SHOW

Copyright © 2014 by Kristine Rolofson

All rights reserved. Except for use in any review, the reproduction or
utilization of this work in whole or in part in any form by any electronic,
mechanical or other means, now known or hereafter invented, including
xerography, photocopying and recording, or in any information storage
or retrieval system, is forbidden without the written permission of the
publisher, Harlequin Enterprises Limited, 225 Duncan Mill Road,
Don Mills, Ontario, Canada M3B 3K9.

This is a work of fiction. Names, characters, places and incidents are
either the product of the author's imagination or are used fictitiously,
and any resemblance to actual persons, living or dead, business
establishments, events or locales is entirely coincidental.

This edition published by arrangement with Harlequin Books S.A.

For questions and comments about the quality of this book,
please contact us at CustomerService@Harlequin.com.

® and TM are trademarks of Harlequin Enterprises Limited or its
corporate affiliates. Trademarks indicated with ® are registered in the
United States Patent and Trademark Office, the Canadian Trade Marks
Office and in other countries.

Printed in U.S.A.

KRISTINE ROLOFSON

USA TODAY bestselling author Kristine Rolofson has written more than forty books for Harlequin. She and her husband of many years call Rhode Island, Idaho and Texas home depending upon the time of year. When not writing, Kristine quilts, bakes peach pies, plays the fiddle and sings in a country blues band. She collects vintage cowboy boots and will not tell you how many are in her closet.

Books by Kristine Rolofson

HARLEQUIN HEARTWARMING

11–THE HUSBAND SCHOOL
24–THE HUSBAND PROJECT

SILHOUETTE TEMPTATION

ONE OF THE FAMILY
STUCK ON YOU
BOUND FOR BLISS
SOMEBODY'S HERO
THE LAST GREAT AFFAIR
ALL THAT GLITTERS
THE PERFECT HUSBAND
I'LL BE SEEING YOU
MAELEIN'S COWBOY
BABY BLUES
PLAIN JANE'S MAN
JESSIE'S LAWMAN
MAKE-BELIEVE HONEYMOON
THE COWBOY
THE TEXAN TAKES A WIFE
THE LAST MAN IN MONTANA
THE ONLY MAN IN WYOMING
THE NEXT MAN IN TEXAS
THE BRIDE RODE WEST
THE WRONG MAN IN WYOMING
THE RIGHT MAN IN MONTANA
BILLY AND THE KID
BLAME IT ON COWBOYS
BLAME IT ON BABIES

A WIFE FOR OWEN CHASE
A BRIDE FOR CALDER BROWN
A MAN FOR MAGGIE MOORE
THE BABY AND THE BACHELOR
A MONTANA CHRISTMAS
THE BEST MAN IN TEXAS
MADE IN TEXAS

With thanks and love to Ellie, Connie,
Ann and Neil, of the Hope Mountain Blues band.

CHAPTER ONE

AURORA VANDERGREN JONESTON Linden-March, otherwise known as Aurora Jones, picked up her buttercup-yellow Western boots—special ordered from a boot maker in Austin and worth every dollar—and carefully placed them inside an oversize shopping bag, along with her purse and the small box that contained a wedding gift. She'd wear her water-resistant, mud-proof UGGs until she arrived at the ranch, and then the yellow clipped-toe, stacked-heel beauties would make their debut in the recently cleaned and decorated barn.

She was late. She hated being late. Especially today, when everyone—everyone—was gathering at the famous Triple M for the wedding of the year.

The wedding of the decade, actually.

Who knew when the last wedding had taken place in Willing, Montana, home to too many bachelors and too few eligible women?

Before my time, Aurora decided, grabbing her car keys off the polished wooden counter of her bar. Way *before my time*.

Willing was not known for weddings, but if the mayor had his way, that was going to change. Aurora and her bar, the historic Dahl, would be thriving in the center of the Romance Capital of Montana before summer began. And Aurora was going to be ready for the influx of tourists.

She shrugged on an ivory down vest and had one freshly manicured hand on the door, ready to push it open and step out onto the sidewalk, when the door was pulled open from the outside. Aurora caught herself from falling forward into the weak Montana sunshine.

"Excuse me," came a deep male voice.

"We're closed," she said, looking past a denim-covered chest as a truck honked on the street. She waved absently, assuming it was the annoying mayor honking his perpetual enthusiasm toward one and all. She'd deal with him unofficially this afternoon and officially tomorrow morning. She could hardly wait.

"But—"

"Closed," she repeated, her keys in her hand. "For the holiday."

"What holiday?"

That's when Aurora looked at him. Really looked at him. He was tall, late thirties, with dark brown hair that appeared a little too long and a face that should advertise male grooming products in upscale magazines. Hazel eyes, sexy stubble and a casual how-can-you-resist-me smile completed the picture. He was taller than Aurora, who was easily five foot ten, but by just a few inches. A child stood next to him, a young girl with white-gold hair who was bundled into a blue hoodie and jeans. The child stomped her sneakered feet as if she was freezing to death.

"A wedding, but I'm running late and don't have time to—"

"A holiday for a wedding?" He seemed baffled, but his eyes twinkled as if he knew he was being charming. "Must be some wedding if the whole town is celebrating. Or are weddings that rare around here?"

"As rare as my being on time," she grumbled, wondering how to get past him. She started forward, assuming he'd move back. Which he did, reluctantly. "It's the first unofficial *Willing to Wed* wedding," she said, knowing how ridiculous she sounded. "It's not one of the official ones."

"The what?"

"Jake," the child begged. "Please?"

"Look," the man said to Aurora. "I have an emergency—"

"It's not an emergency," the girl said, hopping up and down. "I just need to use the loo. This is so embarrassing."

"Could my daughter—" He gestured toward the child and smiled again, but this time Aurora saw that the smile didn't quite touch his eyes. He was in a bind and Aurora guessed it was an unfamiliar one. And the girl called her father by his first name?

Aurora frowned as she studied the man. She ignored the sexy stubble, the square jaw and the wrinkled denim shirt. Who the heck was he and why was he here in town, today of all days, when the whole place was practically deserted? She wondered if she should be afraid.

"If this is some kind of trick and you're actually intending to rob me, you should know that the cash went to the bank last night." She gave him a look guaranteed to intimidate. She'd practiced that look in front of the mirror for years and was very proud of it.

"Jake" held his hands up, palms out. "No weapons, see? I'll wait outside," he said. "If you have a sawed-off shotgun behind the bar, feel free to wave it around. I promise to be terrified."

"Well—" Aurora stepped back into the bar and flicked on the light switch. She felt sorry for the child, who, unless she was an excellent actress, certainly seemed distressed. But if this was a robbery attempt, the man was in for a fight. She had a can of Mace attached to her car keys and the sheriff's number on speed dial. Just to be on the safe side, she pulled her cell phone out of her purse and made sure it was on.

"Go to the end of the room, down the hall— over there to the left—and two doors down on the right."

"Thank you." The child scurried toward the back.

"I appreciate this," the man called through the open door from outside. "There was a café on the main road, but it was closed. So was the gas station."

"I told you," she said, moving closer to the doorway. "It's a town holiday. And it's Sunday. Things are very quiet around here on Sundays."

"Right. The wedding."

She saw him take in her dress with its floaty skirt and violet flowers. The look was ruined with the down vest and thick suede boots, but a woman living in Montana needed to be practical.

"And you're late."

"Yes."

"How late? Will you miss it?"

She looked at the clock hanging over the center of the bar above the mirror. "No. Not if I drive fast. And they'll never start on time."

"I suppose you know everyone in town."

"Pretty much."

"What about Sam Hove? He moved here a few months ago."

"Why?"

"Uh, I think he was writing a book. I'm not really sure."

"No, I meant why are you looking for him?" She liked Sam. Everyone did. He and Lucia were together now, planning to get married sometime this summer. The former adventurer and documentary filmmaker had fallen in love with the nicest woman Aurora knew, and no one deserved happiness more than the widow and her three little boys.

"I'm done," the girl called, hurrying back to the door. "Thank you."

"You're welcome." Aurora couldn't help smiling. The child was very serious and composed. With her round cheeks and light coloring, she looked nothing like her father. Aurora couldn't put her finger on it, but she knew something wasn't quite right. The two didn't seem to mesh like a father and daughter. The child wore expensive clothing, but the father certainly didn't. She stopped the girl before she reached the door and leaned down.

"Are you safe?" she whispered.

"Safe?" The girl's blue eyes widened.

"Yes," Aurora said, feeling foolish but unwilling to let the girl leave with someone who didn't seem to be her father. It was none of her business, of course, but still…. "You know, do you need help?"

"You mean, am I being *abducted*? Really?"

"Call me crazy," Aurora replied. "But I have to make sure you're not in some kind of trouble. I can call the sheriff and keep you safe."

"It's fine." She rolled her eyes. "Jake's my father but I just met him last week. He's okay."

"Oh."

The girl surprised her with a quick hug.

"Thank you. It was really nice of you to be so considerate."

"You're welcome." Aurora grabbed her shopping bag and followed the girl outside, but she wavered between feeling foolish and feeling protective. She just met her father last week?

"Yes," the man—Jake—said, obviously hearing his new daughter's words. "Thank you for your help."

Aurora pulled the door shut and locked the dead bolt. "Well. Have a good day."

He hesitated. "So, everyone in town is at this wedding?"

She took a deep breath of spring air. It was warmer than she'd thought it would be. And the sun was out, thank goodness. "I would think so."

"Including Sam?"

"What do you want with Sam?"

"He's my brother. I'm Jake. Jake Hove." He looked at her as if he thought she would recognize the name.

"I didn't know Sam had a brother."

Something flashed in his eyes. "We're not close. But we're working on it."

Aurora wanted to go to the ranch. She wanted to get into her great big SUV and head out to the Triple M, where she would help celebrate. She did not want to stand out in the wind and discuss bizarre family issues with a total stranger.

"Well," she said, moving away. "Good for you."

"Where is this wedding?"

She stopped, turned around. "That's private information."

"Not exactly." He pointed to a poster in her front window. Sure enough, he'd noticed the "Meg and Owen" wedding announcement, Meg's solution to inviting the town without accidentally leaving anyone out. "I gather this is the special event. Where is the Triple M?"

"Ninety miles from here."

"I guess that's why my brother isn't home. He's gone to an unofficial *Willing to Wed* wedding."

"Yes." Aurora ignored the charming smile he gifted her with. "Does he know you're in town?"

"When you see him, tell him I'm here, would you?"

"Sure." But she didn't know whether to believe he was related to Sam. This man was too handsome, too sure of himself, too accus-

tomed to having his way. Not at all like Sam
Hove, who tended to slip quietly into crowds
and not attract attention. Both men were dark-
haired and tall. And there could be a resemblance around the nose and mouth. Maybe. She
didn't want to stare.

And she was late, she thought, hurrying to
her car. Late, when she should have been early,
except that Bill sent an email with the updated
designs attached and she'd had to send changes
back to him, because it all had to be perfect for
tomorrow's meeting.

"Thanks again for your help," he called after
her.

She opened the driver's door, tossed her bag
inside and scooted behind the wheel. The wedding and barn-dance reception was the social
event of the season, and she didn't intend to
miss a minute. She'd ordered very good champagne, she'd helped decorate the barn yesterday
and today she was going to party.

After all, she hadn't been to a wedding since
her own. But she wasn't going to think about
that. She was going to think happy thoughts.

She'd chosen a dress covered with violets
for the occasion because the bride had gently
hinted that she hoped her two friends would

wear either violet or yellow, if that wasn't too much trouble. Meg was the least fussy bride that ever walked down the aisle. After sixteen years apart from her first love, the rancher Owen MacGregor, Meg had found true love once again with Owen when, last October, he'd finally returned to the town his ancestors founded. It hadn't taken him long to decide to stay.

Meg was the kind of woman who didn't care for shopping and didn't like a lot of fuss made over her, something that amused her friends. Lucia was the queen of thrift stores and Aurora was no stranger to online shopping and discreet shopping trips to New York.

"Of course, we'll wear whatever you want us to," Lucia had promised, knowing full well that she and Aurora would use every resource to find the perfect outfits.

"We'll match the cupcakes," she'd said, giving Aurora a wink. Lucia was Meg's best friend, their having met in culinary school, and was the town's baker. She was baking the wedding cake, plus crate loads of cupcakes so that no one in town would miss out on the wedding dessert. Aurora couldn't imagine how the woman managed it. Baking was a mystery, and

Aurora was on the outside looking in when it came to that particular skill.

In fact, most of her domestic skills were non-existent.

Despite a knack for shopping, Aurora had never dressed to match bakery products before, but in the past four years she'd done a lot of things she'd never done before. She bought a bar, she ran a business, she quilted—quilted, how odd was that!—and she had girlfriends.

Girlfriends. Imagine.

Wait until they heard that someone who claimed to be Sam's brother was in town.

"Hurry," Jake said.

"Why?"

"We're going to a wedding."

"We can't go to a wedding without being invited," his prim daughter declared.

"We're not actually going to *attend* the wedding," he said, hustling her back to the truck. "We're going to meet your uncle Sam. Unless you can think of what else we can do in a town that's closed."

"We could go back to Lewistown. Or Billings. We could go to the movies."

Three logical suggestions, and he didn't even

consider them. He wanted to see Sam. Needed to see Sam. He was so close, and after all these years he didn't want to wait until tomorrow.

"We could wait until tomorrow," his daughter continued. "When we could arrive at a more opportune time."

"A more opportune time? Someone should monitor your time spent watching *Masterpiece Theatre*."

"That would be you, I guess."

"Got that right."

"There's nothing wrong with *Downton Abbey*. Are you not aware how popular it is? The whole world—"

"She's heading north. Keep your eye on the car."

"You're going to scare her if you follow her. She might even call the police."

He sighed. The woman was stunningly beautiful. He'd almost fallen off the sidewalk when he'd opened the door of the bar and she was right there. She had the oval face and flawless skin of a model; those cool blue eyes had assessed him with the aloof attitude that beautiful women often have.

He had not impressed her, and she didn't care if he knew it. "I don't think she scares easily."

"She asked me if I was being kidnapped." Winter made a big show out of making sure her seat belt was fastened correctly.

"The woman has a big imagination."

Winter turned that serious blue-eyed gaze upon him, a look he'd grown used to in the four and a half days since he'd become her father. "She said she'd keep me safe and call the police. No, the sheriff."

"That was nice of her," Jake said, impressed that a stranger would go to the trouble. She would have rescued a little girl and risked missing that important wedding she was in such a hurry to get to.

"I liked her hair. Maybe I should grow mine long."

"You could." Ah, yes. The hair. Silver-blond and fashionably long and straight. Dangly earrings that appeared to be flowers, the same flowers on her dress. A body that stood out, despite being covered by a puffy vest. Even the ugly suede boots did nothing to detract from the woman's beauty.

"She looked like a movie star. Like someone famous."

"Maybe she is." He'd seen that long, silver-blond hair before, he thought. Onstage where he'd performed? No, he couldn't picture her singing country. Or rockabilly.

His serious child thought for a moment. "What would she be doing here? Would some-one famous own a bar?"

"Probably not," he conceded. "Someone fa-mous might own a bar, I guess, but not work there. She looked like she worked there."

"I guess." Then she paused. "I want to go home."

"Yes," he said, keeping his eye on the red Subaru SUV flying along the road. "You've said that before."

"I don't want to be on a road trip."

"I know."

"I don't know you."

"Which is the point of the trip." He thought about the virtue of patience, and how he'd never known he'd had any until two weeks ago, when he got the phone call from Merry's lawyers. Another short week came and went and then he'd gassed up the truck and ushered his new daughter into the front seat.

"I want to go home," she repeated, this time louder.

"Which is a problem," he pointed out, hop-ing he sounded paternal and calm.

"You don't have to rub it in," she muttered. "I know I'm a problem."

"I didn't mean it like that." Jake despaired of getting this fatherhood thing figured out. "I meant the fact that you want to go home is a prob—an issue—something to figure out."

"I'm sorry." She fiddled with the zipper on her jacket. When she was stressed she couldn't keep her hands still. He wondered if she'd ever picked up a guitar.

"You don't have anything to be sorry about." He was sorry for her. Winter. And why had Merry named the child after a season?

As for Merry Lee, ambitious and beautiful, it was hard to empathize with the woman who had kept his child's existence from him for eleven and a half years.

Merry's first album had gone platinum, as had the second. She'd married someone in Europe, had a child, was rich, he'd heard. But Jake hadn't paid much attention. They'd had a three-month affair when he filled in for her guitar player on a summer tour, ended up married in Vegas and then they'd gone their separate ways. Merry wasn't so merry and had a mean temper when she wasn't in front of an audience. The quick divorce had been a relief, and the brief marriage to Merry Lee was something in the distant past.

Until now.

Winter was now digging through the console. "What about the GPS?"

"Try it," Jake said, grateful for the change of subject. "Maybe the Triple M Ranch is on there."

"Like an address?" She reached into the console between the seats and retrieved the GPS.

"Yeah. If not, look it up." He gestured toward his cell phone, a state-of-the-art iPhone he'd bought for the trip. "Try texting Sam again. Maybe he'll answer and give us directions."

"I don't think it's right to crash a wedding," Winter huffed, typing into the device. "We could be escorted from the premises."

"Excuse me, Miss Manners," he said, making her smile just a little bit. "If you can find a store between here and this ranch, we'll buy a gift and make the whole thing legitimate."

They both eyed the expanse of open land ahead of them.

"Fat chance," she muttered, frowning at the screen. "There's nothing between here and the Triple M. It's a historic ranch and was founded by a man from Scotland named Angus Mac-

Gregor. There's even a picture." She held the phone up so he could see.

"MacGregor," Jake repeated. "That's the name of the groom, so we're heading to the right place. Are there directions?"

Winter looked stricken. "We can't go there. We really could get in trouble."

"We won't get in trouble," Jake promised his overly serious child. "We'll owe them a gift, which we will buy tomorrow. You can pick it out. We won't stay for the food or the dancing. We'll find Sam, get the key to his house and get off the road. We'll ask the butler to give him a message." He grinned. "What do you say?"

"Not funny. I'll text him again. Getting off the road would be okay," Winter agreed, setting the GPS device into its dashboard cradle. "But we're not going into the reception."

"Unless the bride requests a song," he added, and then wished he'd kept his mouth shut. He'd learned, over the past six days, that she didn't care much for teasing. She didn't think he was all that funny, and she had little use for music. He suspected she was tone-deaf, which was odd considering that her parents were musicians.

His daughter rolled her eyes. "Oh, *please*."

"Hey," he protested, "she might be a fan."

"You are so not going to sing."

Trying to make her laugh, Jake broke out in a bluesy, off-key version of a seven-year-old hit song.

She ignored him, something she was good at. She didn't care to answer too many questions. In fact, in the week he'd known her, she'd said little about her mother, even less about her childhood. Apparently her mother's cousin had acted as nanny early on, but she'd married and had her own children. Winter had spent the past six years in boarding schools and summer camps.

Except for this year.

This year she had a father.

For better or for worse.

And whether she wanted one or not.

AURORA DIDN'T CARE if Jake Hove—if that's who he really was—followed her out to the Triple M. The male guests at the wedding—and there would be a lot of them, considering that the town's population was overwhelmingly male—were more than capable of taking care of a stranger who might want to cause trouble.

If he turned out to be Sam's problem, then

Sam could deal with him. If he was really Sam's brother—and Aurora had had time in the car to ponder the resemblance between the two men, deciding they did share certain physical characteristics—then Lucia would no doubt explain the situation to Meg and Aurora the next time they met for coffee or lunch or a glass of wine.

Planning this wedding had given Aurora what Lucia called "girlfriend time." Now that she'd experienced it, Aurora intended to continue the practice. Between girlfriend time and quilting lessons, she was slowly filling the lonely hours with friendships instead of compulsively scrubbing woodwork in the bar.

In the past four years since moving to Willing, she'd discovered it was easy to cry and scrub at the same time. Aurora thumbed her iPod and listened to Joshua Bell's new release.

Three young men flagged her down after she'd navigated the long road to the main house, a large white building that looked as if it were a ranch house on a movie set.

Les, the youngest member of the town council and a sweet young man, stepped over to her car.

"Hey, Aurora."

"Hey, Les."

"We'll park it for you," he said. "The yard's still a little muddy, so Owen has asked everyone to walk on the gravel and go straight to the barn. Unless you're going to the house…? You can go on the grass to the front, because it's not so bad. Ms. Loralee and Shelly are in there with Meg."

"All right. Thank you." She stepped out, ignored the appreciative looks from the young men and retrieved her bag and her purse, then trudged across the grassy yard to the front steps of the wide covered porch. She stepped out of her muddy boots and left them off to the side before opening the heavy door and walking inside.

One of Lucia's little boys greeted her. "Hi, Miss 'Rora. You look nice."

"Thank you, Matty."

"The baby won't stop crying," he said, peeling paper from a frosted cupcake. All dark hair and dark eyes and wearing a white button-down shirt and black pants, six-year-old Matty was adorably rumpled. Aurora suspected the shirt wouldn't be clean for very much longer.

Sure enough, a baby wailed from another room. "Uh-oh. Is that Laura?"

"Yep." He carefully licked the frosting violet from the top of the dessert. "Grandma says she needs a nap. My mom made a lot of these."

"How many have you eaten?" She suspected this wasn't his first. She also suspected his mother didn't know he'd been sampling the dessert.

"Today?"

She nodded.

He frowned in concentration, trying to remember accurately. "Four."

"Wow." Aurora had little experience with children and absolutely none with young boys. Lucia's three children often seemed like strange, energetic creatures who made a lot of noise and couldn't sit still.

"I ate seven last night," he confided. "Without frosting. For supper."

"Aurora!" The cupcake eater's mother came rushing into the hall. "We were getting worried about you."

"I was delayed. Sorry. I had a—"

"Matty! I thought I told you no more cupcakes." She plucked the half-eaten cake from her son's sticky fingers. "Go to the barn. Now. Tell Sam you're all supposed to stay with him now."

"Okay."

"And *stay* in the barn this time," she said.

"Where's Mama?" Mama Marie was Lucia's mother-in-law and a devoted grandmother. Well known in town for her Italian cooking and generous nature, she was known to everyone as "Mama Marie" or simply "Mama." Aurora was a little afraid of her. She often had the impression that Mama Marie looked at her and disapproved of what she saw.

"She's keeping Loralee from driving Meg insane."

"Is the mother of the bride giving the bride more advice?"

"She keeps fussing over Meg's hair, wants her to put on more mascara. You know the drill."

"Right." Loralee was not known for subtlety. Flamboyant, softhearted and outspoken, she was best experienced in small doses. "What can I do, besides guard the dessert and distract Loralee?"

"We're going to get everyone out of the house and into their seats in the barn. I imagine the groom is getting edgy."

"The groom has been edgy for weeks." Aurora wondered if Owen thought Meg would change her mind again, the way she had done when she was eighteen and refused to run away with him for the second time. According to Meg, the first elopement hadn't gone according to plan.

"And please tell Meg she looks beautiful. She's stressing over her hair."

"I'll bet she's gorgeous," Aurora said, following Lucia up the wide mahogany staircase to the second floor.

"She is," Lucia said. "Even if she doesn't think so."

"Does Sam have a brother?"

Lucia stopped at the top of the stairs. "Yes. Why?"

"I think he's in town."

"In town? This town?"

"You weren't expecting him?"

"He and Sam have talked a couple of times, but Sam didn't say anything about him coming here. They've wanted to reconnect, though. It's been a long time since they've seen each other." She seemed puzzled. "I thought we were going to fly to Nashville this summer, after the—"

"I told him you were here," Aurora said. "He wanted to know why everything in town was closed, so I explained about the wedding."

Her friend looked thoughtful. "I'll tell Sam to call him right away. I made him turn his phone off this morning so we could get out here early. Otherwise it's insane. The phone never stops ringing with business calls."

"Is he planning another trip to, um, the jungle?"

"He's always planning another business trip, another documentary," Lucia said. "And then there's the book project. But we have a wedding and a honeymoon in Belize first. At least that's what Sam says now."

"I think he's more than ready for the wedding," Aurora said. "When is it going to be?"

"Soon. But we'll do something small," she confided. "Something this summer, after school is out. By the way, I love your boots."

"Thank you."

"Vintage?"

"No."

"They're so original I thought maybe—"

"Aurora! Thank goodness." The bride, who looked stunning in a simple ivory scoop-necked lace dress that skimmed her slender body and stopped below her knees, fairly flew out of her room to where they stood at the top of the stairs. She'd refused to consider a tradi-

tional wedding gown and had instead ordered
her dress from Nordstrom, online.

A bold move, Aurora had thought at the time.
But typical Meg and totally beautiful.

"What do you need?" she asked the bride.

"What time is it?" Meg smiled, but she
looked a little harried. "Time seems to be moving very slowly this morning."

Lucia checked her watch. "You have five,
maybe ten, minutes. Guess what. Aurora found
a man this morning."

Meg seemed impressed. "What kind of
man?"

"Sam's brother, or so he says," Aurora answered, following Meg back into the bedroom,
Lucia trailing behind them. "They do look
alike. A little."

"What did you do with him?" Meg went over
to the window, as if by looking outside she
would spot him. The large, freshly painted pale
blue room faced the back of the house, with
three tall windows facing the barns and the
hills beyond. Lace curtains hung to the polished wood floors and an enormous bed, its
mattress covered in an exquisite blue and white
Irish chain quilt, took up most of the space.

"I left him in town, but I wouldn't be surprised if he followed me here. He knew that Sam was at the wedding."

"Wow. What does he look like?"

Aurora frowned. "Handsome, of course. Like his brother. And he's very confident."

"Confident," Lucia repeated, frowning a little. "What does that mean? He's obnoxious?"

"No," Aurora said quickly, not wanting to insult Lucia's future brother-in-law. "He seems very self-assured, as if there isn't anything that bothers him." She threw up her hands. "I don't know how to explain it. It's as if any kind of trouble would slide right off the man." She sat on the bed and ran her hand along the delicate stitching.

"Sam's calm like that, too."

"Maybe it runs in the family," Meg suggested.

Lucia joined her at the window. "It could. They had a pretty rough childhood and haven't seen each other in years. Sam's going to be thrilled he's here."

"He's here, all right," Aurora said. "His daughter is—"

"Daughter?"

"You didn't know he had a daughter?"

Lucia shook her head slowly. "I didn't even know he was married."

"Not exactly a prerequisite," Meg pointed out. She smoothed the front of her dress nervously.

"No, but Sam didn't say anything about Jake having a daughter. How old is she?"

"Eleven, twelve, maybe? It's hard to tell with kids these days." Aurora had absolutely no experience with children, unless she counted the rare times she was with Lucia's boys. And they were special, sweet children who had excellent manners. She secretly adored the littlest one. There was something about those big dark eyes that got her every time.

"Eleven," Lucia mused. "I can't wait to meet her. We could use a girl in the family."

"Chances are he's in the barn talking to Sam right now." She wouldn't be surprised at all to discover he'd made himself one of the wedding guests.

"Well, let's get this wedding going so we can check the guy out," Meg said.

"You're not supposed to be thinking about men other than Owen," Aurora informed her. "You're supposed to be gazing at yourself in the mirror and worrying about your hair. Which is beautiful. As is the rest of you."

"I've done that and I agree—

I look pretty good."

"More like radiant and gorgeous and very happy," Aurora assured her. "You're the prettiest bride in Montana."

Lucia leaned over and adjusted the seed pearl headpiece that held an elegant lace veil intended to fall down Meg's back. "I like this. It's not too fussy, but it's very bridal."

"The boots are a nice touch," Aurora said.

"I splurged," Meg confessed, looking down at the white pointed-toe Western boots that peeked out from under the hem of her dress. "My mother was beside herself with joy."

Lucia finished fussing with the veil. "When you're marrying a Montana rancher on his ranch, in a barn, you'd better be wearing the appropriate footwear."

Aurora noticed Lucia's own deep purple boots, along with her long-sleeved, formfitting brilliant yellow dress. She was a petite woman, with black hair that could only come from her Lakota Sioux grandmother. Intricately beaded purple-and-yellow earrings hung almost to her shoulders. She had great taste, an eye for color and, as a widow and single mother of three, needed to live frugally.

Aurora hoped that the "frugal" part would change once she married Sam, but she doubted her friend would quit going to secondhand stores. She liked the thrill of the hunt too much to stop.

Aurora wondered what Lucia would think of her new future brother-in-law.

There was a mystery here, but if anyone could get to the bottom of it, Lucia would. And Aurora couldn't wait to find out.

"WILL YOU TAKE this woman to be your lawfully wedded bride?"

"I will," Owen MacGregor declared amid impromptu male cheers. There was shushing and sniffling and a baby cried.

Aurora didn't know whether to laugh or burst into tears. Since she never cried in front of people and wasn't much for bursts of laughter, she sat quietly next to Loralee and hid a smile. Leave it to the rough-and-tumble men of Willing to cheer during a wedding ceremony.

She opened her little yellow purse and pulled out a tissue, which she handed to Loralee, the weeping mother of the bride. She, Loralee,

Shelly, Lucia, Sam and the children were seated in the front row as Meg and Owen exchanged simple and moving vows.

"And will you, Margaret Ripley, take Owen MacGregor to be your lawfully wedded husband?"

"After all this, she'd better say yes," Loralee muttered.

"I will," Meg said, prompting another burst of cheering from the congregation gathered in the historic and enormous barn. Aurora wondered how Owen had cleaned the place so quickly. He didn't own cattle or horses yet, but she assumed that as he revived the once thriving cattle ranch, he'd use the barn for practical purposes.

Or rent it out as a wedding venue.

The rings were exchanged as the crowd watched in respectful silence. Aurora had heard that Owen's mother was too ill to attend the ceremony, but Meg had confided that the woman had never approved of Meg and her relationship with her son. And that some things in life never changed.

So Loralee, the only family member, continued to sob quietly into Aurora's tissue. Tony, Lucia's youngest, climbed over his mother, stirring up a little cloud of hay dust, and settled himself against Aurora to examine the charms on her gold bracelet. Aurora held her arm still so he could peruse them to his heart's content.

Someone from the church sang while Meg and Owen held hands and smiled at each other.

Yes, Aurora decided, all cleaned up like this, it was the perfect place for a wedding. Her own bar, the Dahl, was overdue for a makeover, too. But something more extensive than the good scrubbing Owen had given this barn. She'd been working on reno plans for months, not telling anyone what she intended. It was to be a surprise for the women in town.

We'll have a patio, she mused. *And a lovely room for bridal showers and bachelorette parties.* The bathrooms, which she'd upgraded when she bought the place, would be enlarged and brightened. She wouldn't do anything to change the log walls, of course, because the original building had an ambiance that was impossible to replicate, but she would definitely replace the stinky old wood paneling.

"I now pronounce you husband and wife," the minister announced. "You may now kiss the bride."

The crowd roared its approval. Loralee

pumped a fist in the air. Tony climbed from his seat beside her on the hay onto Aurora's lap and surprised her with a wet kiss on her neck.

Life in Willing was about to improve in all kinds of ways.

CHAPTER TWO

As THE GATHERED guests began to stand and mingle and the bride and groom signed official papers, the mayor of Willing, Jerry Thompson, sat trapped on a bale of hay between the town's teenaged unwed mother and the infamous mother of the bride, a woman married so many times she'd lost count. As a young man deeply committed to improving the small town, Jerry was accustomed to being in situations where the utmost tact was called for. He was the master of small talk, of mingling, of schmoozing.

Unfortunately he was not comfortable sitting next to a woman who was feeding her baby in a very, um, natural way. There was a blanket, there was no skin showing, but still…

Awkward.

"Oh, for heaven's sake, there's another one." Loralee, mother of the bride and self-appointed grandmother to Shelly's baby, wore a slinky purple dress and pale pink boots with purple embroidery on the shafts. She was sixty-two and, as she'd told Jerry earlier, not ready to wear a polyester housedress and serviceable shoes.

"Another what?" Shelly shifted her lump of baby against her chest. Little Laura didn't make a peep.

"Another man hoping to meet women from California. Some of these men think that single women by the busloads are running rampant on Main Street."

"So?" Jerry entered the conversation against his better judgment. Like eating half a chocolate cream pie, he would regret he'd done it. He didn't bother to notice who Loralee was staring at, having decided to look straight ahead and avoid any risk of seeing the breast-feeding process.

"The word's out."

"That was the whole idea to begin with," Jerry muttered. "Attract people? Make the town viable again? The word being out is a good thing, remember? Besides, he's probably a friend of Owen's from Washington. There were quite a few coming, weren't there?"

"Not with a child. I pretty much memorized

the guest list, having gone over it so many times with Meg."

"He's very handsome, too," Shelly murmured. "He seems a little familiar. Are you sure we don't know him?"

Jerry finally turned to look. An unfamiliar tall man stood inside the barn door and looked around as if he was hoping to see someone he knew. A young girl with gold short hair stood close to him. The stranger leaned over and said something to her and she shook her head.

"I've never seen him before. Maybe he's another reporter," Jerry said. "I'll go find out."

"Don't give him an interview. This is a private party." Loralee sniffed. "Publicity is okay, but not at my daughter's wedding."

Jerry paid no attention to Loralee's complaint. He lived for publicity. He'd engineered the town's involvement in the reality dating show and he'd welcomed the Hollywood crew to Willing. His girlfriend produced the show, which had resulted in at least one of the town's bachelors finding the woman of his dreams, and the show was due to be aired the last Monday of April. He'd had many calls from many reporters, but he hadn't talked to anyone who'd intended to come to Willing six weeks early.

He hadn't talked to anyone who was interested in the MacGregor wedding, either, because it had nothing to do with the upcoming show.

"I'll check him out." Jerry lifted himself from the bale of hay and brushed off his pants. The barn, decorated in a real Western flavor, could be used for many wedding receptions in the years to come. They'd filmed one of the big moments of the show here this winter, and since then Owen had kept it empty. It was a huge space, undivided by stalls or stanchions or whatever barns had inside them. It would have held a lot of hay, if that's what it was originally used for.

The wooden floor was faded and worn, but it had charm and character. The huge beams sparkled with ropes of tiny white lights.

"One whole day," Les said, pointing to the beams as Jerry paused beside him. "That's how long it took us to string those lights. We strung some for the show, but Meg wanted more. A lot more."

"It looks good."

The young man glanced toward Shelly, who was now holding her baby upright and patting its little back. "It's a good place for weddings."

Jerry agreed. "Owen and Meg could do a nice business here, with the barn and the catering and the whole rustic Montana historic ranch thing going on."

"It holds more people than the community center, or the café," Les added.

"If it looks good on the show, they've got it made. You can't buy that kind of publicity."

"No, sir, you can't." Les's attention moved back to Shelly. "I'd sure like to get married. This wedding is pretty big, though. And it sure must cost a lot. It would take me a real long time to save up for a wedding."

"Your money's best spent elsewhere," Jerry agreed. The young man's love for the once homeless teenager was sweet, but Shelly had issues. She was only nineteen, had a baby with a rodeo charmer who'd turned out to be married and lived with Loralee in one of Meg's cabins. She worked as a waitress and lived off tips, plus the extra money she made cleaning houses.

She wasn't Jerry's idea of the perfect love interest, but to each his own.

"I'm saving up for a house," Les said. "I'm thinking about building something small, out at my grandparents'."

"It's good to have a plan." Jerry pointed out the man near the doorway. "Do you know who that is?"

"Nope."

"Well, I'm going to go find out. Loralee doesn't want any wedding crashers."

"I saw that movie. She's right. Owen wouldn't like that." Les narrowed his eyes. "Whoa! The guy's talking to my grandfather."

Sure enough, Lawrence Parcell appeared to be helping the stranger out, pointing to the tables where the food was being set up. "He could be one of Owen's city friends, but Loralee doesn't think so."

"Why would a wedding crasher bring a kid?"

"Good point." Jerry edged away. "Let's go see."

He didn't really think the guy was trouble, but it was as good an excuse as any to move through the crowd, shake some hands, spread goodwill and accept congratulations for the success of the filming of the TV show.

Jerry wanted to bask in the glory of the first of many Willing weddings. In fact, he'd offered to give a toast before dinner. To the first of many Willing weddings, he'd say, lifting a glass of champagne. To the first of many blissful couples, to happy brides and brave grooms and to populating the Willing school with more students. To new businesses. To tourists. To increased tax revenues.

No, he couldn't go that far. But it was tempting.

He'd been advised by Owen to keep it personal. No campaign speeches, the groom had ordered. Keep it simple.

Jerry wasn't fond of simple. He was up for reelection in a year and a half.

He eased past his constituents, a boisterous group who talked to one another as if they hadn't been out of their homes in months. Well, winter could do that, make you feel as if you lived in a cave with a television set and a phone and a freezer full of fish, beef and maybe some venison. Thankfully he lived in the middle of town and could get out whenever he wanted. He could walk to the café, to the Dahl, to the community center for the various meetings and social activities.

Tracy had wanted him to come to California for the winter, but he couldn't get away for more than a week at a time. And once a month, if he was lucky. He played bingo with the seniors on Saturday nights, competed in the Dahl's Trivial Pursuit contest, organized the annual film festival—a collection of local residents' home movies—and managed every detail of his town's involvement with the television show.

Tracy thought he was insane.

"Really? Charles Russell?" the stranger was saying.

"They've got a museum in Great Falls," Mr. Parcell said. "You can see where he painted. Pretty impressive, if you like art."

"I like art," the man replied. "Maybe my daughter—"

"Ever heard of Charles Russell, young lady?"

The child nodded. "I studied artists of the American West last year. Charles Russell was known as one of the greatest and produced over four thousand works."

"Well, now," Les's grandfather drawled. "I'm impressed with your education. Where'd you go to school?"

"I used to attend Lady Bishop Pettigrew's," the little blonde girl replied. "But I was recently expelled."

"Why?" Jerry interrupted, stepping into the small group. He couldn't help himself. This angelic-looking child didn't seem at all like a troublemaker. But maybe Lady Pettigrew's had a stricter code of conduct than the schools in Montana.

"I have severe psychological issues."

"Don't we all?" Jerry said into the following silence. He held a hand out to what looked like the girl's stunned father. "Jerry Thompson, mayor," he said. "Since we haven't met, I assume you're a friend of the groom?"

"Not exactly," the other man said, flashing a quick smile. "I'm Jake Hove, and this is my daughter, Winter."

"It's a pleasure to meet both of you." Jerry shook hands with them. The man seemed friendly enough, though he kept scanning the crowd as if he was looking for someone. Winter didn't seem severely disturbed. Jerry thought she seemed like a nice enough kid. She didn't have any obvious piercings or tattoos. She was expensively dressed, in designer jeans and a hoodie. Growing up in Los Angeles had taught him to recognize high-end clothing. "Did you say Hove? Any relation to—"

"Sam," Jake said. "My brother. We're not attending the reception," he added quickly, glancing at the girl. "We're in town and I wanted to see—"

"We waited outside during the wedding," Winter broke in. "We didn't wish to be rude."

"The bride and groom wouldn't have cared or even noticed," Mr. Parcell said. "The whole town was invited. Of course, they know everyone in town, so it was only right."

Winter nodded. "We saw the poster at the bar."

"We weren't *in* the bar," Jake quickly assured them.

"I was," Winter said. "I needed to make use of the facilities."

The old man frowned. "What?"

"She talks like that sometimes," Jake told him.

Jerry wondered if severe psychological issues manifested as speaking with a British accent. Maybe the child had different personalities, like Sybil in that movie he'd seen when he was a kid. Jerry shuddered.

Jake scanned the crowd. "Is Sam here?"

"He'll be up at the main house with Lucia getting the food ready," Jerry said. "She and Marie Swallow are organizing the potluck in the tent."

"I'll check there. Thanks."

"It's the big white Victorian," Jerry added.

"You passed it when you walked in, and of course, you'll have seen the reception tent. It's almost as big as the barn."

"Thanks." Jake put his hand on Winter's shoulder. "We'll head over there."

"How long are you going to be in town?"

"I'm not sure. We're on our way home. To Nashville."

"That's quite a drive," Jerry said, glancing toward the child again. "I hope you'll enjoy your stay in Willing. We have a lot of things going on in town right now, with the television show about to air."

"Television show?" Now that caught the girl's interest.

Jerry nodded. "Oh, yeah. We're about to become famous. Your uncle can tell you all about it. He was at most of the filming."

"But I thought he makes documentaries," Winter said. "In South America." She turned to her father. "You didn't tell me he filmed a show *here*."

"I didn't know," her father said. "We didn't talk very long and—"

"Oh, this wasn't one of Sam's fishing films. This had nothing to do with him. Ours was a reality show," Jerry explained. "We took twenty-four of our most eligible men here in town and created a dating show."

"Willing to Wed?" Jake grinned.

"Yes! You've heard of it?" The money spent on publicity was paying off already.

"A woman at your local bar told us about it."

"Tall? Silver hair? Attitude?"

Jake grinned. "Yes."

"Watch out," he warned. "That's Aurora Jones. She can emasculate you with one look. The woman makes my life miserable."

"You're, uh, involved?"

"No! There isn't a man in town who would take her on." He looked around the room, half expecting Aurora would pop out from behind a flower-covered post and badger him about her building permit again. "We have a professional relationship."

"I thought she was nice." Winter glared at him as if he'd just said Cinderella was an evil witch who stepped on mice and punched princes.

"I suppose she can be," he offered. "When she wants to."

Les's grandfather leaned forward. "Did you see the grizzly bear inside the Dahl?"

Winter nodded. "It was a grizzly bear?"

The old man nodded. "Owen MacGregor's grandfather shot that bear and had it mounted for the Dahl. There are some people around here who think a grizzly would be easier to get along with than Aurora Jones."

"I beg your pardon," Winter said. "But I must disagree."

"So does my wife," the old man declared. "She says she's clever with a needle."

"What does that mean, 'clever with a needle'?"

"Quilting," he explained. "The women around here spend hours cutting up fabric and sewing it back together."

"I think we'll go find my brother now," Jake said, urging the child toward the door.

"Watch out. Aurora's probably gone back to the kitchen with the rest of them."

"The kitchen?" Mike Peterson, standing nearby, chuckled. "I hope she didn't cook anything."

"She didn't," Les assured him. "She donated the champagne instead."

"Well, good," Jerry muttered. "We won't need the Red Cross tomorrow."

ALL HE'D WANTED to do was find his brother. That's all. He had Sam's phone number. He had his address. Who would have thought an entire town would be closed for business on an April Sunday afternoon?

Now he was at a stranger's wedding, on a ranch, in the middle of nowhere. He'd met the mayor and some of the locals and seen for himself the historic MacGregor Ranch. But he wanted to see Sam. Ten years was a long time. Ten years was pretty stupid.

"*Brigadoon,* that's what this is," his daughter said, following him out of the barn and into the sunshine. "Have you ever seen that movie?"

"No." He started along a gravel path toward the main house, easily sixty yards away. A large addition jutted out from the back of the house, where a door was propped open.

"That's where we are," she said, hurrying to keep up. "In a land that time forgot."

"You're mixing up your movies. I saw *The Land That Time Forgot.*" Women kept disappearing into that opened door, which meant that's where the food was.

"No, *Brigadoon* is when two people end up in a town where it's two or three hundred years—well, a long time—ago, only it's not. It's modern day, but they're not, you know, *modern.*" She looked back at the barn. "Do you think they'll square-dance?"

He shrugged. "I don't know what you're talking about."

"You've never heard of square dancing?"

"I've heard of square dancing," he said, taking a deep breath as they approached the open door. Two laughing older women carrying casseroles stepped out. Jake said a silent prayer for patience. He was nervous, he realized. And that realization sent another stab of nerves into his belly. Guilt, fear and excitement warred for space in his chest. Jake didn't often feel nervous, and he sure as heck didn't like the feeling.

His life had changed beyond recognition recently, and he wasn't sure he liked it all that much.

His guilt flared up again. He should have known Merry was up to something when she'd insisted on an annulment, a quick one. She was off to Europe, she wouldn't meet with him and she hired a lawyer to handle the situation so Jake wouldn't have to bother.

He'd been on tour, having gotten a job playing rhythm guitar in a band opening for Faith and Tim. His big break. He'd felt nothing for Merry but relief when she was gone.

"Tomorrow," his suddenly talkative daughter continued, "this place could be enveloped in a mysterious mist and we'll all disappear. Maybe we should escape while we can."

Jake thought he might prefer to talk about *Downton Abbey*. "Do you really think Lady Mary will marry again?"

Winter giggled. That was a first. Jake stopped walking in order to see it for himself. The child looked younger when she smiled. "You look so funny," she said. "And you don't know who Lady Mary is!"

"Oh, yes, I do," he grumbled, just to keep her smiling. "You talked about her all the way from Seattle to Spokane. She's the oldest sister and she was supposed to inherit Downton Abbey but— What?"

Winter pointed to the door. "There she is!"

"Who?"

"The lady from the bar. See?"

Oh, he saw, all right. She would be hard to miss, Jake thought. Once again he realized that she was easily one of the most beautiful women he'd ever seen, with the kind of beauty that should be on magazine covers, except she wasn't a bone-thin model. The dress hugged her curvaceous body in all the right places, yet floated around her legs to give her room to dance. In his experience playing in about five thousand bars, the women wearing floaty skirts always intended to dance.

The yellow boots were sexy as all get out, too.

And then there was the hair, platinum waves that fell well past her shoulders. She'd pinned back the sides, exposing a face that would be considered angelic, except that Mayor Jerry had warned him that she was anything but.

And he'd experienced her brusque manner himself, though she'd been kind to Winter and protective of her friends' privacy.

An interesting woman.

Not his type.

The interesting woman who was not his type saw Winter and smiled, then looked at Jake. Her smile collapsed as they approached.

"You found it," she said, not sounding the least bit happy to see them.

"We did. I was told Sam might be over here." He gestured toward the door.

"He's inside." She hesitated. "Be careful."

"Of what?"

"People carrying food. We're setting up dinner in the tent. The bride and groom are having their pictures taken in front of the house and by the barn. When they're done, we'll eat."

"I won't keep Sam long," Jake promised.

"Meg said you're welcome to stay and enjoy the party." She turned to Winter. "And you, too, of course. Lucia and Sam are really looking forward to meeting you."

"I've never had an uncle before," Winter confided.

"You'll have three cousins after he gets married," Aurora pointed out.

"He's getting married?" This was news to Jake. All Sam had said over the phone was *I've met someone.* Someone special.

She stared at him. "He didn't tell you?"

"I didn't know it was official," he bluffed.

"Hmm."

"Well," he said, attempting to move past her and go into the kitchen. "We have a lot of catching up to do. If you'll excuse me…."

"Three cousins," Winter repeated. "How old? Boys or girls?"

"Boys," Aurora replied. "Younger than you."

"Oh." She didn't bother to hide her disappointment.

"They're not all that bad," Aurora assured

her. "And you'll like your future aunt. Come on, then. I'll help you find them."

With that, they were ushered inside a large room set up like a dining hall. One part of the room held worn tables and benches, while the other was a large old-fashioned kitchen.

"I told you," Winter muttered. "It's like a hundred years ago."

"How would you know?" He was curious; after all, she'd spent her life in Europe and he wouldn't expect her to know a lot of American history.

"I've seen Westerns," she told her father. "This is where the cowboys eat."

"You're right," Aurora said. "This is the summer kitchen."

The summer kitchen was filled with very busy women organizing platters of food. But in the middle of all the activity was a tall, dark-haired man who hurried through the crowd toward him.

Sam.

Jake swallowed the sudden lump in his throat. His little brother looked good. They shook hands and stood there for a moment, not sure what to do. Then they embraced. It could have been awkward, but it wasn't. It was reassuring. Sam seemed glad to see him.

"What's it been," Jake's younger brother asked, "ten years?"

"Something like that," he replied. "I was performing in that show in Miami."

"And I was coming back from Brazil."

They grinned at each other.

"Ten years?" A petite black-haired woman hurried up to Sam's side and smiled as she tucked her arm through his. "Shame on both of you!"

"I'd like you to meet my fiancée," Sam announced. "Lucia Swallow."

She released Sam and gave Jake a hug. "I'm so glad you're here."

"I am, too," he replied, and put his hand on Winter's shoulder. "My daughter, Winter. Winter, meet your uncle Sam and…Ms. Swallow."

"Aunt Lucia," Lucia corrected, giving Winter a hug. "I've never had a niece before."

Sam shook Winter's hand and grinned. "And now I'm an uncle. I didn't know that until a little while ago. I'm really glad to meet you."

"Thank you. I'm a bit of a surprise," she informed them. "Jake didn't know about me, either."

Sam looked at Jake, with an expression that said *we have a lot to catch up on.* Jake nodded. He saw Lucia glance at Aurora, who had watched the family reunion with undisguised curiosity.

"You need to meet my sons," Lucia said to Winter. "They're with my mother. They'll be so excited to know they have a cousin."

"Stepcousin," Winter corrected her, the familiar serious expression on her face. "I'm only a *step*cousin."

"That's good enough," Aurora said, joining the conversation. "You're still part of the family, aren't you?"

Winter considered that. "I suppose that's true."

"You're very fortunate," Aurora continued. "I don't even have stepcousins."

"You don't?"

The silver-haired woman shrugged. "Not a one. No uncles, aunts or anyone else."

"Like me," Winter said.

Aurora shook her head. "No, you're in much better shape."

Jake thought the whole conversation was strange, but his daughter gave Aurora a quick smile.

"Come with me," Sam said. "We're going to track down the kids for Aunt Lucia and introduce you."

"I hear you're getting married?" Jake said casually.

"Yeah." Sam glanced at Lucia and smiled as they left the two women standing there. "She's made me settle down."

"That's hard to believe."

"It was time," his brother declared, but he looked happy about it.

Jake wasn't sure if settling down was anything to celebrate, but he kept his thoughts to himself.

CHAPTER THREE

"Wow."

"Yes," Aurora said, watching the two men guide the child around the women organizing food onto platters. "Wow."

"He's famous, you know," Lucia said. "He was in some big country-western band years ago. Sam said they toured with Faith Hill and Tim McGraw."

Aurora wasn't impressed, but she tried to look as if she was. She knew little of country music and much preferred classical. All that wailing about trucks and beer didn't do anything for her.

"And now," Lucia continued, "he turns up here with a daughter."

"I thought something was strange about it," Aurora confessed. "I even asked Winter if she was all right. I thought she might have been kidnapped or something."

Lucia turned to look at her, eyes wide. "How

do you think of these things? I guess you do have a dark side we don't know about."

"I do." She sighed.

"But it was good of you to check," her friend said. "Just in case."

"I sensed something was a bit off," she explained. "And I was right. She doesn't know him, and now he's her father? I feel bad for the kid."

"What kid?" Owen put an arm around each woman. He was gorgeous in a black suit, a white shirt and a gold and ebony tie. "Who do you feel bad for?"

"Hi, Ranch King," Lucia said. "Where's your wife?"

"Hunting down Loralee for some pictures," he replied. "What kid do you feel sorry for?"

"You're not going to believe this," Lucia said, "but Sam's brother—"

"I heard he's in town." Owen released them to take a wheat cracker from the tray in front of them. "Does that mean we're about to be inundated with groupies and wild musicians?"

Aurora shuddered. "I hope not."

"A concert would be fun," Lucia mused. "To celebrate the TV show."

Aurora gazed at her in horror. "You're obviously spending too much time with Jerry. It's exactly what he'd think to do."

Owen chuckled. "Think of the beer you'd sell."

She laughed. "True." Business was business, but there was something about Jake Hove that made Aurora want to run in the opposite direction. He was too good-looking, too sure of himself, too…charming. It was a facade—she was sure of it. And the daughter? The poor child seemed overwhelmed.

"Why *do* you feel sorry for the little girl?" Owen helped himself to a piece of cheese. "What's going on?"

"I don't know," Lucia said. "We don't know anything about it. What are you doing? We'll be serving in a few minutes. Go out to the tent. There are appetizers there."

"I will in a minute. I'm starving. We had to do pictures. I'm supposed to find Mrs. Hancock and drag her out of the kitchen for one last photo."

The elderly woman had taken charge of the food immediately after the wedding ceremony. "She should be around here somewhere," Aurora said. "Did you hire her for this?"

He laughed. "She worked for my family

years ago. In fact, she was here, in this room, when I met my bride. Meg was working for her that summer."

"That's very romantic," Aurora acknowledged, "but I just arranged those crackers in nice neat rows and if you touch them again I'll have no choice but to become violent."

His hand stopped three inches from the platter and returned to his side.

"Where's her mother?"

Lucia shrugged. "I don't know. I imagine Jake will tell Sam all about it as soon as he can." She frowned as Owen hurried off to complete his assignment. Aurora assumed he'd spotted Mrs. Hancock directing the troops. "Where am I going to put them?"

"In Sam's house?" As of two months ago, the couple had been engaged and living next door to each other. Sam had bought the neighbor's house after mean old Mrs. Beckett was unfortunately discovered dead by Lucia's oldest son.

"Uh-uh. The place is a disaster. Sam's cleaning out forty years of mess—he's rented one of those Dumpster things—and he's made a bedroom out of the living room, but it's not okay for company."

"Maybe Jake could stay with Sam, in the living room, and Winter could stay with you."

"We could do that, but I'll bet that's the last thing she'd want to do, share a room with one of the boys. No," Lucia said, frowning. "I'll see if Iris has room at her place. It's better they stay at a nice B-and-B than have to deal with the chaos at home. Sam's already taken part of a wall down."

"You're still going to put an addition between the houses?"

"Yep." Lucia grinned. "We're going to completely renovate Mrs. Beckett's house and turn half of the downstairs into a professional kitchen. It will be twice as big as I have now."

"We'll both be remodeling at the same time," Aurora said, pleased with herself for having arranged the sliced cheddar cheese sticks into an attractive fan. "I'm glad winter's over."

"Me, too." Lucia smiled at Aurora. "Though it certainly was an exciting one."

"Who knew Willing would become such a romantic place?"

"I'd be careful if I were you." Lucia laughed. "You could be next. There's romance everywhere."

"I'll manage to resist."

"Are you sure about that?"

"Absolutely positive."

"I believe you," Lucia said. "But—" Her gaze drifted past Aurora's shoulder. "You *did* see Sam's brother, right?"

"I did."

"And he is spectacular."

"Agreed." The man was certainly a sight to behold. "If you like the type."

"What is your type, Aurora?"

"I once fell in love with a skinny Frenchman," she informed her. "But I was thirteen. He played the viola."

"And what happened?"

"He dumped me for Renee DuBois, who played the flute."

"And you're permanently scarred, poor baby." Lucia handed the finished tray to a waiting teenager. Half of the high school students in town had been hired to run food and dishes from the tent to the house to the barn and back.

"I'm not like you," Aurora said. "All warm and kind and fluffy and loving."

"Fluffy?"

"Cuddly," Aurora corrected. "Men look at you and think of apple pie and cinnamon rolls and cozy nights by the fire. You're a truly nice person and, well, I'm not."

"Who says?"

Aurora sighed. "Most everyone in town. And I'm not cuddly."

"No, you're not. Which is why I like you so much."

She couldn't help laughing at that. "Well, at least someone around here does."

WINTER PRETENDED SHE was in a movie. It was the only way to deal with the weird *thing* she found herself in. Seriously, it was just like a movie. John Wayne himself would fit right in.

Not that anyone knew who John Wayne was, except for Robbie Middlestone. She and Robbie were the only two members of the Lady Pettigrew Film Society to share a love of American Western films. She would try to text him later, if there was any chance of cell reception, to tell him she'd gone to a party on a real Montana ranch.

She walked between her uncle and her father as they made their way to the other side of the crowded room without finding her so-called cousins.

"They've probably gone to the tent," Uncle Sam said.

So off the three of them went to the tent, with Uncle Sam catching Lucia's eye and pointing to the door as they left. The black-haired woman nodded and handed a large pan to a tall teenaged boy. Winter liked her and wondered if she was part Native American. Imagine having a Native American in her "family."

Winter was hustled back outside into the cool afternoon air. Music, something old-fashioned and country-sounding, blasted from the barn. No one was really dressed up, but everyone seemed pleased to be at the ranch.

She heard parts of conversations as they walked past clumps of people.

"—maybe that Cora gal and Pete will be next."

"He bought that old John Deere off Lawrence Parcell, all right. Said it had a lot more years in it."

"She told him she'd give him one last chance and then? Over. So, it's over, as of last Friday. Her mother is *furious!*"

"Gonna clean it up and drive it in the parade. What about you?"

"Monday nights, I heard. Ask Jerry."

"They won't even consider that legislation until fall. I told him—"

"Who's that with Sam?"

Winter knew the answer, even if she didn't know the woman who asked the question. *That's his brother, who he hasn't seen in years. And that's his daughter, who he didn't know existed.* In a place like this, the information would spread quickly.

She'd heard small towns were like that. Gossipy.

Well, they could gossip all they liked. Winter lifted her chin and stared back at two older girls who eyed her curiously. She gave them her best haughty Lady Mary of Downton look, but they didn't seem impressed.

Winter hurried to keep up with Jake. For all she knew, he could forget about her and disappear into the crowd, leaving her to fend for herself.

Not that she couldn't do exactly that, but she wasn't in the mood to find out how to survive by herself in the Wild Wild West.

Not yet, anyway.

The inside of the tent was decorated with little white lights, long tables and benches. The tables were covered with yellow-checked fabric and glass jars filled with white-and-yellow daisies. About a third of the tables held food in casserole dishes or plastic bowls. There was food everywhere, with more coming in all the time. Three young cowboys were busy opening champagne bottles in the corner closest to the door. Giggling girls filled champagne flutes and set them carefully on large silver trays.

Winter sucked in her breath. It was truly lovely and not at all what she had expected. She'd pictured more hay bales and a bunch of picnic tables.

She couldn't wait to meet the bride and groom now that she no longer thought she and Jake would be kicked out. Being with an uncle made everything okay.

"Hey!" Sam waved to a herd of black-haired boys who were gathered near an old lady. She was round and sharp-eyed, though. Winter assumed she was a grandmother, because she'd met a few of those and they weren't easily fooled. Robbie's grandmother had called his mother a twit and his father a rotter, much to Robbie's joy.

"Money doesn't buy class," she'd cluck. Robbie's grandmother had not been impressed with his parents or with his parents' piles of money, obviously, no matter how much there was of it.

Winter stayed close to Jake as they crossed to the other side of the tent. He was the only person she'd known longer than fifteen minutes.

"Marie," Sam said, grinning. "I'd like you to meet my brother, Jake, and his daughter, Winter. Jake and Winter, please meet my future mother-in-law, Marie Swallow."

To Winter's surprise, she was enveloped in a hug. As was Jake.

"Welcome to the family," the woman said. "And here are the boys." She pointed to each one from tallest to shortest. "Davey, Matty and Tony. My grandsons."

Winter eyed them. The tallest stared back. He didn't look much older than eight or nine. The middle one had cake frosting in his hair. The little one leaned sleepily against his grandmother's side. They were all dark-haired and dark-eyed. Despite wearing dark pants and white shirts, they looked as if they'd get into trouble given a little freedom.

Not exactly an impressive group of cousins. But then again, she reminded herself, she had no experience and had no expectations. For all she knew, everyone had disappointing cousins.

And they didn't seem too thrilled with her, either, except for the tallest boy, who appeared somewhat fascinated. As if he'd seen a space alien.

Jake shook hands with all three boys, which seemed to impress them. She wondered where their father was, then decided it didn't matter. Everyone was divorced; sometimes their parents stuck around and sometimes they didn't. Robbie's parents were still married, but he'd said there were dreadful rows and his father had a girlfriend in Chelsea.

"So," Mrs. Swallow said. "Are you a fisherman, too?"

"No." Jake chuckled. "I'm a musician."

"Ah," she said. "Another Hove who can't stay in one place."

"Up until now, no," Jake answered, still chuckling a little. "I travel a lot, though. I guess it does run in the family."

"Well, I'm glad you're here," she said. "Family's important."

"Yes, ma'am," Jake said. "And I'm glad to meet yours."

Mrs. Swallow looked pleased.

"Your Uncle Jake has come to visit," Uncle

Sam told the boys. "We'll have to show him around."

"We could ride horses," the middle boy suggested. "Owen has 'em."

"Not now, he doesn't," his older brother said. "They're not back yet."

"Where did they go?" She hadn't intended to speak, but Winter couldn't help herself. She'd always wanted to ride a horse, but every time she'd suggested a summer riding camp her mother had shuddered and muttered, "Broken bones, no way."

And that had been the end of that.

"To Les's ranch," the boy explained. "They usually live there, but when they come back here we can go riding."

Well, hallelujah. Something to look forward to. Winter glanced up at Jake to see if he was going to object, but instead he cupped her shoulder and said how that sounded like fun and he'd have to meet Owen and talk to him about it.

"Let's go find Owen, then," Uncle Sam said. "Want me to take the boys?"

Mrs. Swallow shook her head. "Not right now. The food's coming and we'll be eating as soon as the bride and groom say the word. I'll save room for you here at our table. Tell Lucia everything is ready out here."

Still stunned about the possibility of riding horses, Winter let herself be led away from the Swallow family and back toward the opened flap door of the tent. She didn't know how long they'd been here, but they'd done a lot of wandering around the place.

Teenagers carrying large containers of food blocked their way out. It all smelled really good. Better even than the make-it-yourself waffles at the Super 8 this morning.

Jake put his arm around her shoulder and guided her past the staff and into the fresh air. The picnic tables were beginning to fill up now, as wedding guests gathered around plates of appetizers and big vats of lemonade and iced tea. A group of little girls chased each other across the lawn while larger boys, Winter's age, huddled together and looked self-conscious. *Was* the whole town here?

"The whole town is here," her uncle explained, unknowingly answering her question. "You're going to meet a lot of people."

"Will they square-dance?"

Sam shot her a curious look. "Why? Do you?"

"No, but I've heard about it. And we *are* out West."

"I hate to disappoint you," he said, "but I don't think there's going to be square dancing today. Maybe a two-step. There might be a few callers in Billings, but I've never heard of square dancing here in Willing."

"Callers?"

"The people who call out the directions for square dancing. Callers. It's a lost art, or so I've heard."

"Oh." She would have to Google that.

"My daughter has spent her life in France and London," Jake explained. "This is all new to her."

"Well, it was all new to me, too, last December. I'd never been to Montana before, either." Her uncle smiled. "I hope you'll stay awhile so we can get to know one another."

"Well," Winter said, "that would be interesting, considering that you must have very exotic stories about the jungle. And it's not like I have anywhere else to go."

"No place else to go?" Her uncle didn't hide his surprise. He gave Jake a weird look. "Are you homeless or something?"

"We're heading back to Nashville from Seattle," Jake said gently. "I have a place there."

Sam didn't look happy to hear that. "Are you in a hurry?"

"No," Jake said. "But—"

"Good," Sam said. Jake had told her he was a zoologist and made movies about catching fish, but today he looked more like her biology teacher at school. "I've never had a niece before. And I haven't had a brother in a long, long time. We need to catch up."

Winter could have summed it up for him: *divorce, unknown daughter, dead ex-wife.*

Maybe her so-called father should write a song about *that.*

"He bought thirty picnic tables for the wedding," Meg said, walking with Aurora to the tent. They'd received strict orders from Lucia to head there immediately. "Who does that?"

"That's a lot of picnic tables." Aurora thought it made the ranch yard look festive. The whole wedding should have been photographed for a magazine spread, she decided. Jerry had missed the boat on that one. Friends and neighbors clustered at the tables, stood in groups, walked in and out of the barn, gathered around the entrance to the huge white tent. She guessed four hundred people had showed up for this wedding, though they were scattered between the tent, the picnic tables, the yard and the barn. And as she'd told Sam's brother, it was a much-deserved holiday for the town.

"Owen insisted they'd come in handy."

Aurora couldn't help being curious. "Come in handy for what? I can see that you'd need them now, with this many people, but unless you're turning the Triple M into a county park, what are you going to do with them?"

"We may decide to use the ranch as a wedding venue. We've talked about it," the bride said. "We've talked about it a lot, but I want to keep our privacy, too, you know?"

"Really?" It was a beautiful place, and where better to get married than a historic ranch with its own party barn? "You could cater, Lucia could do the wedding cakes, I could provide the bar. Les could park cars and your mother—what would Loralee do?"

"Babysit," Meg pronounced. "Because I intend to have at least three children."

"Good for you." Aurora gave her an approving look. "You'll be a great mother."

"We don't want to wait too long," she said.

"We want to have lots of little MacGregors running around the ranch."

Aurora laughed. "That's going to keep Loralee busy."

That was ambitious, but Aurora admired a person who knew what she wanted. "You're spending your wedding night here or in Billings?"

"Here. This is home."

"Owen knows about all of these future babies?"

"It was his idea." Meg laughed. And blushed.

"Maybe my new addition will be finished for the baby shower," Aurora mused. "If the weather's nice we can open up the new patio."

"I want to see those plans," Meg said. "I can't wait to see what you've decided."

"After the honeymoon," Aurora promised.

Meg shuddered. "You and Lucia are really brave. I'm not sure I could take that kind of mess around me. Just the cleaning and painting in this house has been more than enough work."

They reached the tent, where Loralee waved anxiously. "Come on," she called. "We're ready for the toast!"

Aurora followed Meg inside, then hurried

over to the young men in charge of opening the champagne. Meg and Owen had wisely decided that would be the only alcohol at the party, considering that it was a family-oriented event and that most people had to drive ninety miles back to town.

"We'll do it outdoors," Owen said, coming up to give Meg a kiss and a glass of champagne. "And then everyone can help themselves to food."

Lucia met them just outside the tent. "We're ready!"

Aurora stood to the side and watched the happy couple accept congratulations from the crowd.

"Here," Jerry said, stepping next to her. He handed her a percussion triangle and a beater. "Hit this, will you? It's to call in the cowboys."

"You must be joking." She dangled the large triangle from its chain.

"No. Hit it as hard as you want. Take out all of your anger and aggression," he said, looking out at the groups of people walking toward them across the lawn. "No doubt it will be good for you."

"I'll pretend it's your head," she said sweetly.

JAKE ENDED UP sitting inside the tent at a table with his brother, Sam's fiancée, her three children, Mrs. Swallow, Winter and the gorgeous Aurora Jones.

An odd assortment of wedding guests, he mused. But he liked looking across the table at the three little boys sitting next to his brother. Oddly enough, Aurora sat to his left and Winter to his right. Lucia sat next to Winter and engaged her in a discussion about school in France. It seemed that Lucia had attended a baking school in Paris one summer and spoke some French. Winter chattered away as if she'd known the woman forever.

Jake hoped his daughter wouldn't bring up the severe psychological issues revelation again.

Sam happily surveyed the mound of assorted food on his plate. "This town sure has its share of good cooks."

"You like it here, then."

"You will, too," his brother assured him. "How long can you stay?"

"I haven't decided. We're taking our time, getting to know each other."

"And her mother?"

"Died."

Sam stopped chewing and stared at him. As did Aurora. Jake looked over to make sure that his daughter was engrossed in her conversation with Lucia. He lowered his voice. "I only found out two weeks ago. It took a while to get the paperwork squared away so she could come here. There was a stepfather, but he wasn't involved in her life."

"And you didn't know anything about her?" This question came from his brother.

"No," he admitted. "I had no clue. It was a short marriage, and she left me to go back home to France. I figure she wanted out of the marriage and if I had known about the baby, things would have become very complicated." And Merry didn't do complicated. She had been a free spirit, a beauty whose smile gave her everything she wanted. And when she didn't want Jake any more, she left.

Sam put down his fork and studied his brother. "But you have her now. And that's a good thing."

"For me," Jake said. "But I don't think Winter thinks she got a very good deal."

"Then you'll have to prove yourself," Aurora

said. "You'll have to prove you're good enough to be her father."

"I don't have to prove anything," he all but snapped. "I'm already her father."

"Biologically," the irritating woman said. "But that doesn't mean anything."

"It does to me," Jake retorted, turning toward her.

She blinked. "I'm sorry. I shouldn't have said anything."

"Hey," Sam interjected. "You're both right. This isn't going to be easy, but you're Winter's father now. You're all she has."

"And I'm scared to death." He didn't care if the woman next to him heard it.

"You'll do good," Sam assured him. "I'm still learning how this parent business works, but it's a pretty good deal."

Aurora faced Winter. "Do you think you'd like to stay here for a little while and visit with your new family?"

Winter considered the question carefully while Jake listened for the answer. He had no idea what she would say. "Well, I'd like to stay and learn to ride Mr. MacGregor's horses, but my mother died and now Jake is stuck with me and we're going to Nashville."

"I am not stuck—"

"You are," she interrupted. "But it's not your fault." She looked up at her uncle. "Have you ever been to Nashville?"

"I have not," he replied. "But we'll certainly visit you there."

"You will?"

He smiled. "Of course. All of us. Maybe we'll get to hear your dad sing somewhere."

Jake laughed. "Are you forgetting how my guitar made you crazy when you were a kid?"

"It was pretty bad at first," Sam admitted. "But you got better at it."

"I'd like to stay here, but just for a little while," Winter told Aurora. "I'm in no hurry to go to a new school."

"That's right," Aurora said in realization. "You should be in school."

"I'll need to take a placement test for seventh grade, but there shouldn't be any problem. I excelled in everything at Lady Pettigrew's."

"Really? Everything?"

"Well," she said, looking down at the fried chicken on her plate. "Except deportment."

"Now, that runs in the family," Jake muttered, glancing toward Sam.

"DID YOU BRING your shotgun?" Jake thought that was about as good an opening line he'd ever used, but Aurora Jones looked less than impressed.

"Please," she drawled. "Don't bother flirting."

He wasn't even thinking of flirting, not really. He couldn't help looking at her, though. And wanting to tease her until she relented a bit and smiled at him. "You're a beautiful woman. Why isn't flirting allowed? Are you married? Engaged? In a relationship with the local sheriff? What?"

"You can forget the charm," she said, waving her hand as if to wave him away. "It's wasted on me. I'm immune."

"All right," was the only reply he could manage. "I'm flattered that you think I'm, uh, charming, but that's not—"

"And the whole country-singer thing? Forget it. I'm not the groupie type."

"I didn't think you—"

"Don't," she said.

"Don't what?"

"You're doing it again. That smile."

Jake sighed. "You are a lot of work, you know that?"

She had the gall to look affronted. "What exactly is that supposed to mean?"

"Never mind. I just wanted to thank you again for helping Winter this morning.

She looked doubtful, so he continued.

"She told me you thought she was in some kind of trouble, that you'd offered to call the police and protect her from me. I appreciate that."

She almost smiled. "It could have caused you a lot of trouble.'

"It could have caused you to miss the wedding."

They both went silent for a long moment.

"Your daughter has been through a lot, am I right?"

"Yes."

"Is any of it your fault?"

He thought about that. "Technically, no. I didn't know anything about her," he said. "But I keep thinking I should have."

"Maybe," she said. "But you're with her now, so don't screw it up."

"All right."

"I meant what I said, about proving yourself.

Being a father. You won't know if you did a good job for a long, long time."

"Do you have children?"

He caught a flash of pain in those blue eyes. "No," she said. "But I was eleven once."

"And you remember how hard it was?"

"It wasn't hard at all. I was a pampered and adored only child, but I was a natural worrier. Just like your daughter."

"She's had a lot to worry about," he said with a sigh. "Would you like to dance?"

"No."

"Aw, come on." He gestured toward his daughter, laughing as she learned to two-step with her uncle Sam. "I promised Winter I'd meet her on the dance floor."

He held out his hand and she hesitated before taking it. "You're going to scandalize the entire town," she said. "Dancing with Aurora Jones just isn't done."

"Why not?" He led her through the dancers and stopped close to Sam and Winter. "Is it against the law?"

"No, but I tend to scare people. We had dancing lessons at my bar last fall. To prepare for the television show." She went into his arms, but reluctantly. "I didn't dance. I should have taken lessons, but I hid behind the bar."

"You are a little scary," he teased. "Beautiful women can be."

"You're flirting again?"

"Sorry." He watched his daughter and his brother dance to "San Antonio Rose." Sam had lost that permanently haunted and exhausted expression he'd carried around ten years ago. Jake had blamed his brother's weariness on his jungle life, but now he realized that Sam had been lonely. And now he wasn't.

"Tell me about Lucia," he said to his dancing partner.

"She's the nicest woman I've ever known," Aurora replied. "Your brother is very lucky."

"They're good together?"

"Yes."

Jake believed her, and the relief that swept through him made the whole trip worthwhile.

"ARE YOU THINKING what I'm thinking?"

"What are you thinking, Jerry?" Meg took a break from dancing and stood next to the mayor. They'd become friends, he realized. Together they'd managed to put the town on the map. Together they'd turned a group of scruffy bachelors into television stars.

"Check it out," he said, pointing to Aurora dancing with the newest arrival in town. "She almost looks human."

"She's a good person," Meg said. "The two of you really should stop bickering."

He snorted. "That'll be the day. The woman was put on earth to annoy me. Look who she's dancing with."

"Sam's brother? He seems nice enough. Do you think they look—"

"For heaven's sake, Meg. That's Jake Hove. *Jake Hove.* I can't believe I didn't recognize the name when Sam got here. Hove isn't exactly a common name."

"He's a singer, I heard."

"I looked him up on Google. He hasn't had a hit in six years, but he did all right before that. When he was younger."

"And your point is?" She waved at her husband, who was bouncing around the room with Loralee, his mother-in-law. Jerry shuddered. Owen MacGregor was a brave man.

"We're attracting celebrities now, Meg. Sam Hove, adventurer and filmmaker. Your husband, descendant of ranching royalty. He doesn't really count, though, because he lived here before the show. But now we have Jake Hove, Nashville star. Look at him! He's making Aurora smile!"

"She smiles sometimes," Meg said, but Jerry noticed she stared at the dancing couple with new intensity. "When she feels like it."

"Oops, guess I spoke too soon." Jerry sighed. "We have to find him a nicer woman."

"Why?"

"So he'll stay," Jerry said. "He'll attract other famous people."

"I don't think—"

"And," Jerry announced, the thought coming to him in a flash of inspiration, "he can write the town a theme song!"

"Have you been drinking? We specifically told everyone that there would be no alcohol except for the toast—"

"No, no." He waved off her frown. "Who would be a good match? Patsy? She's outgoing enough. Or Iris. He could stay at the B-and-B and they could get to know each other."

"Maybe," Meg said, obviously unconvinced. "Iris is seeing a teacher from Lewiston, I think. I don't know about Patsy, but if she's interested she'll make it known."

"We do need a theme song. Do you think he'd do it for free?"

"I'm not asking him. And you shouldn't, either."

"All he can say is no."

"You'll embarrass Sam. And Lucia."

Jerry considered that for a long moment. "Sam and I get along just fine. Next time we're having breakfast at the café, I'll casually bring up the subject and see what he says. No pressure. Just a man-to-man conversation."

"I suppose," she said, smoothing her lace dress. "Lucia will be the next bride in town. Maybe Jake will stay for that wedding."

"Don't forget Mike and Cora." They were the successful *Willing to Wed* couple. Their romance would be played out on television in just a few short weeks. Jerry expected a busy summer as the show caught on and women around the country realized the appeal of Montana bachelors.

"And you and Tracy?"

"Next time I'm in L.A. I'm going to take her shopping for a ring. I debated about the surprise aspect, but I think she'd prefer to pick it out herself. She's very particular about her jewelry."

"Congratulations."

"Well," he said, wondering if Tracy would actually agree to marry him, "it's not a done deal."

"Does that mean you'll leave Willing?"

The very question filled him with horror. "No way, Megsy-babe. I'm working my way up to state senate, maybe even governor."

"Good luck with that. With everything." She gave him a quick hug before Lucia's little hellions ran over to ask her for more cake.

CHAPTER FOUR

AURORA DROVE HERSELF home, the way she'd driven herself to the ranch. She'd left quickly, slipping out after dancing with Jake Hove, after giving Meg and Owen quick hugs, after shaking off their thanks for the champagne and wishing them a happy honeymoon.

She'd exchanged her fancy yellow boots for the staid waterproof boots she'd left outside the house, retrieved her vest, waved to Lucia and trudged across a field to find her car parked with dozens of others half a mile away.

She didn't mind the walk. Or the fresh air. Or the darkness that was fast approaching. The music and laughter faded as she crossed the dirt driveway and searched for her car, but she could still hear the sound of happy people in the distance.

She had to laugh at herself for dancing. Who would have thought such a handsome man would track her out to the wedding and crash the reception? And who would have thought he'd pick her to flirt with?

Oh, those types were dangerous, she knew. All charm and smiles and lingering looks. But it had been fun to dance. He'd laughed when she had given him a hard time about the flirting. Any other man she'd met here in town would have cringed and run away, but not that one.

He was like Jerry, unafraid. But unlike the often pompous and ridiculously ambitious mayor, Jake Hove had a certain appeal. She hadn't felt that way about a man since Alex walked out, which had been four years, ten months and six days ago.

Aurora didn't like remembering, and she didn't like to dwell on the past.

Tonight she would watch the latest episode of *The Amazing Race,* thanks to her DVR having recorded it while she drove home to her apartment above the bar. She would put on her yoga pants and old Cabela's T-shirt and she would carefully stuff her new boots with tissue and set them neatly in their box.

She would review her plans for tomorrow and make sure that nothing—absolutely nothing—would hinder her expansion of the Dahl. The men in this town liked things to stay the same, she knew. Even Jerry, with all his bluster and big plans for Willing, expected certain institutions, such as the Dahl and the Willing Café, to never change.

But it was long past time to update the bar, and it was time to do something to attract women to socialize there. The A client base wasn't being served. The women of Willing had to have a place of their own.

Aurora parked her car behind the bar and climbed the stairs to the second floor. Owning a Montana bar in the middle of nowhere wasn't the life she'd expected, but she was determined to make the most of what she'd created for herself.

"TOMORROW," SAM SAID. "We'll figure it out tomorrow, but tonight you'll stay here."

"I'd planned to stay in a motel," Jake said, stepping into Lucia Swallow's well-equipped kitchen. He'd heard she was a baker, but now he understood that the woman took her business seriously. "There's a Super 8 in Lewiston."

"Which is filled with the wedding guests from D.C.," Lucia said. "As are the two B-and-Bs in town."

Sam frowned. "Who'd have thought there'd be a problem at this time of year?"

Jake looked at his brother. "It's not a problem. We could drive to Billings. Or Great Falls."

Winter started tapping at Jake's cell phone. "I'll find something," she said, serious and focused.

"You'll sleep here tonight," Lucia said. "Winter, you can have Davey's room, and, Jake? You have your choice of the couch here or a sleeping bag at Sam's house."

"Pick our couch," Davey whispered. "Sam's house stinks."

Sam winced. "It was owned by a reclusive old lady," he explained. "I'm still filling Dumpsters with junk."

"I can help with that," Jake said.

Winter looked up from the phone. "We're staying here?"

Jake couldn't tell if his daughter was pleased or horrified. He supposed that was one of those things he'd learn soon enough. He watched her tuck the phone into her pocket and wait for instructions, so he assumed that was a good sign.

"School night," Lucia said to her boys. "Go upstairs and get ready for bed. Davey, take your blankets and pillow and camp out with your brothers."

"Okay," he said, glancing toward Winter. "Do you like to read? I've got a lot of books."

"Thank you," she said, using her polite British accent again. "Your hospitality is very much appreciated."

Lucia shot Sam a look, but she managed to hide her smile when she replied, "Go upstairs with Davey, then. He'll show you his room and I'll be up in a minute with sheets and blankets."

The four children ran up the stairs, with the two smaller boys squealing with laughter.

"She does that thing with the accent when she's nervous," Jake offered. "She's a big fan of *Downton Abbey*. And going to school in England, well, it's what she's grown up with."

"It's okay," Lucia said. "I love Mrs. Patmore."

"She's the cook at *Downton*," Sam explained when Jake did a double take and stared at him. "Come on. I'll show you my place."

"I appreciate this," Jake said. "But I didn't intend to stay here."

"You can check out the B-and-B tomorrow," Lucia said. "Iris only has a few rooms, but it's lovely."

"If you like flowers and ancient furniture,"

Sam muttered. "It's like an old bordello in there."

"It was an old bordello," Lucia informed him. "It's a historic building."

"Yeah," his brother said, rolling his eyes. "Jake might prefer my living room floor."

Jake followed Sam outside and across the yard. Lucia's was the middle house of three identical homes that looked as if they'd been built in the nineteen thirties. The one he was being led to looked as if it needed a fresh coat of paint and new windows.

"The woman who lived here was a recluse," his brother explained, stepping up to the back door. He swung it open and wiped his feet on a mat. "I'm pretty much gutting it and building an addition to make the two houses into one house. The middle part will be a master bedroom suite, along with a windowed hall that will let in lots of light."

Jake stepped inside as Sam flicked the lights on to illuminate a dark-paneled kitchen. "You've got your work cut out for you."

"I've got a crew from Lewistown coming in a couple of weeks. I've spent the winter cleaning stuff out and trying to get the plans right. This and most of the living room will be Lucia's professional kitchen area. It will look like the one she has now, only with more ovens and counter space. She wants to have a place where she can hold baking classes."

"You'll have to show me the plans." His brother looked happy and proud, two things Jake had seldom seen when they were growing up. "You like this place."

Sam nodded. "Yeah. I came here because a stranger on a plane told me this was his home." His eyes darkened. "And now it's mine."

There was more to that story, Jake knew, but he didn't pursue it. His brother would tell him when he felt like talking.

"Come on," Sam said. "I'll show you where we're going to camp out."

"I've got a sleeping bag in the car." He always traveled with one in the trunk, a habit left over from the days of road trips between gigs. He also had his favorite guitar and a thick, battered notebook of songs. A change of clothes and a road map had been all he'd ever needed.

"Good." Sam waved at the nearly empty living room that encompassed the front of the house. A new mattress lay in one corner, obviously where Sam spent his nights, and an old couch sat against the far wall. "I've got a piece of foam you can use if the couch is too uncomfortable. I got rid of the mattresses that were here."

"Don't worry about me," Jake said. "I can sleep anywhere."

"That doesn't surprise me." And then Jake's younger brother smiled. "I'm real glad you're here."

"I should have given you more notice."

"No way," Sam said. "I'd want to see you, anytime, anywhere, but I'm pleased you're here in town."

"Well, it looks like an interesting place."

Sam smiled again. "I like it. Maybe you and your daughter will, too."

Jake was silent for a moment, then cleared his throat. "This fatherhood thing—"

"Is tough," his brother said, completing his sentence. "I'm new at it, too."

"Where's Lucia's ex?"

"She's a widow."

"Ah. So the boys really need a father. How do you do it?"

"It's easy," Sam said, his expression serious. "I just think of what our father would do or say, and then I do the opposite."

Jake thought about that for a long moment.

"So, no drunken rages. No beatings. No showing off at political fund-raisers?"

"You got it."

He nodded slowly. "I keep telling myself I'm not like him."

Sam snorted. "You're not. Neither one of us is."

"Another reason to celebrate."

"THIS IS REALLY bad timing," Jerry muttered, slumping over the latest budget reports stacked on the table near the back of the Willing Café, otherwise known as "Meg's." If he'd had working brain cells this morning, he would have wondered if Meg was going to keep working at the café or move out to the ranch to start making babies with her new husband. "My head is killing me," he grumbled. "I probably should have changed the meeting to next week."

"Isn't that against the law?" Les fiddled with his own copies of the budget and the meeting's agenda, not that he would have read them. Jerry lifted his aching head and frowned at the kid. If his grandfather hadn't gotten sick, Les wouldn't have been on the council. He didn't have a political bone in his body and, as an ex-rodeo participant, had little knowledge of business.

"No," he said, not trying to hide his impatience. "It's not against the law, not if everyone is notified ahead of time and the new date is published in the paper."

"Oh."

"Unless we don't get a quorum." He saw Les's mouth open and hurried to explain, "That's the minimum number of council members we need to have a meeting."

"I know what a quorum is," the other man said indignantly. "I was going to ask how many we need."

"Four out of six," Jerry said, moving his papers aside so that Shelly could deliver his coffee and a carafe. He had high hopes for the caffeine cure. "Owen's not going to be here, because of his honeymoon. And Pete partied just as long as I did last night."

Les smiled at Shelly. "Good morning," he said to her. "That was sure fun yesterday."

"Yes," she said, giving him a shy smile. "It was."

"I'm glad we got to dance."

She blushed. "Me, too."

Jerry sighed. He wished the two would just go ahead and get married. Or at least start dating. Les was crazy about the girl and she needed a husband. Her baby needed a father. Everyone in town could see it was inevitable that the two of them got together and frankly, Jerry found all this unrequited love business exhausting to watch.

"The party at the ranch ended around seven," Jerry said for no other reason than to break the two apart. He took several sips of the hot coffee. "But some of us went back to my house for a while."

"Oh." Les looked over toward the door. "Here comes Mike."

"Great." Mike was known for his quick treasury reports, something they all appreciated. Jerry thumbed through the stack of papers in front of him. He hadn't forgotten about the regularly scheduled council meeting. But he had forgotten that Aurora's ambiguous building permits were on today's agenda. He did not look forward to that particular subject. Telling Aurora she didn't have the space to build whatever it was she wanted to build was a lesson in futility. And quite possibly dangerous.

"And Gary just drove up."

"That's three."

"That leaves Hank and Pete."

Jerry looked at his phone. No one was officially late yet. He drank more of his coffee and thought about ordering pancakes. His head throbbed and his eyes felt as if they'd been rubbed with sandpaper.

"Shelly?"

She turned back. "Yes?"

"Could I get some blueberry pancakes, with a side of bacon?"

"Sure." She scribbled something on her order pad. "Do you want juice?"

"No, thanks." He'd stick with coffee. And ice water, too. He would take another aspirin.

He rarely drank more than two drinks, but perhaps the combination of champagne, dancing, celebrating and the scotch back at his house had given him one heck of a headache. He was tired, too. Maybe he'd spend the rest of the day at his desk, and then take a nap.

Or was he too young to take naps?

"Man, I hope they hurry up," Les was saying. "I've got to get over to Owen's and get the place cleaned up."

"By yourself?"

"No, Hip's gonna come with me. Shelly said she'd come out later and help, if she can borrow Loralee's car."

Jerry watched Aurora enter the room and head in their direction. "Brace yourself."

"Yeah," the kid said. "She looks like she's ready for a fight."

"She always looks like that," he reminded Les as Mike joined them at the table.

"We're not fighting about something?" Les eyed the papers in front of him on the table. "She wants a building permit? Is that a good thing or a bad thing?"

"It depends," Jerry muttered. "On what she wants to build. And how much room she needs to build it." Was she going to raise the roof? That might be legal, if she retained the historic nature of the building. He had no idea how Aurora felt about the historic nature of anything, though. For all he knew she planned to top the building with a deck, hot tub and a neon sign that said Free Beer.

Aurora, dressed in black leggings, tall tan boots, a denim shirt and a khaki fishing vest, approached the table. She eased gracefully into a chair at the head of the table, hung a massive purse over the back of her chair and placed a leather document folder in front of her. "Good morning." She looked at her watch and then to

Jerry. "What's the matter with you? You look worse than usual."

"I think I'm getting a sinus infection."

"Well, please breathe in the other direction," she said. She greeted Les and Mike. "I saw Gary in the parking lot. Where's the rest of your illustrious council?"

"Owen's on his honeymoon." He made a show of studying her. "What happened to last night's glow of wedding happiness?"

"*Glow of wedding happiness?* Lovely. Are you writing poetry now? Are we going to have cowboy poetry parties like they do in Lewistown?" She opened her folder and unclipped a pen.

"I'm not stealing Lewistown's cowboy poetry gathering," he muttered, although he'd thought about it at one time. They got a lot of mileage out of that annual August event but, he thought, no television coverage. At least not national.

He eyed Aurora with some trepidation. Last night he'd thought she was simply mellow from wedding happiness. He'd never seen her look so relaxed. In fact, she'd even smiled a couple of times. Pete said he'd tried to film her with his new phone, so he could put it on YouTube: *Aurora Jones in a Good Mood.*

Shelly appeared with more coffee cups and a carafe, which she set down in front of Aurora and Mike. "Can I get you anything else?"

"Just a little cream," Aurora said. "Thank you."

"Sure." She hesitated. "Al made cinnamon scones this morning. He said to tell you the recipe you gave him worked."

Jerry almost fell off his chair. Aurora exchanging recipes with the café's grumpy cook? The pain in his head stopped him from even thinking about making a joke. If he laughed he might have a stroke.

"I'm glad," Aurora said. "It's a secret recipe from the Highlands, from a castle there. The chef was kind enough to share—"

"You were in a castle?" This was from Les, who looked as confused as Jerry felt. "In Scotland?"

"You know what a *recipe* is?" Jerry couldn't help himself. Mike cleared his throat in warning. Aurora glared at the three of them as Shelly scurried back to the kitchen.

"You may find this hard to believe," Aurora

said to them, "but people have been known to actually have had *a life outside Willing.*"

"Go figure." Les helped himself to more coffee. "I like it right here."

"Me, too," Mike said. "I did an article once about the connection between Scotland and the original ranching ventures in Montana. There's a lot of historic—"

"Here's Gary. And Hank," Jerry announced. He didn't want Mike to launch into the Mac-Gregor ranching history this morning. There were times when he found it fascinating, but this morning he only wanted this meeting to be over quickly. "And the school bus just pulled up, so Pete's coming."

"Excellent," Aurora said. "Call the meeting to order, Mayor, and let's get down to business."

He didn't like the glint in her eyes, but as soon as the other members of the council settled themselves at the table, Jerry did as he was told.

AURORA WAITED ENDLESS minutes for the men to read the minutes of the last meeting—sidewalk repair, potholes, the possible locations for watch parties when *Willing to Wed* began next month—and went over the budget report. She paid little attention to their figures and instead looked at her own proposal for the fiftieth time.

She expected no trouble. Hank was a gifted mechanic and owned his own garage, so he understood what it was like to run a business. A widower in his midfifties, he spent one evening a week at the Dahl, usually on karaoke night. He only drank one beer and was always a gentleman.

Pete Lyons, on the other hand, drove a school bus and liked to party once in a while. He was in his thirties and had been a hit with the women on the show. Lucia had spent a lot of time on his wardrobe, because Pete was a work-in-progress as far as grooming went. Today he wore a perfectly respectable black hoodie and jeans, but Aurora knew that he and Jerry were buddies. If Jerry found a way to oppose her building plan, then Pete would be on the mayor's side.

But he was only one vote.

Gary Peterson, retired, divorced and immersed in his daughters' and granddaughters' lives, shouldn't be a problem. Les would vote yes, because his butt wasn't planted on a bar stool six nights a week. Not since he was saving his money for a future with Shelly, anyway.

Mike, newly engaged and having emerged as a somewhat geeky romantic figure during filming, finished his budget report and waited for comments. Jerry, shoveling pancakes into his mouth, didn't have much to say.

"My turn," Aurora declared.

"New business," Jerry said, wiping his mouth with a napkin. "Is there any new business?"

"Of course there is," Hank said. "Look at the agenda."

"I have to officially call for new business," Jerry explained, turning to Aurora. "You want something?"

Hank looked at his watch. "I've got three transmissions backed up, plus a couple of axles that need a miracle. Can we move this along?"

"Of course, Hank," Aurora said. "As you know, I purchased the vacant lot next to the Dahl last month."

"From Jerry," Les added.

"Yes," she said. "He finally decided to sell a practically worthless lot for an exorbitant amount of money."

"You got a bargain. You beat me down," the mayor conceded. "It was easier to sell you a parking lot than it was to keep hearing you complain."

"Whatever," she said, hiding a smile. He'd made a decent profit on that lot, she knew, and had no reason to complain about the sale. "Now we need to discuss zoning. And a building permit."

"You can't build on that lot," Jerry said, rubbing his temples. "You know that. We've been over and over it. We're not moving water lines—"

"Yes, I know that," she agreed, pulling a neatly folded set of building plans from her folder. "I realize now that zoning is no longer an issue. Would you move your breakfast, please?"

The men hurried to clear a space in the middle of the table.

"I'm applying for a building permit to expand the Dahl."

"Expand how?" This was from Mike who, as the owner and sole reporter for his family newspaper, was always on the lookout for a story.

"With an additional party room, a patio and an outdoor pizza oven."

"Wait a minute," Jerry said. "You can't build on that lot—"

"It will stay a parking area," she assured him.

"But where—"

"I recently bought Chili Dawg," she announced. "That solves my zoning issue. That building will be torn down, thank goodness, as it's an eyesore, and you know it, and my addition will take up that space."

"I don't get it," Les said.

"The Dahl is a historic building," Jerry sputtered. "You can't go changing it. It's a symbol of the West, of our history!"

"It's pretty cool the way it is," Pete added. "I mean, the Dahl has always been the Dahl, you know?"

"I'm not changing the bar itself," she assured them, deciding it was not a good time to tell them about removing the smelly paneling behind the pool table area. "The front of the building will get a new coat of paint, maybe a new awning. And definitely a new window. But the women in this town need a place where they can have a glass of wine or an evening out without feeling as if they're back in the Wild West."

"A wine bar," Gary said, frowning. "You're putting in a wine bar?"

"Well," she conceded, "maybe."

"And a patio," Hank said. "A patio in Willing?"

"They have patios in bars all over the world," she assured him. "And men actually use them."

"I'm gonna miss Chili Dawg," Gary said. "I eat there all the time."

"Then it's a wonder you haven't died," Aurora told him.

Jerry frowned. "Chili Dawg isn't historic?"

"On what planet?" was her response. "It's a nineteen-eighties shack."

He didn't argue, but there were comments from the others.

"Man, this isn't good news."

"Where's old Harve gonna go?"

"Who's gonna make the pizza?"

"Are men allowed in?"

"Will you have hot dogs?"

"What exactly is a *wine* bar?"

"There's nothing wrong with the Dahl the way it is. Women do go in there," Jerry said.

"Rarely," Aurora said. "Because there's no other place."

"You've had parties," he insisted. "Meg's

wedding shower, remember? The place was filled with women."

"It doesn't have the atmosphere I want," she said. "I really don't understand what the problem is. I'm expanding my business. It's my right."

Jerry sighed. He was probably just upset he hadn't thought of it first. But the questions from the others continued.

"You're not going to take the TV away, are you?"

"What about the pool tables?"

Aurora tapped her index finger on the plans. "See for yourself. I'm keeping the historic integrity of the building, but I'm adding an area that is more feminine. It can be reserved for private parties." She looked at Jerry. "For wedding-related activities. Isn't that what you've wanted? To attract women to Willing?"

She had him there, she knew.

"Not at the expense of history," he said, his attention diverted by his phone. "Give me a second here."

"You're reading a *text*?"

He held up a hand and stood. "I'll be right back." With that, Jerry and his phone left the building.

"Well?" Aurora eyed the town council. "I've followed the law. You've seen the plans. And you can't possibly object, because this will improve Main Street."

This declaration was met with silence.

"It will look better," she said, then lowered her voice in a Mafialike imitation. "The grizzly is safe with me."

"Some things are sacred," Hank said, surprising her. "This is, uh, pretty fast. Maybe we ought to give this more thought."

"I need to have it done for the summer, before tourist season." She looked over her shoulder to see Jerry walking slowly across the room. He looked as if he'd been given bad news. He took his seat and cleared his throat.

"Where were we?" he said.

"My building permit," she prompted. "To improve Main Street. To upgrade the look of downtown. To attract customers. To attract female customers."

"To change the Dahl," Mike muttered. "That's not right."

Gary nodded. "I agree."

"Yeah," Hank said. "I'm attached to that place. I'd hate to see its, uh, personality altered."

"That's three votes no?" Jerry looked surprised.

"I vote yes," Les said. "If we're voting."

"Yes," Pete said. "I guess I can't see what's wrong with having more women at the Dahl." He looked at the plans again. "Or next to the Dahl. Whatever."

Jerry's phone beeped again, and he twitched. Yet he didn't look at the screen. "I think we need to postpone any official vote."

"Postpone?" Aurora stared at him in amazement. "What on earth are you talking about?"

"Well," he drawled, not meeting her gaze.

She wanted to grab his phone and toss it into his coffee cup. She couldn't believe he would propose delaying her permit, not after all of the hard work and planning she'd put into this project.

"Considering the circumstances," Jerry said, "all those in favor of tabling this issue until next month's meeting say aye."

They said aye.

"Aye?" Aurora repeated. "Really? Aye?"

Jerry stared at his council members. "This has turned out to be a really bad day."

Aurora frowned at him. "You think?"

WINTER SLEPT IN a bed made up of Spider-Man sheets and a faded old *Star Wars* blanket. When she woke, she didn't know where she was and had to think about it for a long minute. Montana, she remembered. A small town. She looked around the tiny room and saw a hundred little action figures and stacks of books. A chest of drawers was covered with rocks, its drawers open to reveal jumbles of clothes.

She was staying with her uncle's girlfriend, who had three boys.

Three boys who weren't really her cousins, no matter what anyone said.

And she had a father who wasn't really a father, no matter what anyone said about that, either.

Seriously, this was weird. One day she'd been at Lady Pettigrew's and the next thing she knew, her mother was dead and Mr. Tate, the family solicitor, was explaining how her life was going to change. Then there'd been that semiviolent scene in the parlor with Pippa, the most irritating girl in her class who had made terribly rude remarks about her mother dying. And Winter had thrown a fit—a massive, screaming, hysterical fit— and had been removed from school before the term was over.

And now she was trapped with an American father she'd never even known about.

No wonder she was having abandonment issues. Lady Pettigrew's headmistress had recommended counseling. That didn't sound like fun. Was she supposed to talk about her mother, a beautiful woman she rarely saw? Was she supposed to complain about her father, a man who practically lived out of his car?

Was she supposed to be sad? And if so, how sad? Would a counselor tell her how she was supposed to feel?

If so, that would be a relief.

"YOU'RE GOING TO love this place," Sam told him. He turned to Winter. "What do you want for breakfast? Pancakes? French toast? Bacon?"

Winter shrugged. "I quite enjoy bangers."

"Sausages?" Sam's smile remained undiminished. "I'm sure Meg's has them, too."

"Meg was the bride," she said. "Correct?"

"Right." Jake didn't care what emotional issues his daughter had; he was growing tired of the British accent. "This is convenient," he added, noting it was a short walk to the café. Just one block up and two blocks over. He wasn't much of a cook, which was another thing that concerned him when it came to fatherhood. He was supposed to provide nutritious meals and on schedule, too.

He'd never been good at schedules.

Tony, Lucia's youngest boy, held Sam's hand and bounced along with a cheerful expression. Lucia had elected to stay home and "get things done," whatever that meant.

Jake hadn't slept well. His life was a mess and had been a mess for a long time. He'd sung his songs and traveled the country and done what he could to make a living.

And he'd made a pretty good living.

But he was a father now. Was he supposed to take Winter along on tours? No way. That was no life for an eleven-year-old girl. He needed to find a school for her. She was used to boarding schools and seemed to like the one she'd gone to in England. He'd Googled a couple online that were possibilities for the fall. But what was he supposed to do in the meantime?

"This is the center of the town's social life," Sam was saying. "Jerry took me here for breakfast the day after I arrived. I wasn't used to walking in snow and ice." He chuckled. "I was so cold all I could think of was getting out of here and going someplace warm."

"Back to the jungle?" Winter asked. "Is that where you wanted to go?"

"I didn't care," his brother explained. "I just wanted to be warm."

"But you didn't go," Tony announced, bouncing a little as he walked beside his future stepfather. "You stayed!"

"I sure did," Sam agreed. "And I'm real happy that I did." He looked at Jake and smiled. "You might feel that way, too, you know."

The restaurant looked like a hundred others he'd seen, one level on a main road through town, an oversize gravel parking lot ringed with motel cabins. These cabins looked well cared for, though. As if its owner actually rented them out and made a profit.

"Maybe I—we—could stay here for a couple of days," Jake said. "Or are they only open in the summer?"

"I can ask," Sam replied. "Meg's out of town, but someone will know."

"They appear to be incredibly small," Winter said. "I'd prefer my own room."

"Well, I'm sure you would, Lady Mary,"

he told his daughter. "But there's not a lot to choose from around here."

To his amazement, Winter giggled.

"We'll stop at the B-and-B on the way home," his brother said. "Iris might have something now that the wedding is over." He opened the heavy glass door and ushered them inside.

Jake smelled coffee. And bacon. And everything else good to eat. They'd walked into a large room lined with windows and booths, its center filled with small tables and chairs. On the opposite wall was a counter and stools, and beyond that, Jake assumed, was the kitchen. The place was noisy and warm, the kind of place you wouldn't mind having breakfast in every morning. There were three elderly men at the counter who swiveled to see who had just arrived and whose faces lit up when they saw Sam.

Jake's brother had found a place here in this town. Jake followed him across the room and he and Winter were introduced to the three seniors who took a great interest in him and his daughter.

"I saw you out at the ranch," one of them said. "I'm John Ferguson. My wife and I didn't stay for the dancing, so I didn't get a chance to meet you. Glad you're here. How long are you two staying?"

"Not long," he heard himself admit.

"You're a singer," another man, George Oster, said. "You gonna sing about Willing?"

Jake grinned. "You never know."

"Well, if you sing at the Dahl some night, I'll be there."

"Thanks."

"We have a real nice school," sharp-eyed Martin Smith said to Winter. "Have you seen it yet?"

Winter shook her head. "I'm finished for the term."

The old man's gaze sharpened. "I heard you lived in Paris or somewhere like that."

"My mother resided in Paris," she explained. "But I attended Lady Pettigrew's, in London. Until I had a fit and was expelled."

Jake closed his eyes briefly and prayed for patience. Winter was brutally frank and seemed to have no problem announcing her so-called issues to anyone who'd listen.

"Expelled, huh?" He shrugged. "Well, you tell your father to take you over to the school and get you enrolled there. We're not London," he said, giving her a wink, "and one little fit isn't gonna get you kicked out."

"That's good to know," Winter said, sounding relieved. "I'm thinking about staying here for a while. And I suppose if I did stay I'd have to enroll in school."

"You sure would," Mr. Smith agreed. "Tell your father here to get himself organized."

"I will," she said. "If you'll excuse us, we're going to have breakfast now."

"See you tomorrow," the man said, swiveling back to his coffee. "Let me know how it all works out."

"I'm in over my head," Jake muttered to his brother.

"Your daughter has a mind of her own," Sam agreed. They watched Winter and Tony cross the room to study the rotating display of pie and cake slices. "Is there any reason why you can't stay here?"

"Work," he said. "I found a replacement for the summer tour that was scheduled, but I still have a lot to do in the studio. And then there are some charity concerts I'm not sure how to handle."

"Your fans won't be disappointed?"

"The kid who's replacing me is a bigger name

whose record just hit number two, a surprise for a lot of people in the business. It'll work out fine."

"All right. Leave Winter here, with us, while you're away. You know she'll be fine, and Lucia would love it."

"That would be the easy way out," Jake said, not that he hadn't thought of it himself. "I took the easy way out when Merry wanted a quickie divorce. I didn't even ask her why she was in such a hurry, because I was so relieved to be out of it." He watched Winter take Tony's hand before he could disappear behind the counter where a thin, blonde teenager fiddled with a coffeemaker. "She needs a father. And I'm all she's got."

"She also has an aunt and uncle," Sam reminded him. "Don't forget that."

"I can't take the easy way out this time," he said. "You and Lucia have three boys and a wedding and a honeymoon coming up. Another child, especially one like Winter, adds a whole lot of extra baggage."

"We don't mind," his brother said. "We talked about it this morning, before you were up. Lucia's worried about the girl."

"Yeah," he said. "So am I."

"And I'm worried about you, too," Sam added. "I think you should stick around here. We've got a lot of catching up to do."

"I need to make a home for my daughter, Sam."

"Looks like you need to make a home for yourself, too. You've got family here. Don't run from it."

"I'm not running," Jake insisted, looking at Sam's worried expression. "I'm going home, to make a life for my kid."

"Make it here," Sam repeated. "Give us a chance to be a family." He shot Jake a sheepish smile. "Hey, there's a first time for everything."

CHAPTER FIVE

"MEETING ADJOURNED," Jerry croaked. "All those in favor?"

They were all in favor. Everyone but Les fled from the restaurant. Jerry had never seen Gary move so fast, while Mike looked as guilty as someone who'd just been caught robbing a bank. Hank muttered something about brake oil while Pete mumbled, "Sorry" and fled. Les took one look at Aurora's murderous expression, grabbed his coffee mug and headed to the safety of a counter stool. Jerry wanted to do the same thing, but he sat frozen in place.

"You can't do this," Aurora said.

"*I* didn't do it." He rubbed his face with his hands. *How fast can I get to L.A.?*

"You're the mayor. You're supposed to be in charge."

"Jeez, Aurora." He actually felt faint. "I'm not *king*."

"It's illegal. I'm calling my lawyer."

"Your permit wasn't denied." There was a midafternoon flight out of Billings. He'd taken that before, but maybe there was something earlier? Was there? He pulled out his phone and saw the latest text from Tracy.

Long distance doesn't work, she'd typed. He ignored the stabbing pain in his head and called up Travelocity. "Your permit was *delayed*," he said, knowing there was nothing he could do to stop the coming explosion.

"There was no reason…"

He looked up. Aurora Jones was a beautiful woman, in her own way. She wore expensive clothes and stocked a bar with the finest liquor. She paid her bills on time and donated generously to every school fund-raiser. But she was also cold, unapproachable and self-sufficient to a fault. She didn't make friends easily and she didn't inspire loyalty. Jerry assumed she was a decent person, but he didn't want to invite her over for dinner or anything like that.

"They're afraid," Jerry said. "Give them time."

"I don't *have* time."

"And you don't have a building permit, either." He went back to his phone. Could he make the one-fifteen flight? Sure he could.

If he left right now. He ignored the choking sounds coming from the head of the table and booked the earlier flight.

"Aurora," he said finally, having secured the reservation and the chance to convince his future wife not to dump him. "Would you like some advice?"

She glared at him.

"Advice," she repeated softly, sending a chill down his spine. "Of course, Mayor. I would certainly appreciate any advice you'd care to bestow upon one of your loyal constituents."

He decided to take the high road and ignore that snarky remark.

"Schmooze them," he said. "Go to each man and listen to what he has to say. Show him the plans again. Make him understand this is not going to hurt the Dahl in any way, shape or form."

"Isn't that *your* job?"

"Not today," he said. "And not this week." Jerry gathered his papers together and stood. Aurora Jones needed patience. And tact. He wondered how on earth she would get them.

"MAY WE JOIN YOU?"

Aurora looked up to see that the request

came from Jake Hove's odd little daughter. The girl stood politely next to the booth where Aurora was sampling Al's cinnamon scone and sipping a cup of Kona coffee that the cook had brewed especially for her.

Aurora was attempting to calm down. She'd wanted to stomp out of the café right after the idiots had voted, but she hadn't wanted to hurt Al's feelings.

"Of course," Aurora replied, sounding as pleasant as she could manage as she scooted over toward the window to make room for Winter. "Would you like a scone?"

"Yes, please."

Her anger dissipated as Aurora felt the almost overwhelming desire to wrap this girl in her arms and promise her that everything would work out, that she would be okay. The child looked lost and alone, but so brave. *Keep being brave,* she wanted to tell her. *You need to be brave.*

Winter slid into the booth and unzipped her hoodie before her father and uncle caught up with her. Tony clung to Sam's hand and grinned. That little boy would grow up to be a colossal flirt. Aurora smiled back at him. After all, she liked children. Until they grew up to be politicians.

"Good morning, gentlemen," she said as they stopped awkwardly at the booth.

"Good morning. Winter," Jake said, "what are you doing?"

"I'm going to have a scone with Aurora," she said primly. Aurora met Jake's gaze and shrugged.

"You're all welcome to join me," she said, hiding the fact that she was flustered. She preferred to eat in the privacy of her own home. She should have taken Al's scone with her and eaten it there, at her little table, with her jasmine tea in her favorite oversize mug, except that she'd appear to be unappreciative of his effort to create the perfect Scottish scone for her.

Did Al know Gary or Mike or Hank very well? Could he put in a good word for her?

And Sam was popular, despite having only lived here a few months. Had he done any male bonding while eating breakfast at the café every morning? It was a thought.

To her surprise, the men and the little boy squeezed into the opposite side of the booth as if it was no big deal. Men were social creatures in the morning, she decided. The café was filled with the proof.

"What are you up to this morning?" Sam looked content with the world as he reached over for the menus tucked behind the napkin dispenser. He handed one to Jake and one to Winter.

"I had business with the town council," she said.

"And did you get what you wanted?" This was from Jake, who seemed to have no qualms about making small talk.

"I did not," she replied, keeping her voice even. "Not yet."

Jake looked surprised. "Should I ask what happened or would you rather talk about the weather?"

"Nice day," she said. "But it might rain tomorrow. Where's Lucia?"

"Taking advantage of a quiet house," Sam said, waving at Shelly. "Meg's wedding wore her out."

Jake grinned. "When's yours?"

"Whenever she says it is," his brother replied. "The sooner the better. You can be the best man."

"Okay, folks," Shelly said, skidding to a stop at the end of the booth. "What'll it be?"

"I'd like a cup of tea," Winter said. "Please. And a scone."

"Me, too," chirped Tony.

"He'll have milk and pancakes," Sam said.

"And a mushy egg," the child added.

"One mushy egg coming up," Shelly said, jotting it down. She blushed when she looked at Jake. "I heard you. And your band. One time. At the rodeo in Boise."

"I hope you liked the show." Jake closed his menu.

"Oh, I did," she said. "We did. My friends and I did. You sang that song about the summer wine and the hill with the flowers and how you remembered that time when you were young."

"Yes," he said. "That's one of my favorites."

She kept blushing and staring at Jake until Aurora decided to put the girl out of her misery. "Shelly," she said. "Honey, would you bring Jake and Sam some coffee? They look like they could use it."

"I'll be right back," the girl promised, and rushed off.

Winter stared across the table at her father. "What was that all about?"

"Get used to it," Sam said, chuckling. "Your father's a star."

"What's that mean?" Tony sprinkled pepper on his napkin and sneezed.

"That's disgusting," Winter told the little boy. "Put the pepper back."

"It means," Jake said, removing the pepper and the napkin, "that people like my music."

"Huh." His daughter didn't look convinced.

Aurora watched the proceedings and thought of her tiny kitchen table and flowered tea mug. Shelly raced back with the coffee and seemed to be more in control of herself. Les, lurking at the counter, waved.

Sam waved politely back, and the young man interpreted that as an invitation and came over to say hello.

"We're surrounded," Aurora told Winter.

"You must be very glad I'm here," the girl stated. "Or you would be the only girl."

"I am very glad you're here." Aurora ignored the men's conversation with Les, who looked as if he was about to pull up a chair and join them for breakfast. They were discussing the weather and fishing season. Fascinating, as usual. Tony, busy unbuttoning his shirt, hummed a little song.

"I'm thinking about staying for a while," Winter said.

"Really?"

She nodded. "I don't think I have a lot of other options."

"How old are you?"

"I'll be twelve in July."

"And why are you thinking about staying in Willing?"

"Well, I have decided it's time I took charge of my own life."

Jake stopped listening to the fishing speculation and stared at his daughter. "What?"

"I don't want to be on a road trip. I don't want to live in Nashville," she said.

Aurora shrugged. "Who does?"

Jake's eyes narrowed. "I do. I have an apartment—"

"And you said you're never there," Winter cut in. "So who's going to take care of me? I have my own money. I should be able to do what I want."

"That's a very interesting theory," her father drawled. "But you're a minor. And you're stuck with me until you're eighteen."

"I barely know you." She sniffled, and Aurora couldn't help herself. She put an arm around her and hugged her to her side.

"You've had a tough time lately," she whispered. "I'm sorry."

"I'm okay." Winter sat up and composed herself. "I just want my own bed. And my own room. Without *Star Wars*."

"You can have those in Nash—" He stopped at the look Aurora gave him.

"What kind of bed do you want?" Aurora asked as Shelly returned to the table with a tray of drinks.

"Something fluffy. Blue. Light blue. With lots of pillows."

Aurora took a sip of coffee, but it was almost cold. "You'd better get busy, Dad. Get thee to a Target."

"The waitress wants to know what you would like for breakfast," Jake said, softening his voice.

"I'm going to have a scone, please, and scrambled eggs. And bacon."

"Aurora? Anything else for you?"

"Just a little more coffee," she said.

The men ordered their breakfasts, Les said goodbye and Sam told Tony to put his shirt back on.

"I'm a wrestler," he said, protesting. "They don't wear shirts."

"They do," Aurora said, "when they're in restaurants." She'd been around Lucia's children enough to know that they paid attention to adults and rarely had temper tantrums. At least not in public. And, of course, she had that soft spot for Tony, whose big brown eyes showed every emotion in his heart.

"Man, I wish now that we hadn't torn up the house," Sam said. "We could easily put beds in the rooms upstairs, though. Give me three or four days and you'll be perfectly comfortable."

"No," Jake said. "You're in the middle of a construction project. Heck, half the time you won't have water. And you're replacing the electricity, too, right?"

"Well—"

"Jake," Winter said, "we can stay at the bed-and-breakfast place." She turned to Aurora. "It used to be a bordello and it's very historic."

"Oh, it's definitely historic." She took another swallow of cold coffee. "You should go see it. It's like something out of the Old West."

"Like in the movies?"

"Absolutely." Iris had done it up in velvet and silks, with dark overstuffed furniture and all sorts of Victorian accents. It was a little claustrophobic for Aurora's taste, but the tourists loved it. Some of the women from the television filming had stayed there, and it had been a favorite place for Tracy, the producer, to film romantic dates.

"You're going to hate it," Sam murmured to his brother.

"I've stayed in a lot of strange places."

"Not like this, I'll bet." He grinned. "Unless you have a wilder life as a musician than I thought."

"I get food poisoning," Jake said. "More times than I can count. Other than that, it's just a lot of late nights and a lot of highways."

"There you go," Sam said, "writing another song. 'Late Nights and Highways.' Has a certain country appeal, right?"

"Yeah, automatic hit, all right. You ever actually catch any fish on that show of yours?"

Aurora watched the two men joke around together. Tony, stuck between them, watched for Shelly to return with his meal. Winter tapped Aurora's arm.

"They're funny," she said, but she wasn't smiling.

"They are," she agreed.

"Matty said that Sam told his mom he had a bad childhood."

"You'd never know it to look at them." And what defined a "bad childhood?" If Jake was anything at all like Sam, then he was a pretty solid man who could be trusted. Owen liked Sam, which meant a lot. Meg thought he walked on water, and Meg was finicky. Even Lucia's mother-in-law had given her approval, and that hadn't come easily.

"I think we should stay here," the girl said. "Don't you?"

"I don't know. I imagine that depends on your father." Shelly arrived with a tray piled high with plates of food and set them out in front of them. Aurora shifted her coffee and moved her empty plate to give them more room.

"He's not really my father," she said.

"I don't—"

"I just met him," she continued. "He doesn't know me. And I don't like him."

Aurora stopped what she was doing and studied the child. She didn't know much about children, but that seemed like a very odd thing to say. Jake might not be perfect father material, but he seemed likable enough. "You don't?"

Winter shook her head. "I might like him someday. But at the moment I'm undecided."

"He seems okay" was the only thing Aurora could think to say. "He seems to be trying hard to be a good father."

The girl shrugged. "I might go back to Lady Pettigrew's, if I have proof of having had counseling and have no lasting psychological problems."

"Would you like to go back to England?" Somehow she'd thought the girl was enjoying seeing this part of the world. But maybe she missed her friends. She was at that age where friends mattered.

She shrugged. "Perhaps. Or not really. I haven't decided."

Aurora doubted if Winter would be the one doing the deciding, but she kept quiet.

"Aurora?"

"Yes?"

"Have you lived here forever?"

"No."

Winter waited for more of an explanation, so Aurora continued.

"I…came here a few years ago and decided I would stay."

"Why?"

She realized that Sam and Jake looked at her as she contemplated the answer to that question. She'd given the usual responses before, almost three years ago now, when people asked. *I wanted to get out of the rat race* seemed to be a favorite. Another lie, *I used to visit my grandparents out here when I was a kid,* was easily accepted. *I saw Willing in a magazine* only confused the person asking the question, because no one could remember Willing ever being in a magazine.

"Well," Aurora said, looking into those clear blue eyes and knowing she couldn't lie. It wasn't fair to lie to this new little friend. "Just like you, I had a broken heart. And this seemed as good a place as any to wait it out."

"Did it work?" This came from Jake, who seemed almost desperate for a positive answer. So desperate she felt sorry for him.

"It did," she said. *Until now,* she wanted to add. When she was so frustrated she wanted to kick gravel in the parking lot and curse the political system. When she wanted to corner Hank in his garage and then yell at Mike while he cowered behind his desk at the newspaper.

"And where were you before?" asked Winter.

"Back east. With my parents. And then I traveled," she said. "Just like your father."

"Did you sleep in your car and sing in bars?"

"No," Aurora said, trying not to laugh. "But then again, I wasn't a star."

JAKE QUICKLY LEARNED that Iris recently renamed the B-and-B More Than Willing to play up the building's original use. She also sold Welcome to Willing T-shirts and a map featuring the various locations of the *Willing to Wed* dates, "soon to be aired on national television."

Winter wanted a map and a T-shirt, plus the Blue Lace Room with its blue satin-covered queen-sized bed and matching lace-trimmed pillowcases. Jake took the Red Room, despite its slightly raunchy decorations, because it was next to Winter's and had a connecting door that Iris unlocked for their convenience.

His daughter also bought a postcard featuring the town center and a marble statue of a bull that had something to do with the ranching history of the area. She said she couldn't wait to send it to her friend Robbie, who would be *so jealous*.

Winter had certainly perked up. One minute she was feisty and independent, and five minutes later she would look so sad and lost. He had a hard time adjusting.

"You can stay for ten days," Iris said. She was a tall, no-nonsense woman of about forty, with curly dark hair and green eyes. She was slender in her jeans, pink slippers and a faded sweatshirt that had "Just Married" scrawled across the front in silver lettering. "But then I'm all booked up for the start of the show. That's the last Monday night in April. Put it on your calendar. Some of the Californians are coming back for the party."

"Thanks." Jake gave her a credit card and signed the guest register.

"I've heard you're a musician, so if you want to practice you can use the living room. The place is empty now except for you, so feel free."

"I won't be—"

"I serve breakfast between seven and nine, but if you have a specific time you want, just let me know. Write it down on a Post-it note and stick it here on the counter."

"Thank you, we'll—"

"I have a ten p.m. quiet zone policy, so if you're out late partying at the Dahl, be quiet when you come in. Except for Thursdays, which is karaoke night, and I'm out late. I suspect you'll be there, anyway, so don't worry about making noise when you come in. I'll tell you if we have any guests, but I don't have any reservations, not yet, and you'll probably know someone's around as soon as I do." She looked at Winter. "No rap music. No hip-hop. Unless you're using earbuds, and even then, well, that stuff is atrocious."

"I agree," Winter said solemnly. "Do you have the internet?"

"Sure do. Wireless, of course. The password is gopanthers. That's the high school basketball team."

"Go Panthers," Winter repeated.

"No caps."

"No caps," Jake repeated. "Got it."

Iris rang up a receipt and handed it to him. "Will you be singing at the Dahl? Aurora usually has a band on Saturday nights."

"I don't think so. I don't have my band with me right now."

"Too bad. We could sure use a change of pace." She hesitated. "Karaoke on Thursdays. Don't suppose you'd be interested in that, either?"

Jake chuckled. "Man, I haven't done that in years."

"Say no," his daughter said, as if she would die of embarrassment at the thought of her father singing karaoke in front of a bar filled with people.

Iris answered for him. "Never mind, honey," she said to Winter. "Your dad would just make all of us amateurs look bad."

"I don't know about that," Jake said, smiling. "I've been to some pretty good karaoke bars. You might have a star hidden right here in town."

Iris laughed. "I think you're the only one we've got, Jake."

CHAPTER SIX

"YOU DID WHAT?"

"I closed it," Aurora declared, not without some pride in her voice. She stood on the sidewalk in front of the Dahl and admired the sign she'd made for the door of her bar. Thick black letters on a piece of white cardboard stated the simple truth.

Closed Until Further Notice.

"And I mean it," Aurora added. "I'm going to be busy with the demolition. And I'm going to do some renovating inside the bar. I hadn't intended to close it down, but...well...I don't like what's being done."

Lucia studied the sign and then turned to her friend. "I just heard about the meeting from Shelly, who heard about it from Les. This is going to cause quite a commotion once people see this. Can you survive financially for a few weeks? Do you know what you're doing?"

"I absolutely do." She'd walked home from

the café this morning and she'd fumed the entire time. She'd stood on the sidewalk and eyed the shack that was once the Chili Dawg. Surely no one could come up with a reason for that eyesore to remain. The cracks in the windows had been covered with duct tape and the *C* and *D* on the sign were faded so much they weren't even there.

The Dahl looked much better, but it needed a new window and a fresh coat of paint. She'd thought of installing a new sign, too, one with more old-fashioned lettering. But that was before three men told her what she could and couldn't do.

"I want my addition," she added. "And there's no reason for them to deny me my right to build onto the Dahl."

"You're declaring war," Lucia said.

"I didn't fire the first shot. The town council did."

Lucia sighed. "I can't believe Jerry let it happen."

"He told me to be nice, to talk the men into it." She put her hands on her hips and smiled as she studied her sign once again. "I think I'll let this do the talking."

Lucia laughed.

"Do you want to come up for coffee?" Aurora had never invited anyone into her living quarters upstairs. She entertained in the bar and preferred it that way. She found herself holding her breath, half afraid Lucia would accept and yet nervous that she'd say no.

"I can't. I'm walking to the school to meet the boys." She looked at her watch. "I've got to go. But ask me again, okay?"

"Okay."

Lucia tilted her head. "How long are you going to be closed?"

"Until I get my building permit," she said. And then she added, "They hurt my feelings."

To her surprise, Lucia gave her a quick hug. "They're idiots. The Dahl is not just a bar, it's a meeting place. What's going to happen to karaoke night and the TV watching parties for the show? I'll bet they didn't think that far ahead."

Aurora blinked back tears. "I still have plenty of work to do. They can't stop me from tearing down the hot dog shack."

Lucia looked at the building again. "I'll come over with my sledgehammer. Just say the word."

The thought of tiny Lucia Swallow swinging a sledgehammer made Aurora smile. "Thanks for the offer, but I've got a crew coming from Billings. Demolition is their specialty."

"Good." She started to walk away, but hesitated. "Are you free for dinner Saturday night? You know, now that you're not working?"

Aurora didn't know what to say. She'd kept her socializing to the bar and to town events. She'd only recently become more friendly with Meg and Lucia, two friends who'd met in culinary school and who'd known each other through lots of hard times. It was the bad times that showed you who your friends were. Unfortunately Aurora had had the bad times, and got through to the other side, but her profession back then had left little time for friends. She'd had her music, her teachers and her husband. And when the smoke cleared, she'd been alone. But now she thought that Meg and Lucia would be the kind of people who would be there for her, no matter what. She was doing her best to learn how all of this girlfriend business worked.

"All right," she said. Maybe closing the bar was going to have more positive results than she'd imagined. "I'd love to. What can I bring?"

"I have no idea what I'm cooking, but bring a bottle of wine. It'll be casual. Meg and Owen get back on Friday, so hopefully they can come and we can talk about how great the wedding was."

"The wedding *was* great," Aurora said, remembering dancing with Jake. "Your future brother-in-law practically swept me onto the dance floor."

"He's a charmer." Lucia grinned. "You two looked good together."

"No matchmaking," Aurora said. "We've had enough of that around here."

"He's probably not your type, anyway." Lucia started walking toward the school, which was on the other side of the grocery store, past the parking lot and the ball field that backed into the alley.

"My type?" Oh, yeah, she'd said she had a type. Hmm. She wondered what that might be. "Very funny."

Lucia waved, leaving Aurora to contemplate the fate of her business and what kind of man her friend pictured her with. She opened the door to the bar and locked it behind her.

"It's just you and me now," she said to the grizzly mounted on its wooden base in the corner of the room. "If we get lonely I'll turn on the karaoke machine and we'll sing."

"I'M NOT TRYING to fix anyone up," Lucia told the men standing in her kitchen. Sam handed Jake a beer and opened another for himself. "I'm not," she insisted, stirring something in a big pot. "I just thought it would be nice to welcome Meg and Owen home, and since Aurora's not working—"

"You're a romantic at heart," he said.

Jake laughed at the expression on Lucia's face. "It's okay," he assured her. "I like her."

"You do?"

"Sure. She's interesting. Mysterious."

"Remote," Sam countered. "She's got the whole town riled up, though."

"Yeah," Jake said. "What's with that? Iris just about had a stroke when she found out that there wasn't going to be karaoke Thursday night. She ended up going to movie night at the senior center, even though she said she'd seen *Hangover* six times."

"Iris isn't a senior," Lucia said. "She's in her forties."

"Well, she was desperate enough to pretend to be retired," Sam pointed out. "I'm not sure closing the Dahl is such a good idea. Maybe Aurora should rethink it. I don't drink, but I liked going down there once in a while. And the nights when they filmed the *Willing to Wed* episodes there were a riot."

"Don't bring it up unless she does." Lucia set a sauce-covered spoon in a dish on the stove. Jake watched, fascinated with how efficient she was. Nothing seemed to faze her, not the three boys running in and out of the kitchen, or Winter's questions about basil and parsley, or the little black dog that kept chasing the boys around the house, or the phone ringing with orders for cakes and cupcakes and various desserts.

Sam couldn't stop looking at his fiancée and touching her in small, protective ways. He hovered, as if he were afraid she would disappear if he looked away. And Lucia beamed at him, as if she felt the same way.

Jake had been in love a few times, but the glow had quickly faded. He envied his younger brother for having found someone who obviously adored him. He envied Sam's ability to commit to someone.

He assumed Sam's months in the Amazon had come to an end. Compared to his brother,

Jake felt practically homeless. Here he was, living in a bordello with a daughter who was a stranger, in a Montana town in the middle of nowhere with a lot of people who seemed half-crazy. He liked them, but still…it was a lot to get used to in one week. And he didn't know where he'd be a week from now.

The last thing he needed was a date. The last thing he needed right now, with his life turned upside down, was a woman. Especially a woman who looked right into his eyes and made her opinions known. Who challenged him.

He had a daughter who did that, which was just about all he could take.

"Aurora's here!" Davey ran into the kitchen, Boo barking at his heels. "I can get it!"

"He likes her," Lucia said to Jake. "She bought a ton of rafflc tickcts from him at the last school fund-raiser."

"High praise," Jake said, following Sam and Lucia into the living room. Davey had already opened the front door and invited Aurora inside. She was listening to something the boy said and nodded her agreement.

"What's he hitting you up for now?" Sam asked, taking her leather jacket from her.

"Tickets to the ham dinner."

"You don't have to—"

Aurora shrugged and handed Lucia a bottle of wine. "I like ham."

"They're gonna raffle a quilt," Davey told her.

"I know. I helped make it."

Jake decided he liked ham, too. Because the silver-haired woman in the black jeans, black sweater and black boots studded with crystals looked appealingly nervous, as if family dinners weren't her usual Saturday-night activity. Silver bracelets jangled from narrow wrists, sparkly earrings hung halfway down her neck, and her makeup was flawless.

And she looked as if she wanted to run out of the room and down the street.

Intriguing, he thought, stepping closer to greet her.

"Hey," he said, resisting the urge to kiss her cheek. He wondered if she wore perfume, and if so, what kind. "I hear you're out of work, too."

"Yes. I suppose you could say that."

"Well, that's one thing we have in common."

"Thank you for the wine," Lucia interrupted them. "Come on in and we'll open it right now."

She gave Jake a warning look to be on his best behavior.

The dog began barking wildly, wagging its tail as it ran into the kitchen.

"Meg and Owen must be here," Sam said, as the dog's barking increased in volume. "Boo! Cut it out!"

Bedlam ensued, much to Jake's amusement. Winter appeared in the kitchen, hovering close to the stairs as if she were reluctant to get too close to the action and wanted to be able to escape upstairs at any given moment. The three boys jumped up and down as they each tried to speak at the same time. The newlyweds gave hugs to everyone before Owen took Boo outside to the backyard.

Aurora and Jake hung back and watched the show.

"Is it always like this?" he asked her.

"I wouldn't know, but I suspect so."

Jake retrieved the wine from the kitchen counter and, using the opener that Lucia had set down, quickly opened the bottle. "Does this have to breathe?"

"Not as far as I'm concerned" was her reply, so he filled two wineglasses half full of red wine and handed one to her.

"You come here often?" It was an old pickup line, but he thought it might make her smile. It didn't, though she gave him an appreciative look before Meg greeted them.

"Did you have a good time?" This was from Aurora, who looked pleased to see the dark-haired woman.

"Fabulous." She turned to Jake. "I'm Meg," she said. "I know we met briefly at the wedding, but I'm sure you met a lot of people that day."

"None of them was wearing a gown," he said. "Of course I remember you. And Owen. Thanks for letting me crash the party."

"Me, too," his daughter said, sidling up next to him. "You looked beautiful," she told Meg. "I liked your barn."

"I'm glad," she said. "We're thinking of renting it out for weddings, but I'm still not sure if that's a good idea."

"But what about the horses?"

Owen came in and shook Jake's hand, greeted Aurora and said, "What about the horses?"

"Where will the horses go if they can't use the barn?"

The rancher looked taken aback. "I have

more than one barn," he said. "I have a number of outbuildings that—"

"Owen," his new wife interjected. "Sam is trying to offer you a beer."

"That'd be good," he said, distracted.

"Davey said you give riding lessons, Mr. MacGregor," Winter said.

"Unofficially," the large man explained. "The horses actually belong to Les Parcell, one of my neighbors. I borrowed them a couple of times last fall when the boys wanted to ride. I'll be getting my own soon, though. And Les is going to move his horses onto my place."

"For riding lessons?"

He looked at Jake, who nodded. "Sure. And now that I'm back home and the wedding is over, I can get back to work and start buying stock."

Aurora took a sip of wine. "For heaven's sake, MacGregor, take the child horseback riding next week. Get a horse from Les, load it into the trailer—or into whatever you load horses into—and show Winter the ranch." She turned to the girl, who had finally appeared in the kitchen to stand next to Aurora. "Do you have boots? You'll need boots."

Winter's gaze dropped to Aurora's crystal-dotted Western boots. "Not like those," she said. "Not even close."

Aurora looked at Jake. "Take her to Lewistown Monday and get her some boots. Wrangler jeans. And a hat."

"Shopping?" Winter's face lit up.

"Shopping," Aurora declared. "And if your father doesn't cooperate, call me. I know all of the stores."

"Yes," Jake murmured, glancing again at the sparkly earrings. "I'm sure you do."

"And you," Aurora said, turning back to Owen. "You need to get a very nice horse for this girl. A pretty horse."

Meg, who had been distracted by Davey's sales pitch about the ham dinner, returned to the conversation and handed Owen a bottle of beer. "That's a great idea."

"A nice, *pretty* horse," Owen echoed, looking at Winter's excited expression. "I can do that."

"A really old horse," Jake added, picturing the bucking broncos at his last rodeo gig.

"Not too old," Winter said. "And maybe not too big."

Meg smiled. "Owen, you must know of a nice, attractive, medium-sized, middle-aged horse, right?"

"No problem," he said seriously, as if he actually had a horse in mind.

"There." Aurora took another sip of wine. "That's settled, then."

Owen looked at Jake. "I'll give you a call after I talk to Les."

Winter produced her cell phone, kept handy at all times in the pocket of her non-Wrangler jeans. "I can give you my number and you can give me yours, Mr. MacGregor."

Meg laughed. "You're very organized," she said.

"It was part of the curriculum last year," his daughter explained. "I received high marks."

"You must get that from your uncle Sam," Jake said. "Scientists are very organized and focused."

"And what are musicians?" This came from Aurora, whose blue eyes were lit with mischief. "What traits do they share?"

"Good question." He pretended to think it over while he held her gaze. He wished he could rattle that calm exterior and pay her back for getting him involved in a trip to town. "They hate to shop."

"True. Most musicians I've met look as if

they're wearing the same clothes they had twenty years ago."

He ignored that comment. He'd bought a new shirt in Seattle, to meet his daughter at the airport. "And we're optimistic."

Her beautifully shaped eyebrows rose. "How so? What about all of that sad music?"

"We're sure we're going to write the perfect sad song and Keith Urban is going to buy it, record it and have a hit."

"Ah," she said. "Who's Keith Urban?"

Jake didn't know if she was kidding him or not, so he ignored her question. "Musicians have tattoos. And are superstitious. And frugal."

"Which is why they hate to shop?" Lucia offered, before moving away to take something out of the oven. The entire house smelled of oregano and garlic, making Jake's mouth water.

"Jake has a tattoo," Winter said. "On his arm."

Aurora didn't look all that impressed. "Superstitions?"

"I'm very attached to my guitar case."

"Frugal?"

"Have you seen my truck?"

"Really," his daughter said. "It's like ten years old, but it's sort of cool."

"I'm glad you think so," he said. She hadn't been all that thrilled when she climbed into it last week.

"So," Aurora drawled, "you're a walking stereotype."

"And proud of it."

He realized the others had drifted away, leaving the three of them standing near the sink.

"She closed *what?*" he heard Owen roar from the living room. "Why?"

"Aurora!" Lucia called her. "Ranch King wants to know what you've done with the grizzly!"

HE OFFERED TO walk her home.

"We could give you a ride," Meg said, "if you don't mind dog hair."

Aurora didn't mind dog hair, but she didn't mind walking home, either.

And she said so.

"We're going your way," Jake insisted, leaning against the kitchen counter. "We're staying at Iris's."

"All right." Anything else would have been rude, but Aurora resisted being paired with

Jake. She didn't want to be paired with anyone, actually. When her marriage ended she'd
decided being alone was preferable to being
involved with a man again. As clichéd as it
sounded, she liked being completely independent and having no one who depended on her,
no one who had expectations of her.

So she'd sat next to Jake at dinner, across
from Meg and Owen, but she'd attempted
to pretend he wasn't there. The children had
elected to eat in the kitchen and then bounded
upstairs to watch a movie. Lucia had bribed
them with cookies and root beer so the adults
could eat in peace.

It hadn't been all that peaceful. The table
wasn't huge and Jake's elbow had bumped hers
several times. She'd liked that, she realized.
She didn't want to be attracted to him, a wandering musician in the midst of a life crisis.
He was a walking recipe for disaster, a groupie
magnet, a charmer, a man accustomed to flashing a sexy smile and having the world drop
to its feet in awe. And, she reminded herself,
she knew the type. Her husband, Mr. Charisma
himself, had loved to be the center of attention.
And once Aurora could no longer give him

that, he'd moved on to manage musicians who also craved the world stage.

Lucia made meatballs and lasagna, which she served with an enormous bowl of Caesar salad and thick slices of garlic bread. Owen and Meg talked about the wedding with Lucia and Sam. Aurora noted that Loralee had danced with Jerry.

"My mother's been married many times," Meg explained to Jake. "Did she flirt with you?"

"Not at all," he said. "But I think she was the person who told Winter that she should always wear blue, to show off her eyes."

"That would definitely have been Loralee," Owen declared.

"But now you're the talk of the town," Meg had said, looking at Aurora. "Jerry must be going crazy with the Dahl closed."

"Jerry had other things on his mind. He's in California asking Tracy to marry him."

Meg's glass thumped to the table as she stared at Aurora.

"You're joking," Meg said, frowning. "I know he has this crazy obsession with her, but I never had the sense she felt the same way about him." She shook her head. "That isn't going to go well."

"No," Aurora agreed. "He left in a hurry, right after the meeting."

"Has he called you?" Sam poured himself another cup of coffee.

"No."

"He won't let it rest," Owen declared. "You have the best televisions in town. And the largest. We'd planned to hold all of the official watch parties at the Dahl. Surely Jerry must be trying to fix this with the council."

But that was the problem, Aurora realized. He wasn't. She refused to call or text him. He knew the situation.

And she knew hers.

So here she was, after several hours of great food, conversation and company. She'd heard Sam's explanation of the ongoing remodeling, laughed at Meg's version of her prewedding jitters and reassured Owen that the bear was in no danger of ever being moved from his corner of the bar. Jake had entertained them with stories of backstage disasters and Lucia had happily made sure they all had enough to eat.

Meg and Owen took Boo and left after Davey hugged the dog about a hundred times and Meg hugged everyone in the kitchen. Marriage already agreed with her.

"Thank you for a wonderful evening," Aurora told Lucia, meaning every word. "I haven't had a Saturday night off in a very long time."

"You should do it more often," Sam suggested, holding her jacket for her to put on.

"I think that's going to happen," she said, wondering if and when anyone on the council would contact her to negotiate a deal. But she didn't want to think about it, because she'd had a different kind of Saturday night. And she'd loved it.

Jake called upstairs for Winter, who descended with an elegant movie star grace, much to Aurora's amusement.

"Finally," the girl groaned. "I'm so tired. Two of them are asleep and Davey keeps counting his money."

"His money?" Lucia looked puzzled, but Sam smiled.

"He's saving for a new bike," he said. "I've hired him to help me in the new house."

They were such a family already, Aurora thought. After only a few months, Lucia and Sam had created something new and strong.

How had they done that? Someday, when she knew them better, she would ask.

"Get your coat," Jake said. "And thank Lucia for dinner."

"I love, love, love your meatballs," his daughter said. "They're better than in Rome."

"You've been to Rome?" Lucia asked.

She shrugged. "Only once. On a school trip."

Jake shook his head. "I should not be surprised by anything she says. But I am." He turned to Aurora. "Have you been to Rome?"

"Many times," she replied. "And Lucia's food is just as wonderful as anything I've eaten in Italy."

"Many times?" Lucia laughed. "You're going to have to tell us all about that one of these days."

"It was a long time ago." She hurried to change the subject before anyone could ask more questions. "By the way, Chili Dawg is going to be torn down next Friday. Tony might like to watch."

"Oh, that would be great. He can wear his hard hat and pretend he's part of it. From the other side of the road," Lucia added. She hid a yawn behind her hand. "Sorry."

"We're on our way," Jake said, ushering Aurora and Winter out the door. He pulled a flash-light from his jacket pocket and shone the way down the driveway to the sidewalk.

"You came prepared," she said. "I'm impressed."

"We do this almost every night," he said. "Take my arm. This part of the sidewalk is pretty rough."

She hesitated, then looped her arm through his. Their strides matched, and Winter scurried ahead of them as if she was in a great hurry to return to the B-and-B.

"How long are you staying?" Aurora thought of it as a way to make conversation, nothing more, but Jake winced.

"That's a big question," he said. "I've been here longer than I intended to be. Iris is kicking us out in another week. The other B-and-B is booked solid for the length of the show, too. I guess a lot of contestants are coming back for a reunion."

"And the TV people are promoting it," she added. She breathed in the cool air. "I love this time of year."

"Not too hot, not too cold?"

"Exactly. It could snow or rain. We had snow on Easter morning the first year I was here."

"And where were you before?"

She saw no harm in telling the truth. "New York."

"City?"

"Yes."

"You're a long way from home."

"This is my home." She kept her voice light, but it was the truth. The apartment above the Dahl was her home now, and she was lucky to be alive to appreciate it.

"So, what happened in New York? You told Winter you had a broken heart, which was very kind of you, by the way. She likes you."

"I like her, too," she said, watching the girl get farther and farther ahead of them. "It was a very ugly, very sad divorce." It was strange to say it in such a matter-of-fact way. Would *I had a breakdown and he left me* have been better? No. Probably not.

"I'm sorry to hear that."

She tried for a lighter tone. "That's why people sing the sad songs, right?"

"Yes, but I write happy ones, too."

They had crossed the park and were close to the More Than Willing house. Jerry's, larger and more ornate, stood next to it. Its windows were dark, which meant that the irritating man was still frolicking in Los Angeles without a care in the world.

Iris's house was lit from top to bottom, including the light on the front porch. Aurora could hear the television from outside. It sounded like basketball.

"I'm going in," Winter said, hurrying up the steps. "I'm tired. And I want to tell Iris about the horseback riding lessons."

"Wait," her father said. "We're walking Aurora home."

"You don't—" Aurora began, but Jake stopped her.

"I do," he said. "It's after ten, and I don't care how small a town this is, you shouldn't be walking alone at night." He called after Winter, "Tell Iris I'll be back in fifteen minutes. Stay in the living room with her until I get back."

"Sure. Good night, Aurora!"

"Good night, Winter."

They watched her until she was inside.

"An interesting child," Jake drawled, tucking Aurora's arm closer to his side when she would have removed it. She didn't want to be the object of such casual charm, the easy flirtatious way this man had of making her feel like the only woman in the world. She knew better, but she enjoyed the protective warmth despite her misgivings. The sidewalk was even here, and there were two streetlights illuminating the way.

"You're lucky to have found her."

"She found me," he said. "Or I should say, the lawyers did. Lucia hasn't told you this?"

"She hasn't said much, except that you hadn't been married long before your wife left."

"Yeah. The thrill of following the band had worn off and she wanted to go home."

"And you didn't want to move to England?"

"I never had the chance," he said. "Our marriage was a ridiculous mistake. I was relieved when she said she was leaving."

"And you didn't know she was pregnant."

"No clue. All I felt was embarrassed to have gotten myself into a mess like that. Merry was bipolar and had stopped taking her medications. She came from a wealthy family and she missed the lifestyle, so she left. She didn't want me to know about the baby because she was afraid she wouldn't be able to move back to England."

"Would you have stopped her?" Or would he have taken the easy way out and gone on with his life as if nothing had happened? She wondered what kind of a man he was, and hoped for his daughter's sake that he was ready to be a father now.

"No," he admitted. "But I would have gone over there to take care of my child. I don't think I would have trusted Merry, not at that time. She told me she'd met someone else and she wanted to go back to her 'real' life."

"Does Winter know that?"

"I've told her, but I don't think she believes me."

"I'm sorry," she said. "I'm sorry for both of you."

"Don't feel sorry for us," he growled. "I don't need your sympathy."

"That's not—"

"I just thought you should know that I'm not a deadbeat dad, that I am not the kind of man who walks out on my kid."

"Why?"

"Because," he said, frowning. "It just… matters."

"All right." She didn't know how to respond to that.

"We're here." He stopped in front of the Dahl. "Do you go in here or around the back?"

"Either way," she said, fishing her keys out

of her pocket. "It seems strange that it's so dark." She grimaced. "It's not a typical Saturday night."

"I'll come in and wait until you get the lights on," he said as she unlocked the door. "Besides, I want to see the bear Owen was so worried about."

She switched on the lights after pushing open the heavy door. The room smelled like furniture wax and stale beer. She blamed the old paneling for the beer. She waited for Jake to enter and then locked the door behind him.

"I don't want anyone to get the wrong idea and think I'm open."

"Wow." He stopped a few feet from the door. "This is a huge place."

"It goes back quite a ways." She gestured toward the back wall, behind the pool tables. "Back there are the bathrooms and storage. And the stairs to the apartment."

"Can I walk you up?"

She shook her head. "That's not necessary. And besides, I'd have to lock the door behind you after you leave." She pointed to the deadbolt lock.

He glanced around the room. "It's a great

bar, Aurora. You can tell it's been around for a long time."

"Since the town began." She ran her hand along the top of the bar itself. "Other buildings haven't survived. The man I bought it from inherited it from his father."

"And the bear," he said, eyeing the beast. "He's bigger than I imagined."

"I like him," she confessed. "I wasn't too sure at first, but now we're great friends."

"Iris said you usually have a band on Saturday nights." He walked over to the distant corner where large black speakers sat on a raised platform.

"I invested in my own sound system last summer," she said, sliding onto a padded leather stool. She watched him walk around the room, look at the two huge televisions that hung above the mirrored walls lined with bottles of liquor and beer taps, check out the two pool tables and eye the moose head next to the wall clock on the back wall.

"It's a great bar," he said, walking over to her. "Why did you buy it?"

"It was for sale," Aurora said. "I know that sounds glib, but it's the truth. I was here and it was for sale and I bought it."

"Just like that?"

"Just like that."

"Any regrets?" He sat on the stool next to hers and swiveled to face the room, just as she had done.

"No."

"You're a mysterious woman, you know that?" He turned toward her and smiled.

"Yes," she said, ignoring the way her body responded when he looked at hcr like that. She didn't want to melt toward him and hope he kissed her. She didn't want to run her palm along the hint of beard on that square jaw. She didn't want any involvement whatsoever. She liked her life the way it was, simple and un-complicated.

Jake looked at her for a long moment and then stood. "I've got to be going. Iris likes horror movies and Winter won't admit she gets nightmares. I'd better go before Iris starts making popcorn."

She slid off the stool and followed him to the door. "Thanks for walking me home."

"Sure," he said, bending to brush her cheek with his lips. He did it so casually and naturally that Aurora didn't have time to react, not that she would have stepped away. "Good night."

"Good night."

She waited for him to leave, then twisted the dead bolt lock shut and turned out the lights in the main room. She walked through the silent, dark room and around the corner to the stairs to her apartment. Her predecessor, Mick, had redone the place just a few years before he sold it. There had been a woman, he'd said, and she was particular.

Aurora thanked that unknown woman every day for the skylights, the hardwood floors and the modern kitchen with its granite counters and stainless-steel appliances. Not that she cooked anything, but they were there in case she ever had the urge. And they were sparkling clean.

At the top of the stairs she turned to walk down the narrow hall that led to the front of the building and its tall, narrow windows that overlooked Main Street. The kitchen took up one side of the room, and the living area took up the rest. What would have been the dining room table was Aurora's sewing space, and she liked spreading out her fabric and designing her quilts. At those times, she thanked Mick's girlfriend again for providing the extra light. She kept her extra fabric and quilting supplies in large plastic totes lined up against the wall. Someday she'd have shelves built for them, but for now she was content.

The far wall, covered in bookcases, the television and all of her audio equipment, concealed her bedroom and bathroom, which were both large and luxurious. There was no old pine paneling up here, just walls painted creamy white and a multicolored Oriental rug Aurora had found in an antique shop in Great Falls.

She didn't have a sofa, but instead used a chaise longue upholstered in ruby chenille and an oversize chair, which both faced the television, and a massive rectangular glass coffee table, something Mick had offered to leave for her when he moved South.

But Aurora rarely used the television. On the table sat a violin case, which housed the most important thing in her life. She loved to play the Pietro Guarneri, but rarely played anything more complicated than scales and simple runs. It was worth far more than the Dahl and the hot dog building. It was her most precious possession, not because she had loved it since she was twelve, but because it reminded her of what she'd had before her world ended.

Aurora bent over and reverently opened the

case to look at the violin. She lifted it carefully, attached the shoulder rest and removed the bow from its holder. Then she tested the sound, adjusted the tuning and practiced her scales for a brief but satisfying hour. Her fingering was a bit stiff, she noted. And she needed to work on her third position. She'd grown lazy.

Tonight, she thought, running through her practice routine, had been a lovely evening.

And yet it was good to be home. Alone.

ROBBIE LIKED TO USE Google. Winter owned an iPad, an iPhone and a small notebook computer, but she'd discovered that the internet service in Willing had its good days and bad days.

She'd give Robbie something to do. He'd be at his grandmother's all weekend and she kept him busy with chores during the day—his grandmother believed in chores—but she went to bed early and Robbie didn't do anything but text and tweet stuff. He also loved to research. He was one of the smartest kids in her school because he was relentless, his grandmother said. She boasted of his "intellectual curiosity," which Winter assumed meant that he was a snoop. He'd found pages and pages of information on Jake for her. She knew the names of his songs, the artists who sang them, the places he'd lived in and the names of his band members (former and present).

Her father loved spaghetti and detested golf. He collected guitars and wished he had a dog, not a cat. There were old rumors about him and Willie Nelson's daughter.

Winter wanted to know more about Aurora. The woman was the coolest person she'd ever met. And Jake smiled at her. And listened to her when she talked. If there was a chance that Jake was going to make Aurora his girlfriend, then Winter wanted to know more about her than that she had really impressive taste in cowboy boots.

What would Lady Mary, of *Downton,* do in this case? She would write to her aunt in London and she would get all of the information on anyone invited into her grand home and estate.

Winter had faith in Robbie. She herself had looked Aurora up on Google and found nothing but a couple of articles about the Dahl, which had its own Facebook page, but she hadn't had a lot of extra time to search. And after failing a few nights in a row, she'd given up.

She owns a bar called the Dahl, she emailed

Robbie. She used to live in New York City. Last name Jones. I think she's rich. She's been to Rome. Who is she? Can you find out?

CHAPTER SEVEN

HARVEY DAWSON'S RETIREMENT party was not held at the Dahl Sunday night, despite many attempts by various men in town to talk Aurora into opening it for a private party. Her Closed sign remained on the bar's door despite numerous complaints.

Aurora told everyone the same thing: until she got her building permit for an addition to the Dahl, the bar itself would remain closed, owing to renovations.

A group of loyal Chili Dawg customers met at the café Monday morning and bought Harve breakfast. Shelly reported to Aurora that there was definitely some hostility toward Aurora for ending people's chili-dog-eating habit. Meg passed out flyers that showed the new plans. And Harve explained to one and all that he was happy to get out of the hot dog business and thought he might get himself some alpacas for his place outside town. It was either that or buy a couple of new pickup trucks, one for him and one for his son, Harvey Jr.

Mike, Hank and Gary stood their ground, with Mike writing an editorial in his newspaper about newcomers not respecting history and tradition. Gary decided it would be a good time to visit a daughter out of state, and Hank kept fixing cars.

Aurora started screening her calls and stopped checking email. She started playing Strauss on the violin, just for fun.

"It's like a vacation," she told Meg. She'd walked to the café Tuesday morning to give Meg more flyers. "I'm working on a huge new quilt, one with lots of strips and tiny triangles. In blue and yellow and white."

"Coffee or tea?"

"Coffee, please," she said, sitting on a stool at the far end of the counter. She looked down the row of stools at the old men, who looked back. "Good morning, gentlemen."

They mumbled greetings but weren't enthusiastic. Aurora hid a smile. She'd dressed in her most outrageous Western boots, along with skinny jeans and a T-shirt that advertised Moose Drool beer.

"Is the demolition still on for Friday?" Meg plopped a cup of coffee in front of her.

"Absolutely. I hope the weather's good. I think we'll have a crowd." She set the stack of flyers on the counter. "I think the tourists are coming in already. Did you see the show was mentioned in *People* magazine?"

"I did. They called the town disheveled, dusty and quaint, and referred to the café as an eatery. You know, that really is a beautiful design." Meg picked up the top piece of paper and studied it. "You've combined the two buildings so beautifully, and I love the patio on the side and in the back."

"The new part will be brick, and set back from the sidewalk fifteen feet," Aurora said. "I'll put a couple of little tables out there, and flowers."

"I love the windows," Meg murmured. "Can I book the first party when it's done?"

"Nope. The first party is a women-only open house. You and Lucia are going to cater it." She smiled. "I hope."

"Definitely." Meg lowered her voice to a whisper. "I hope you're prepared. Jerry texted last night to say he'd be back tomorrow."

"Sure he will," Aurora said, taking a sip of coffee. "The show is going to start."

"He'll be in a panic," Meg cautioned.

"Good. Maybe something will get done. I'm not going to back down. In fact, the quilters are coming on Saturday afternoon for a sew-in."

"What's that?"

"We're making quilts for the Quilts of Valor Foundation, for wounded soldiers. We'll sew all day. I have plenty of tables and we'll set up a cutting station on the pool tables." At Meg's shock, Aurora added, "I'm covering them with plywood, don't worry."

"I still can't picture you sewing," Meg said.

"Really?" Her living room had stacks of fabric decorating every available surface now that she had time to sort and clean.

"You're not the most domestic person I've ever met, Aurora." Meg smiled. "Tell me about the pizza oven."

"Mama Marie is going to make pizzas, which I'll freeze. What else should I have for evenings?"

"I'll work on it." Meg leaned closer and lowered her voice. "I'm glad someone else will be doing food here in town, because I want to spend more time at the ranch. With Owen."

"Marie is your answer," Aurora said. "See if she'll take over the supper business for you. Turn this place into an Italian restaurant at night."

"Are you kidding?"

"Why not? She's talked about opening her own restaurant, but she hasn't done it yet."

"You're brilliant." She smiled. "Not domestic, but brilliant."

"I've had a lot of free time to think," Aurora said. "Owing to my present political difficulties."

George Oster leaned over. "Ms. Jones," he said, "you've closed the only bar in town."

"Yes," she said, bracing herself for another round of complaints, "I realize that."

He shrugged. "Stand your ground, girlie. You've got a right to do business, and don't let anyone tell you otherwise."

"Thank you, Mr. Oster. I appreciate that."

"Too much government," he grumbled. "That's the problem everywhere."

Meg handed him a flyer and winked at Aurora. "There you go, George. Maybe Mrs. Oster would like to see what's happening in town."

"She don't get out much," he said. "But she wants to know if that singer fella is going to perform anywhere around here. She's got a couple of his CDs and says she's waiting for him to do a show. Is he going to do a show? That'd sure make her happy."

"That's a good question," Meg said. "I'll find out."

"You can ask him yourself," Aurora said, feeling the tiniest bit of happiness. "He just walked in with Winter."

George waved him over and Jake shook hands with the man and greeted Aurora and Meg. Winter looked pale and unhappy, though she perked up when she saw Aurora.

"I called you," she said to Aurora. "But you didn't answer."

"I'm sorry. What's up?"

Jake explained, "I had intended to take Winter shopping for riding gear this morning, but Sam needs help. The lumber is being delivered and the construction guys have been delayed by a couple of days. He's going to need some help unloading the trucks."

"We're going riding on Thursday," Winter said. "Because school gets out early. It's Easter break."

"Oh, that's right," Meg said. "Lucia mentioned something about the boys coming out to the ranch. Great!" She smiled at Winter. "I'm glad you're getting to ride."

"I'm going to take lots of pictures." She held up her phone. "My friends in London will be so jealous."

"Not everyone gets to go horseback riding on a Montana ranch," Aurora agreed. "Unless they pay to stay on a guest ranch."

"Have you ever done that?"

"Uh, no," she said. "I've never actually wanted to ride a horse." Broken bones would have ruined her career. Her parents had protected her from any possibility of damaging her hands, arms and shoulders. Thank goodness. "So, what's the problem?"

"We're going tomorrow," Winter grumbled. "But tomorrow Lucia can't go with us."

Aurora wondered where this was leading. "That's too bad."

"I hate to ask you," Jake said, flashing her a smile. "But is there any chance you could go with us tomorrow? Winter refuses to shop with me unless there's another female around."

"He doesn't know what I need," the girl said, looking at Meg. "Maybe Mr. MacGregor could give me a list."

"I don't think you need a list," Meg said.

"Just jeans and boots with heels. A sweatshirt. Owen has riding hats he bought for the boys. One of those would be a very good thing to have."

"We'll buy you a special riding hat as well," she assured the child. Aurora looked at Jake, who stood behind his daughter and eyed the coffee. "Are you going to have breakfast?"

"Yes," Winter answered. "We came to ask you to go shopping with us, and if you weren't available, we were going to ask you which stores to go to."

"I know them by heart," Aurora declared. "Sit down next to me and we'll make a plan."

"You can have my seat," George Oster told Jake. "I'm heading home to take the wife to Billings to see her sister." He looked at Winter. "Are you in school yet, young lady?"

"There's only three and a half weeks left. It simply isn't worth it."

"Well," the old man said, slamming his hat on his head, "I guess there's always next year."

"If I'm still here."

"Well, that goes without sayin'." He said his goodbyes and limped out the door.

Winter settled herself on the stool and waited

for her father to do the same. "Will you go with us?"

"Sure," she heard herself say. "I'm on vacation right now."

Winter beamed. "I knew you'd say yes."

Aurora made the mistake of looking at Jake, who seemed happy that he was off the hook as far as shopping was concerned. He grinned at her. "I owe you," he said.

"Yes," she said, smiling in spite of herself. "I expect lunch. And ice cream."

"That's all? I could take you out to dinner, too."

Winter frowned suspiciously at her father. "Are you asking her out on a date?"

"I just might be," he said, looking somewhat surprised but pleased with the idea. His gaze met Aurora's as if daring her to accept.

"You can repay me in some other way," Aurora said quickly. Why on earth would he think she was going to go out with him? Had she given him the wrong impression?

"All right," the man answered, plucking a menu from its metal holder. "Let me buy you breakfast, then."

"That I accept." There, that was better. She

ran her hands on her thighs and wished he didn't make her nervous.

"Aurora?" Winter asked.

"Hmm?"

"You said we'd make a plan."

"Sure." She pulled her thoughts away from the past and concentrated on the serious child who waited for her attention. "You will pick me up at nine o'clock. By nine-forty we'll be parked in front of store number one."

"Excellent," the girl said. "And you don't have to worry about money." She took the menu her father offered her. "I have my own credit card."

"Which you are not using," her father said.

"My lawyer—"

"Stop it," he said, and his daughter closed her mouth. Aurora was impressed. The teasing father was gone and in his place was a man who meant what he said. He looked at Aurora. "We've had this discussion before," he explained, before turning his gaze back to his silent child. "I can and will take care of you."

Winter gulped and looked very guilty but didn't say anything. Jake sighed and put a hand on her shoulder. "Really, hon. It's going to be all right."

Aurora blinked back tears of her own and picked up her coffee. "I certainly hope you mean that, Jake, because your daughter's boots are not going to be cheap. And do you have any idea what jeans cost?"

Winter giggled and Jake shot her a grateful look.

"We'll stop at an ATM on our way to town," he promised. "I'll clean out an account."

Winter took a deep breath. "I feel like French toast this morning. With bangers."

"Excellent choice," Meg said, returning to the counter with Aurora's omelet just in time to hear her. "What about you, Jake?"

"The number three, scrambled," he said. He had a deep voice, with a sweet roughness that would translate into an interesting vocal quality. She would order his music on Amazon this afternoon and hear it for herself. Just out of curiosity, of course.

This wasn't good, she thought, reaching for the salt and pepper. She'd always been attracted to musicians, from the skinny Jean Benoit in the junior orchestra to a lanky bassist at Juilliard and then there were several crushes on very unavailable cellists. She loved the cello. Almost as much as she loved the violin.

And, of course, there was Sean. With no musical talent except an exceptional understanding of how to manage those whose world consisted only in music, he'd given her his heart and he'd turned her into an international star.

For a while.

She ate her breakfast and listened to Winter chat with her father about the difference between riding English and riding Western. Apparently she'd researched the subject and had memorized the information. Aurora was saved from having to participate when Jake's attention was diverted by the arrival of the drummer from Wild Judith, the local band that often played at the bar. He stopped to say hello to Aurora and introduce himself to Jake.

Jake asked about local jams and Adam—at least that's what she thought his name was— told him about open mike nights in Lewistown and Billings. That led to a discussion about songwriting, a class in Great Falls that Adam hadn't liked, how hard it was to get gigs and the possibility of getting some guys together to play some night.

"Maybe at the Dahl," Adam said, looking at Aurora. "Are you still closed?"

"Yes," she said. "I am."

His face fell. "Oh. Bummer. I was hopin' we could get Jake to play with us."

"Is there somewhere else we can jam?" This was from Jake, who ignored his daughter's groans. "Maybe Iris will let us."

"No way," Winter said. "She's not giving up her TV."

"Sam's house is torn up," Jake said. "How many people are we talking about?"

"I could get about ten or twelve, easy," Adam said. "More, even."

"Where do you practice now?"

"The bass guitarist has a barn we use in the summer. It's still too cold. Harve used to let us use Chili Dawg in the winter, but it was pretty small. Especially for the drums."

"Chili Dawg?" Jake turned to Aurora. "Is that a possibility?"

"It's being torn down. The power's shut off and so is the water."

"Bummer," Adam said once again.

"Come to the Dahl on Thursday night," Aurora said. "You can jam all you want." Because Jerry would be back. And there would be no karaoke, no musical entertainment in downtown Willing for the public to enjoy. She'd bet a lot of people would be calling their town councilmen to complain.

What a lovely thought.

"It will be a private gathering," she continued. "You'll have to come in the back."

Adam grinned and Jake looked excited.

"That'd be good," he said. "I've been going crazy wanting to play."

Winter rolled her eyes. "He practices all the time, but he doesn't sing. He just talks to himself and writes stuff down in an old notebook."

"That's called 'writing songs,'" Jake said, laughing. "That's how it works, hon."

He was handsome, charming and liked to laugh. He was also a man. A man who played a guitar and lived mostly on the road. Even if she liked him, she would keep her distance. Because even a little flirtation could lead to something more, and Aurora had learned a long time ago that it was easier, safer and smarter to be alone.

TIME WAS RUNNING out. He had to either head to Nashville or find a place to live. Iris wished she could let him keep his rooms, but she was booked up starting next Wednesday.

The television show was about to air, and

the excitement in the town had already begun. It was all anyone talked about. The guy who owned the newspaper was the only man who got engaged during the show, though Sam had heard there were other romances that were still moving along. So every edition of the Willing paper was filled with *Willing to Wed* news of some sort. Romantic recipes contributed by Lucia, decorating tips by Iris, beauty advice by the local hairdresser and a countdown to The Big Day.

Cora Crewe, the fiancée and soon-to-be reality television star, wrote a weekly article about antiques. She was about to open a shop on Main Street, Lucia told him. He spent his days helping Sam with his house. The man was determined to get the place under control before he and Lucia set a date for the wedding. Jake wondered why it mattered. Just marry the woman and get on with it, but Sam wanted the house ready. It didn't have to be completely finished, he'd told his older brother, but he wanted the master bedroom done.

With three little boys running around, Jake agreed that a private bedroom was an important part of a honeymoon.

And he was glad to help. They'd gutted the entire downstairs. The concrete had been poured, the lumber delivered and the crew to begin the center addition was coming Monday. Sam had an electrician putting in a new system and a plumber installing new pipes for the kitchen and bathrooms, but he and Sam were framing the kitchen themselves. Jake knew that Sam could have hired someone to do it, but he suspected his brother wanted to push the project along faster. And it was as good an excuse as any to spend time together.

"Spend the summer," his brother suggested. "Better here than in Tennessee."

"I've thought about it," Jake said. He'd thought about it as he drove Winter and Aurora south to Lewistown. He'd thought about it when he checked out the local music store and read the flyers on the bulletin board. *Keyboard player wanted for country-rock band. Spring concert to benefit the Arts Council on May 3. Open Mike Night every Wednesday at the Purple Cow.*

"What's to think about?" Sam wiped his hands on a rag provided by Lucia. "It's a great town. Winter's happy. There's a beautiful woman down the street."

"Meaning Aurora Jones."

"You two seem to get along." Sam chuckled. "Not everyone can say that."

Irritated, Jake tossed his hammer aside. "I don't know why people think she's difficult. She's a good person."

"You're absolutely right." His brother struggled to keep a straight face. "Hand me that level, will you? I've got to check this stud."

Jake did, still grumbling. "I've only been here, what, eleven days? It seems longer than that."

"You miss the music? Get a band together."

"If I'm staying, I need to find a place to rent. Preferably furnished. And right here in town. But I don't know, I'll have to find something to do."

"Is money an issue? You haven't touched the trust—"

"Have you?"

"Not yet, but I've got three boys to send to college."

"Winter doesn't need the money," Jake confided, looking out the window at the quiet street. Spring in Montana was an iffy season, he'd realized. There was rain, sleet and sometimes sunshine that didn't feel all that warm. Sunshine Lite, he thought. And wondered if that was a song title. "Her mother spent most of her own trust fund, according to the solicitors, but Winter's grandparents left her set for life."

"Lucky girl."

"Not so lucky." Jake turned from the window and surveyed the gutted room. "She's missed out on a lot. That goes without saying, I suppose. At least you and I had each other. And we lived at home."

"Though we wished we didn't."

"Yeah. Boarding school would have been a good deal."

Sam cleared his throat. "I'd be glad to pay you, Jake. You know I need the help and I want to get this addition done so Lucia and I can get married and get on with our lives."

Jake laughed. "Sam, do you have any idea how much money a hit song can make for the guy who wrote it?"

Sam shook his head. "Haven't a clue, big brother."

"If a big star records it and it's a hit? Easily a million."

"A million dollars," Sam repeated. "A million dollars?"

"Yeah."

"And you've had some hits?"

"Yes," he replied. "I have. Not with my re-cordings, but with the songs I wrote for other people. The big stars." He picked up the hammer again and prepared to knock out more studs in the dividing wall that was to be removed.

"So why aren't you in Nashville writing songs?"

"I like to tour. I like being on the road. I love playing music. And meeting the people. I can write songs anywhere," he explained. "Some are good and some suck. Some are pretty brilliant."

"So you could live anywhere you want," Sam said, brightening. "Then live here."

Jake shook his head. "That's the problem. I'm not sure I could stay in one place without going crazy."

"You've got a daughter now," his brother said. "Going crazy is the least of your problems."

"I need a plan," Jake said, banging the stud to loosen it. "I need to figure this out."

"I told you we'd keep Winter with us," Sam said. "But I don't think that's the best thing for either one of you. The kid needs her father."

"Yeah." Jake pulled the stud free and set it aside. "I just wish I knew how to be one."

"I CAN'T FIGURE out how to make him turn."

"Rein on the right side to turn left, rein on the left side to turn right," Mr. MacGregor said. He stood just inside the corral and watched the four of them maneuver their horses in the same direction.

Winter remembered that part, but she wasn't sure the horse, whose name was Icicle, knew the routine. Icicle, a gray mare with a white tail and mane, looked like a star. But she moved as if she was half-dead and seemed unable to walk fast.

Icicle finally responded to the touch of the rein on her neck and turned in the proper direction. Winter was almost grateful for the slow-motion turn, because it would be really embarrassing if she fell off a horse the first time she rode one.

Davey and his brothers trotted around the corral like miniature cowboys, much to Winter's envy. She longed to be that comfortable in the saddle and to feel so confident that she could actually speak to another person while guiding Icicle around the ring.

"You're doing great," Mr. MacGregor called. "You have a nice, light touch. Keep it up."

Easy for him to say. Meg at the café said he'd been riding since he was two. But having a "nice, light touch" sounded like a decent compliment. She would text that to Robbie tonight. Winter shivered, despite her hoodie and the warm socks she wore inside her new boots. They were Tony Lamas and they were aqua, with pointed toes and riding heels.

She loved them. Every few minutes she'd glance down and look at her boots in the stirrups because she couldn't believe she was actually riding. Her new American-made jeans were stiff, but Aurora had offered to soak them in fabric softener and make them more pliable. Her baseball cap was dark brown, with "The Dahl" embroidered across the front in red letters—even though she'd had to take it off to wear the riding hat Mr. MacGregor had supplied. A hard hat for first-timers, he'd said. Davey had whistled when he saw the new baseball cap and asked her where she got it.

She just knew he would try to get one, too. She kind of hoped he did, because he was a pretty nice little kid. She'd gotten accustomed to having three boys as her cousins.

They were loud and silly and mostly dirty, but they were okay.

Icicle snorted and bobbed her head.

"Give her a little kick with your heels," Mr. MacGregor said. "She's starting to slow down."

"Okay." Icicle's ears were pointed straight up and her attention was on something outside of the corral, toward the hills. She began to prance, so Winter grabbed the saddle horn to keep her balance.

"Squeeze your thighs and knees, that's right. And keep her heading around the ring."

Icicle obeyed, giving Winter such a thrill she thought she might start laughing. Just a few weeks ago she'd been expelled for her severe psychological issues, and today she was riding a horse in Montana while wearing real cowboy boots. She leaned over and patted Icicle's soft neck.

"Good horse," she murmured. "Could somebody take a picture?" she hollered. Her father, leaning against the fence, pulled her cell phone out of his pocket.

"Lookin' good, kid," he drawled, and held up the phone.

Winter smiled for the camera. She didn't know how long her father would stay here, but she wasn't going anywhere without a fight.

CHAPTER EIGHT

FOR ONCE THE lights on Main Street held no welcoming appeal. Instead, Jerry thought the town was almost pathetic in its dark and rain-misted state. There wasn't a soul around at ten o'clock, and except for the glow of lights at the Dahl, nothing indicated that anything was going on.

He slowed as he turned the corner and saw the Dahl. He stopped the car in the middle of the street and saw that the Closed sign was still on the door, but he heard music coming from inside. Aurora was up to something, maybe a private party. Well, there was no law against that.

She hadn't convinced Mike or Gary or Hank to ease up a little and vote for the permit, either. He wondered if there'd be some mean, high-powered lawyer sitting in his office in the morning. He'd bet Aurora knew a lot of mean people.

She would fight. Just the thought of tangling

with that woman made Jerry lean his head back against the leather seat and moan, which he did for several long, fulfilling minutes. The show was going to air in eleven days. He'd spent months publicizing it, planning the watch parties, inviting the press, readying the town and yet...

Jerry turned on his cell phone for the first time in three days. He'd taken a break from politics and publicity, from budgets and council members, from smiling and hand-shaking.

It hadn't helped his mood. He was alone and unloved. Tracy wouldn't take him back, wouldn't leave the Canadian director/former stuntman and ski champion and return to her Montana politician.

For all his pleading, he'd only proved that he was a pathetic excuse for a man. It was a miracle he still grew whiskers and spoke in a baritone.

The cell phone showed no calls or messages from Tracy. He sat there blocking the street, his headlights shining on the empty street in front of him, for long minutes. How long, he wondered, could he sit here without anyone noticing?

He should ask the county sheriff just how

often he patrolled the main street of Willing, but then again, who really cared? The music at the Dahl stopped suddenly, then started up again. He heard a drum riff and laughter, but then quiet. So it was a live band. Maybe those crazy Wild Judiths were practicing, getting ready for the festivities next week. Maybe they'd learn how to sing in tune.

Wouldn't that be something to look forward to?

Jerry knew he was anything but festive. Not only was his heart broken, but it had been trampled upon and then picked up like roadkill and fed to the hogs, just as old Lawrence Parcell described his ranching days back in the fifties. According to Bob, a lot of garbage was eaten by those enormous prize-winning hogs.

He closed his eyes again, knowing that his headlights were on and anyone who decided to actually get out of the house and drive down Main Street would see him and avoid a collision. Would the sheriff give him a ticket? Test him for alcohol?

There was nothing but coffee in his bloodstream. Miserable black coffee from two different gas stations between here and Billings. And candy bars. Snicker's Dark, to be exact.

He would explain his broken heart and resulting low blood sugar to any law enforcement individual who decided to make an issue out of the mayor sitting outside the local bar.

"Jerry?"

He didn't open his eyes. "What?"

"Are you all right? Should I get my emergency kit?"

"I'm fine." He opened his eyes to prove it, then turned his head to see Hip's face in the passenger's-side window. Horatio Ignatius Porterman was a decent man, tall and lanky, with an unfortunate drinking problem. He'd served time in Iraq as a medic and was the town's EMT, but he never drove a vehicle. His cousin Theo, a collector of used cars, took him wherever he needed to go.

"You might want to park. You know, along the curb?" Hip opened the door and peered in. The interior light hurt Jerry's eyes.

"Yeah, well, I was just checking on the Dahl. What's going on?"

"A jam." Hip smiled and lifted a narrow guitar case. "We might do a little Johnny Cash."

"Have a good time." When Hip hesitated, Jerry made a show of putting the car in gear. "Really. Go on. I'm leaving, moving on down the road, putting pedal to the metal and all that."

"You're sure?"

"Sure."

"Okay." Hip shut the door and Jerry stepped on the gas.

"Go have fun with the rest of the traitors," he muttered. "See if I care."

"NOT BAD," JAKE said, nodding to the bass player. "You did a great job with that, Hip."

The man, perched on a chair with his guitar in his lap, played a bass lick. "Like that?"

"Exactly like that." Jake eyed his band of musicians. Adam, the enthusiastic drummer, had called all of the members of a local band called the Wild Judiths, plus several local men who wanted to jam with a guy from Nashville.

"The name of the band came from the Judith Mountains and the river," one of them explained. "Seemed natural."

"It's a good name," Jake agreed. "I like it."

They'd played for three hours, taking turns with their own songs from their set lists to Jake's suggestions. He felt good, felt as though he'd come home. Here he was, in a bar, with guys playing music. His daughter was with

Lucia baking cookies for a Saturday-night fund-raiser at the school and would spend the night. She hadn't protested staying with her future aunt and the little boys, having spent several hours out at the ranch riding a horse.

Jake wanted to write a song about that old horse. He was that grateful for its apparent inability to move fast and therefore toss his daughter to the ground. Yes, there should be a hymn to old horses, because they made fathers breathe a little easier.

Adam looked at his watch. "I gotta go. Work tomorrow."

"Me, too," Hip said, turning off his guitar.

There was a chorus of groans from the rest of the jean-clad, unshaven crowd. Jake liked each one of them. They didn't have a lot to say, but they stayed in tune and with the beat. Not one of them could sing, but the lead singer and rhythm guitarist managed to stay in tune and remember most of the words to the songs.

"We'll do it again," Jake promised, setting his own guitar aside.

"I sure wish the Dahl would open," Adam muttered. "I talked to Hank and he said he's kind of embarrassed by the whole thing, but

Gary Peterson is the one who's really ticked off."

Jake leaned back in his chair. "Why? I mean, why would adding on to the bar be such an issue?"

Hip shrugged. "Gary's a traditionalist."

Adam snorted. "He's an old stick in the mud, that's what I think. The guy should be voted off the council. Heck, we're supposed to play after the show opens, you know? Now what are we supposed to do?"

"Mike's coming around," someone said. "I heard that from Maxine, who's helping Cora set up her shop."

Jake didn't know any of those people, but he knew he shouldn't be surprised that in a town this small there were few secrets.

Adam eyed his guitar. "I've been wanting to ask you all night. Is that an old Martin?"

"Yeah." He lifted it again. "A 2-44. From the nineteen thirties."

"Sweet." One of the other guitarists whistled. "I've never seen one before, but I've read about them."

"I've had it for years," Jake said. "It goes where I go."

"No kidding. If it was mine I wouldn't let it out of my sight."

Hip leaned over. "They don't make them like that anymore."

"No," Jake agreed. "They don't. There aren't many people creating instruments one guitar at a time."

Jake handed it to him.

"Go ahead. Try it."

It was another half hour before the men left the Dahl. Jake's rare guitar was examined and complimented. It was carefully held and played by four of the guys, including a shy eighteen-year-old whose father brought him along as a treat for studying hard on his midterm exams.

Jake was the last one left in the bar, and after he'd helped Adam carry parts of his drum set to his truck, he thought he'd better thank Aurora. He hadn't seen her since he'd arrived at seven. She'd unlocked the back door for him and seemed distracted. Plus, she'd had bits of thread stuck to her black T-shirt.

"I'm sewing," she'd explained, brushing at the thread. "Tell the guys the liquor's off-limits."

"I will. Thanks."

She'd disappeared back up the stairs. Somehow he couldn't picture Aurora Jones behind a sewing machine stitching up anything. He wondered if she'd mind if he came up just to say good night and thank her for giving him his sanity back.

He saw a light under the door at the top of the stairs and heard the television, so he knocked. "Aurora?"

It took a minute for her to come to the door, and when she opened it she blushed. "I'm sorry," she said, gesturing to her pink sweat pants and black T-shirt. "I didn't expect— Well— I thought everyone had gone home."

She looked adorable. Her silver hair was clipped into some kind of knot on top of her head and she was sprinkled with bits of thread and tiny pieces of fabric. Her feet were bare and she wore no makeup or earrings. Somehow the lack of jewelry made her seem younger. She stepped aside to let him inside.

"Come on in," she said.

"Sure." He followed her down a hall and into the large room that served as a living, dining and kitchen area. Fabric was piled along the back of an oversize chair in front of the television, and a large table near the kitchen held the sewing machine and several mountains of fabric and sewing tools.

"I've interrupted you," he said, fascinated by the mess. He'd expected her to live in a place that matched the dark knotty pine of downstairs, but this apartment was bright, with light walls and modern furniture. He noted the large windows and the updated kitchen.

"That's okay. My back was starting to hurt." She shrugged. "I've been sewing for hours." She picked up the remote from the kitchen counter and switched off the television, which had been featuring the weather. "Tomorrow's demolition day," she explained. "I'm hoping for sunshine."

"And will you get it?" He noted the quilted, intricately pieced wall hangings, the photographs of what must be her parents, standing in front of the Parthenon, and the shelves filled with books.

"According to the local weather channel, yes." She stood awkwardly near the table and then gestured toward an open bottle of wine on the counter. "Would you like a glass?"

"Sure." The invitation surprised him. Aurora seemed more relaxed here in her own place. He liked this side of her. He watched her retrieve another wineglass from a cupboard above the sink and then fill it halfway with a deep red wine.

"Chianti," she said. "A Classico. Enjoy."

"You like wine, then?"

She looked a little embarrassed. "Lucia and Meg tell me I'm a wine snob, but I grew up with parents who knew wine and liked to talk about it."

"I grew up with parents who liked wine, too," he said, smiling a little in self-deprecation. "And whiskey, rum, vodka and whatever else they could drink."

"I heard it was pretty bad," she said. "Lucia didn't break any confidences, but I got the impression you and Sam couldn't wait to leave home."

"It's no secret," he said. "I've given interviews and I've never tried to hide the fact that I ran away from home. My parents lived the high life, with enough money to buy all the booze they wanted and enough social standing to prevent anyone from questioning their children's bruises." He took a sip of the Chianti, which was surprisingly light. "It's why I don't write drinking songs."

"What kind of songs do you write?" She

started to clear a space at the table and then stopped. She gestured toward the chairs on the other side of the room. "I guess we'd better sit down away from the sewing."

He eyed the piles of blue, white and yellow rectangles and blocks. There seemed to be some kind of organization to the piles, but there were other small stacks of fabrics that were just piled up. "What are you making?"

"I'm not sure yet," she said, somewhat shyly. "I just keep sewing until it makes sense. It will be a quilt. Maybe a large one. I don't know."

So she was an artist or incredibly disorganized. Interesting.

"Where's Winter?"

"Spending the night at Lucia's. They're baking."

"Baking?" Her perfect eyebrows rose. "*Winter* is baking?"

"Reluctantly," he confessed. "She'd rather be on her iPad or texting or whatever it is she does to stay in touch with her friends, but Lucia needed help and Winter volunteered. There's no school tomorrow, so she's spending the night and Sam promised to take everyone out to breakfast."

"And to the demolition?"

"Oh, yeah. Matt, the middle one, probably won't be able to sleep tonight. He can't wait."

He followed her over to the living area. She gestured toward the large chair and perched on the chaise.

"Oh," she said, reaching for the violin. "I need to put this away."

"Wait." He set his wineglass on the coffee table and touched the fiddle. "You play?"

"A little. A long time ago." But she didn't meet his gaze. He lifted it, weighing the elegant instrument in his hands. The wood was exquisite, as was the craftsmanship.

"This is beautiful," he said.

"Yes," she said, her voice soft. "It is."

He tipped it in order to see inside for a clue as to who made it, but the light wasn't good enough. "What is it?"

"It's very old," Aurora explained. "It was a gift from my parents on my sixteenth birthday."

Jake didn't know a lot about violins, but he knew fine woodwork and he knew age. He knew beauty. And he knew this was no ordinary instrument. "And the sound?"

"Is spectacular."

"A sixteen-year-old girl with a violin like this? That's interesting." He tipped the violin over to see the flames of wood on the back, then gently righted it and admired the patina. "How old?"

She hesitated. "Approximately sixteen ninety-eight."

He very carefully handed it back to her and hoped his hands weren't shaking. "You said sixteen ninety-eight?"

"Yes."

"And who made it?"

Aurora sighed. "It's not important. And it's not something I want to become public knowledge. It should be in a bank vault, in a special room. But I can't bear to lock it up."

"So you play."

"Yes."

"By yourself."

"Yes."

"Well, that's a shame. But at least you play it and it isn't locked away. Will you play something? I've never heard a violin from sixteen ninety-eight."

"I only play scales," she said. "Just scales."

Jake smiled. "Just play anything at all. Scales are fine. I'd like to hear the sound."

She did not look pleased, but she held the violin and lifted the bow that rested on the table.

"I don't usually keep them out," she said. "But I heard the music tonight—by the way, you made the guys sound better—and I couldn't resist trying to play along a little bit. Just for fun."

"Were we too loud?" He watched her stand, adjust her feet and posture and lift the bow to the strings. The violin nestled under her chin as if it belonged there, as if it was part of her. Jake waited. The woman owned a valuable violin and had played when she was a child. Who gave a teenaged girl a violin like this one?

She'd said she was pampered and adored, he remembered. Obviously.

Aurora played scales effortlessly, bowing faster and faster, her fingers dancing across the strings. He noted the posture and the way she held the violin. She was classically trained. He'd shared the stage with enough fiddlers to recognize the difference between those who had been trained for orchestras and those who had taught themselves some bluegrass tunes.

And then there was the sound, big and rich and filling the room with beautiful, perfect, round notes. He'd never heard anything like it before. And he knew he was listening to an instrument that belonged onstage. Or in a museum.

And the woman, he wondered. Where did the woman belong?

"Please tell me you can play 'Orange Blossom Special.' Between the band and that song, we could bring the house down some Saturday night."

Aurora shook her head. "I've never brought the house down."

He didn't believe her. The speed at which she played the finger exercises—and that's what they were, complicated finger exercises meant to warm up for playing or practicing the hard stuff—meant the woman had serious skills.

"Play something," he said, when she'd finished warming up.

Aurora stopped and dangled the bow from her fingertips. "I don't play. I haven't in years."

"Why not?"

She paled, then removed the shoulder rest before turning around to set the violin and bow carefully into the case on the floor. Jake hadn't noticed it before. "It's no longer a priority."

"What does that mean?"

Aurora returned to the chaise and sat down. She reached for the wineglass she'd set on the floor. "It used to be important. But it's not part of my life now. I can't stop my finger exercises, but I don't haul out my music and run through various Bach pieces."

Jake wondered if that was really true. And if it was, could she be talked into actually playing again? He was curious, but he let it go. For now. "I guess, with the bar and all, you don't have the time."

"It's not that," she said, looking more and more nervous. "I don't love it the way I used to."

He thought that was a strange thing to say, but he drank the wine and pretended to believe her. He'd seen her face when she'd picked up the instrument and placed it under her chin. He'd watched her eyes soften, and her body melt into the notes. She'd only played scales, but she'd played them like a master.

Once again, the mystery of Aurora Jones intrigued him.

"You didn't tell me what kinds of songs you write," she said. "I should order your CDs and find out."

"Love songs," he said. "I write love songs. Slow, fast, in between. Those are my favorites."

She smiled. "Now, why doesn't that surprise me?"

"I've also written songs about dogs and trucks and going home."

He drained the rest of his wine. "And that's where I should go. Home. To Iris and the Red Room."

"How much longer are you staying?"

He shrugged. "Iris has guests coming in, so we have to move out before next Wednesday. Sam wants us to move here, or at least spend the summer, I don't know."

"What does Winter want?"

"She wants to ride horses. She likes it here. I'm not sure how she feels about me, though." He paused. "Do you know of any places around here to rent?"

"You want to stay here?"

"You look as if the idea that I'd want to live in Willing surprises you."

"Well," she admitted, "it is a little odd, considering you travel, and you live in Nashville."

"I have family here," he reminded her. "And I want to stay for a while. But not at the B-and-B."

"You could ask Jerry. Or Theo Porterman. He knows just about everyone in town."

"Theo is Hip's brother?"

"His cousin. He and Hip do odd jobs for a lot of people. Or you could put an ad up on the bulletin board at the café. And at the grocery store."

Jake took his glass over to the kitchen counter and left it there. He eyed the piles of triangles and rows of narrow strips stitched together in long rectangles. "I never intended to stay here for more than a few days. I thought I'd see Sam and move on."

"It's not a bad place," she said, following him over to the counter.

She took the glasses and put them in the sink. "There are a lot of good people here," she said reluctantly. "Your daughter will do fine."

"Yeah." He'd already figured that out. The child accustomed to boarding schools and field trips throughout Europe needed a home. She needed to return to her own house after school, eat supper with her father, visit with Lucia and Sam and the boys, go horseback riding out at the ranch and do all the things a typical kid did. She probably needed a dog, too. "Why did you decide to stay?"

Aurora shrugged and looked away. "It was like no place I'd ever been before. People said hello to me. The town was in the middle of nowhere and yet I felt as if I could be happy disappearing into it." She rinsed out the glasses, tucked them into a dishwasher and wiped her hands on a blue-checked towel.

"Disappearing," he echoed. "Why did you want to do that? Did it have to do with that divorce you were telling me about?"

She surprised him by smiling. "Hey, we all have our secrets, Jake. I'm not telling you mine."

When she would have brushed past him, he caught her by the hand. "You do surprise me." He gently held the long fingers that had lifted the bow and moved it so rapidly across the strings of the violin. "The violin, the sewing, the apartment…" He looked into those blue eyes and saw a woman who hid herself from the world. And he couldn't imagine why she'd want to do that.

"Jake," she said, her voice low. Just that. Jake. It might have been a warning, or an invitation. He didn't stop to think about it. Jake slowly tugged her closer and bent his head. Her lips were soft against his, sweet. His fingers framed her face as he kissed her again; he felt her hands touch his waist. The prickly, distant Aurora Jones was returning his kiss and he found himself reluctant to end what was happening between them.

Slowly, he lifted his head and looked down at Aurora.

"Don't expect me to apologize," he murmured, wanting to kiss the frown from her lips.

"N-n-o," she stammered. "Of course not."

"Nice kiss…. I felt the earth move."

Yes, there was her smile.

"That must happen to you a lot," she said, still smiling. She stepped back and away from him.

"You'd be surprised," was all he said.

She tilted her head and examined him. "Groupies?"

"No." He laughed. "I'm too old for all that."

"Ex-wives?"

"Only one. Look," he said, running his hand through his hair, "I'm on the road a lot."

"Yes," she said. "I'll bet you are."

"No—I'm not what you think I am. I'm rarely in one place long enough to have a relationship. I don't fall in love easily, I don't have one-night stands and…" He paused.

"And?" she prompted, studying him curiously.

"I liked kissing you."

She didn't look as if she believed one single word of it.

"You look surprised. You don't believe that

you've surprised me, too? That I liked kissing you?"

"Actually, no."

"I'm not sure I've ever had to convince a woman of that before," he said, almost laughing.

She blushed. "Well, you're a man, so I'm sure you like kissing, but you don't have to pretend it means anything."

"I don't have to pretend—"

"You don't have to talk about it," she said, urging him towards the hall.

"But I don't want you to think that—"

"Stop," she said, her voice pleading. "It's embarrassing enough. Could we just say good night and forget this happened?"

Not likely, Jake thought, but he said good night and Aurora followed him down the hall and down the stairs. She watched him collect his guitar and notebook and after he left he heard her lock the door behind him.

And there, he realized, walking slowly down the sidewalk, was another reason to stay in Willing.

Aurora leaned against the door and took deep breaths. Why had she encouraged him to stay here? It was pretty clear he was attracted to her, and if he stayed here, she'd have to see him every day. It put her in a very difficult situation. One she didn't want to be in.

She wanted to be alone. She liked her life the way it was. With absolutely no complications.

And no kissing.

"THE SHOW MUST go on," Aurora whispered to Jerry. She'd come up behind him, hoping to catch him off guard. "Isn't that what they say?"

"Yes." He sighed.

"And the show starts in what, ten days?"

"Cut it out, Aurora." He looked up at the sky as if hoping it would rain.

"Approximately two hundred and forty hours," she mused. "That's not a lot of time."

"No." Jerry stood on the sidewalk, staring at the Chili Dawg as if he'd never seen it before. He didn't even turn toward her, which was disappointing. She'd looked forward to seeing the fear in his eyes as he pondered the start of the show without every party, every event, every minute celebratory detail in place.

"It's a shame," she said. "Haven't you sent out invitations to the launch party? And wasn't I supposed to concoct a special drink for the occasion?"

"Love Potion Number 59490," he choked. "Also known as Zip Code of Love."

"Yes," she said, standing next to him in the surprisingly large crowd of people who'd come to see the demolition. "Didn't we work on testing flavors for hours?"

He groaned. "Just open the Dahl, Aurora. Just for the opening night."

"Just give me my building permit." She didn't want to be mean about it, but what the council had done went against everything Jerry wanted for the town, and he knew it. He'd let her down, and he knew that, too. "I've got a construction company lined up. If I can't start on time, they'll move to the next job and I could lose weeks. You know how it is. I want to get this done this summer."

"She wants to get it done this summer," Lucia, joining them, repeated. Meg was with her. "What's wrong with that?"

"Nothing," Jerry said. "I don't have a vote. I'm only allowed to vote to be the tie breaker."

"You can call an emergency meeting," Meg said, winking at Aurora. "You've done it before."

Jerry muttered something about being surrounded, but he didn't move from his spot on the sidewalk. The four of them watched the de-molition crew dismantle the one-story wooden building. Aurora saw Sam and Jake, with the four children, over on the other side of the street where they presumably had a better view. The three boys could barely contain their excite-ment, while Winter looked more interested in people-watching than men banging on boards.

Aurora wondered if Jake would ever kiss her again, which was not what she should have her mind on this morning.

Just because she hadn't been kissed in years was no reason to overreact. She'd chosen to live her life free of relationships, so there was no reason to let a simple kiss bother her when it could so easily be ignored and not repeated. And what was it about Jake that made her for-get her plan to stay alone? She was lonely, that was all there was to it. All of this romance going on in town was affecting her. And not in a good way.

"Can you believe this?" Meg pointed to the four women from her quilting group who car-ried signs that read I Vote For Aurora. Meg held another batch of flyers detailing the plans for the addition and passed them out to anyone who walked by. Aurora wore a pink T-shirt she'd found in Lewistown during her shopping trip with Winter that said Girl Power in broad silver strokes. She'd piped music into the street from the Dahl: a continuous loop of the old gospel standards, "Working on a Building" and "If I Had My Way."

"Inspired," Meg said, laughing as Patty Griffin's voice belted out an old song about tearing a building down.

"How was your trip?" asked Lucia, who stood next to Jerry and smiled at all the activity. "Are we all set for the show?"

"She dumped me," he stated, his voice flat.

"Tracy? Dumped you?" Lucia looked at Meg and Aurora as if to say *Did you know about this?* They shook their heads but didn't look surprised. No one had really expected Tracy to be happy in Small Town, Montana.

"I'm sorry," Aurora said.

"We all are," Lucia added.

"She wasn't good enough for you," said Meg.

"Absolutely not," Aurora said, when Meg elbowed her. "What happened?"

"She met someone else." He stared at the Chili Dawg, which was no longer the Chili Dawg, Aurora noticed with satisfaction. The sign was gone, as was the roof. A pile of old lumber filled a giant Dumpster set up along the curb, and more lumber joined it every few minutes. The four men assigned to the job looked as if they knew exactly what they were doing. Once in a while one of them waved to the crowd.

"I'm really sorry," Meg said. Lucia patted his back.

Aurora finally understood his distress over the text message. "Is that why you were in such a hurry to leave the meeting last week?"

"Yeah," he said, jamming his hands in the pocket of his fleece jacket. "She dumped me with a text. A *text*."

"Brutal," Aurora said.

"That's not very nice," Lucia agreed. "Not nice at all."

"You'll meet someone else," Meg assured him. "Think of all the people who will be coming to town soon. One of them could be the love of your life."

"Speaking of next week…" Aurora said. "And speaking of new women coming to town, and those women wanting a place to socialize, and those women wanting to meet the handsome, charismatic and charming mayor of Willing—"

"You're laying it on a little thick," Meg interrupted her. She turned to Jerry. "Call another meeting, get another vote and issue the permit."

"I'm grieving my loss," he said, then without another word to anyone, turned and walked away.

"He's going *home?*" Lucia was incredulous.

"I don't think he's himself," Aurora said, watching her nemesis trudge down the sidewalk. He owned the largest house in town, a huge white Victorian that fronted the park. Next to it was Iris's bed-and-breakfast, a slightly smaller Victorian with a larger front porch and a bigger array of summer flowers. Jerry had thrown himself into town politics and town improvement since he'd moved from California about four years ago. Or was it three? Aurora couldn't remember exactly, but he'd been here when she'd arrived and he'd been about to make an offer to buy the Dahl when she'd unknowingly beaten him to it.

"Harve is giving away balloons," Meg said, pointing to the man in the blue baseball cap and the white beard. He stood next to a helium tank and filled red and blue balloons for the kids.

"He said he had them left over from the

Fourth of July parade," Lucia explained. "That's nice of him."

Mike and Cora walked over and said hello. Mike looked embarrassed and wouldn't look Aurora in the face, but Cora chatted happily about her store and when she was permanently moving to town.

"Jerry's letting me stay at his place," she said. "Until Mike and I figure out when we're getting married. I don't really want to live together until then."

"I don't blame you," Aurora said. "After all this is over, you may not even want to get married."

Mike sputtered. "No, we're all set!"

"Some things, like marriage, shouldn't be rushed into," she continued. "Cora might realize you're the kind of man who doesn't want a businesswoman, such as myself, to have the right to build her business the way she sees fit."

"It's okay," Cora assured her. "Mike's going to vote for you at the next meeting, aren't you?" She turned to her fiancé. "It's good for business, remember? My business and everyone in town's business."

"I hate to see things change," he grumbled,

but Cora put her arm through his and gave him a kiss on the cheek.

"I know, babe," she said. "But you'd better get used to it."

"You have the votes now," Meg said, watching Cora and Mike head toward the street. Mike had his camera out, so no doubt the photos would appear in the next edition of the paper. "Mike, Les, Pete and Owen will vote yes. Even if Hank and Gary vote no, you get the permit. Congratulations."

"Thanks." She watched as Jake, Sam and the kids headed in their direction. Jake was smiling at her. And she could feel herself start to blush. "It's getting warm out here in the sun," she said, hoping that would explain her flushed skin.

"It is?" Lucia glanced up at the thin clouds above their heads.

"Maybe Owen could talk to Jerry about an emergency meeting," Meg said. "I wonder what the rules are for that."

Aurora forgot all about rules and meetings and votes when Jake caught her eye and grinned. He certainly was a handsome man, she thought once again. No wonder she'd let him kiss her.

Of course, she'd need to be a little more careful in the future. She had a lifestyle to protect.

"Sam wants him to stick around. He's worried about him."

"Why?" Except in his dealings with his daughter, Jake Hove looked like the most confident, self-sufficient man she'd ever met. Owen MacGregor and Sam Hove were a close second, but Jake had a charming smile and a charisma that the other men lacked. Aurora decided not to share that observation with Lucia.

"Jake needs help with Winter. Sam said Jake told him he's not going back on tour."

"Because of his daughter?"

"I would think so. But he's a carpenter. He worked construction for years while he was trying to break into the music business. He and Sam are both pretty good at it."

Yes, they looked like the kind of men that would be pretty good at most anything they set their minds to.

"He told me he's looking for a place to rent."

"Really? He told you that?"

"Last night. After the jam."

Meg and Lucia exchanged glances. Then Meg chuckled. "You're blushing and he's smiling at you and heading this way. What happened last night?"

"Absolutely nothing." But her friends didn't believe her. She could tell by the way they laughed.

CHAPTER NINE

AURORA WAS CLEARLY enjoying herself, he noted. Meg and Lucia stood near her, talking to various people who wandered along the street across from them as the demolition of the building continued. She looked like a Viking queen, tall and silver-haired and regal as she watched her building being taken apart board by board.

"Jake," Winter begged. "Can we go riding again?"

"If you ask me that again I'll take you back to Iris's. She needs help cleaning, she said."

"That's totally unfair."

"Yeah, well, even cowgirls get the blues."

Her brow furrowed. "Is that a song or a book?"

"Both. Maybe." He made his way through the crowd toward Aurora. It was only polite to thank her for the use of the bar last night. Besides, he wanted to see if she'd remembered the kiss. He was curious to see if she'd ignore him or smile.

The woman did not smile enough.

"I need to talk to Aurora," Winter said, striding off ahead of him. Winter had lost that standoffish expression and seemed to be more comfortable around her new family.

He caught up with her as Winter was telling Aurora about her horse and a couple of older men stood by impatiently. Meg and Lucia were occupied with a group of women carrying picket signs.

"Aurora." One of the old men, built like a tank and wearing an old World Series baseball cap, broke into the women's conversation to get into Aurora's face. "Haven't you done enough?"

"Excuse me," she said to Winter, before turning to the man with the square head and short blond hair. "What's your problem, Jim?"

"My problem," he snapped, "is you getting over your hissy fit and opening that damn bar in time for the show. That's my problem, sweetheart. And it's a big one."

Jake stepped into the conversation, getting into the man's face. "Show a little respect," he growled. "There are ladies here."

"Hey," the man sputtered. "This isn't any of your business."

"I think it is." Jake angled his body so that Aurora and Winter were behind him. "You don't talk to Aurora that way."

"You don't look like a reporter." The man sneered. "And you can't be her boyfriend. So who are you? Get out of the way so I can say what I have to say. Someone's gotta teach that woman—"

Jake leaned forward and looked the man right in his gray eyes. "Last chance, bud. *Shut up.*" He kept his voice low, his eyes on Jim, and he curled his hands into fists. He was ready should this rude jerk do or say anything else threatening.

Jim blinked twice, then held up both hands in a gesture of defeat. "Hank doesn't need this sh—trouble," he declared. "He's gettin' calls day and night, people complaining, everyone mad at him."

"Hank's brother," Aurora whispered from behind Jake's back. She attempted to move to his side, but he kept himself between her and the irritated man. "Hank's on the town council, one of the men who blocked the building permit."

"I don't care who he is." Jake watched as Jim took several steps back, well out of range of a pair of swinging fists, and then scurried across the street. "He can keep his mouth shut and he can stay away from—"

"My women," his daughter said, completing the sentence for him.

Jake turned around and looked down at her. "That's not what I was going to say."

"In the movies," she said, her eyes glowing with delight. "In the *movies,* that's exactly what the hero would have said. *Stay away from my women.*" She giggled, for some reason absolutely delighted by what had just happened.

He wasn't sure Aurora was as amused. She stared at him as if he'd sprouted three heads and a pair of antlers. Lucia's boys were jumping up and down with balloons, hopefully distracting her from what had taken place, and Sam gave him a thumbs-up. Meg looked pensive and nodded at him before taking a balloon from the littlest Swallow boy, who looked so happy he was glowing.

"That was…interesting," Aurora said.

"He was bothering you," Jake tried to explain. "I couldn't let him do that."

Those perfect eyebrows rose. Those blue

eyes assessed him. "You think I'm upset with you?"

"Well…" he stalled. He assumed that was a trick question.

"I'm not."

"All right."

"I deal with rude men a lot," Aurora said, her gaze not leaving his. "I pretend I'm used to it, but I'm not." She leaned over and planted a kiss on his cheek. "Thank you. That was sweet."

"Sweet?" Why did that word bother him? His cheek burned.

"Uh-oh," Winter groaned. "Aurora, you're ruining it."

"Ruining what?"

His daughter sighed dramatically. "The scene. That's not how it goes in the movies."

"And how does it go?" Aurora asked, amused by the girl's frustration.

"You're supposed to fall into his arms with gratitude." She giggled. "He sweeps you off your feet and onto the horse and you ride off."

Aurora, her beautiful mouth twitching with suppressed laughter, turned back to Jake. "You don't have a horse," she said. "And if you try to lift me you'll fall down."

He moved closer so he could whisper in

her ear, "Sweetheart, you underestimate me. I could sweep you up and carry you out of here in a matter of minutes. Just say the word."

To his great amusement, she blushed.

IF SHE'D BEEN offered a million pounds, Winter couldn't explain why all these people were interested in watching an old building being torn down. She wondered how she would explain it to Robbie.

An old man gave away balloons while the hot dog shop disappeared.

He wouldn't believe her. Winter pulled out her phone and took a couple of pictures to prove it.

Robbie's grandmother would like this, Winter thought. She liked to say, "Things are not like they used to be," in a sad voice. But here, in Willing, things were the way they were, things were the way they used to be. Winter could blink and picture everyone in old Western-movie clothes and it would be the same.

She wanted to stay here. Jake could go be a singer on the road and live in his truck and write his weird songs, but she wanted to stay. The trouble was that there was no room at Lucia's right now. There would be, though, when the two houses were connected. She'd seen the rooms upstairs in Uncle Sam's house. He planned to fix them up, but not right away. She didn't need them to be fancy. And she only needed one room. And a bathroom, too, of course. And wireless internet, which was only natural.

But until then she had few options. She barely knew Meg and Owen, though it would be cool to live out on the ranch. Jake could pay them to take her in. It would be just like boarding a horse, she thought. But somehow she didn't think Jake would look at it that way.

No, she thought, looking at the tall, elegant woman waving at the men on the roof of the hot dog place. Aurora was her only option right now.

"Save the sign," Aurora called. "Remember? I said to save the sign! And any usable boards!"

Would she care about Winter's severe emotional issues? Maybe, maybe not. Jake worried about things like that, but Aurora seemed like the type of person who would flick them away with a wave of her hand. Like the queen, whose smallest gesture was noted and obeyed.

Flick! Problem solved. Flick! No more tears. Flick! You have a home.

"We need to find a place to rent," her father said, breaking into her fantasy.

"We do?"

"The TV show is going to start soon and Iris is booked up."

"We're going to *live* here?"

Her father misinterpreted her surprise. "For a while," he said. "It's no *Downton Abbey,* but Sam needs help with his house and you can take riding lessons and help Lucia with the boys. It could be a good summer."

"And then what?" She didn't want to trust this sudden good news. "What happens after that?"

"We'll see how it goes," her father answered. But he was looking at Aurora when he said it, and Winter wondered what he was thinking.

Flick!

If Jake liked Aurora, there was an even better chance Winter would be allowed to stay with her. Or when they broke up, would she be tossed aside, too? Or would Aurora keep her, like a souvenir?

"What's the matter?"

"I have a headache," she told her father. "Aurora is cool, isn't she?"

"Very."

"I wish I knew her better." Meaning, *I wish you'd take me with you next time you jammed at the Dahl so I could check out her apartment.*

"Yeah," he said, his gaze on Aurora. "Did you know she plays the violin? I saw it last night."

"Aurora?" Winter couldn't picture her as a musician. A model maybe. Or a skier. Aurora looked like an athlete, not someone who played a violin.

"The violin was very old," he said. "The oldest I've seen outside a museum." He turned back to Winter. "You ready for lunch? We can walk over to the café and get burgers. I told Sam we'd meet him there."

"Sure." The hot dog store was now just a skeleton. Lucia and Sam had moved the boys over to the Dumpster, which was something little boys would be impressed with. Meg was talking to Aurora, who was still giving orders to the men doing the work.

Did she want to live with someone who played the violin? Winter thought about that for the minutes it took to cross the street and head up to the café two blocks away. She could buy earplugs, of course. And she could pretend she liked the music. It would be the least she could do, when Aurora was her roommate.

"JERRY." LORALEE TOOK A seat across from him in the corner booth at the café, even though he tried to ignore her. Was everyone in this town completely oblivious of other people's feelings and pain?

"Jerry," she repeated, her floral perfume wafting toward him. Chanel, he thought. Tracy had worn Chanel, then switched to something organic. He didn't mind either one.

But not on Loralee, of course. He shuddered.

"Jerry, look at me, sweetie," the woman urged. "We have a show to prepare for. You can't quit now after all of your hard work, right?"

He lifted his head from where he'd been pretending to study the menu for the past ten minutes. "It doesn't matter. The show will go on without me."

"No," she insisted, "it won't. People are starting to arrive. Meg's cabins have been booked for weeks. I've had three people this morning ask if this was the town that was going to be on television. We need our mayor to be front and center on this."

"When did you start talking like a soldier?" He finally looked at the woman. She wore her waitress uniform today, with her wild yellow hair pinned up in a mess on top of her head. The dangly earrings were pink, as was her apron. As was her lipstick and the blush on her cheeks. Blue eyeshadow and dark eyeliner completed what he thought of as the Loralee Look. She would be at home dancing with old cowboys in old bars and being driven home by them in old trucks. He didn't want to like her, but most of the time she was harmless. And she was Meg's mother, so she had to be treated carefully. She drove Meg crazy, but Owen didn't seem to be bothered by having her as a mother-in-law.

"I'm repeating what George said this morning," she admitted. "Everyone is worried about you. First you let the Dahl close, then you disappear, now you're moping around town just because that bossy little twit found herself another man."

"Bossy little twit? That's not—"

"That's exactly what she is," Loralee insisted. "Take the blinders off, Jerry-boy, and smell the roses."

He moaned and leaned his head against the back of the booth. "Have you been drinking?"

"Very funny." She rapped him on the knuckles with her order pad. "Mike's going to vote yes. Owen's back from the honeymoon and will vote yes. All you need to do is call a meeting, take a vote and get the Dahl opened. We have a welcome party scheduled there for next Saturday night, with a 'Meet the Willing Men' theme. The guys will all be there to talk to the press and anyone else who is in town and wants to meet them. And then Sunday afternoon the quilting ladies are hosting a tea for the press. Iris has date maps and T-shirts for sale. Janet Ferguson is in charge of the Welcome to Willing goody bags, and your letter to incoming residents has been printed."

"I haven't written a letter."

"Meg wrote it for you," she explained. "It's very, uh, welcoming."

"Have you read it?"

"No." She looked up from her pad. "Does it matter?"

"I guess not."

"The ham dinner's tomorrow night, at the school. You're hosting. Les has the PowerPoint presentation set to run on a continuous loop out in the lobby. Meg has the schedule of events laid out. You want people to see their mayor moping over a *Californian?*"

"No." He hated to admit that she was right. Even though his heart was broken, he needed to pretend it wasn't. He was a man of action, an up-and-coming politician with his finger on the pulse of the town. He was a fool with a broken heart who no longer cared if any of the poor saps in this town found someone to marry, because he himself was heartbroken and alone. He was one of the pathetic, lonely bachelors now. His only hope was to find someone as wonderful and beautiful and smart as Tracy in the weeks ahead, as the tourists flocked to a town they'd seen on television.

"Man up," the waitress ordered. "Grow a pair and get with the program."

"Eloquently put," Jerry muttered, then reached for his phone.

"COME ON," JAKE SAID, grinning. "It'll be fun."

"Fun isn't how I would describe it." Aurora had intended to avoid him, had planned on sitting with the widowed quilting women to discuss the wisdom of assembling an impromptu quilting exhibit at the community center. Janet

Ferguson, president of the quilters association, thought it would show visitors that the women in Willing were a friendly and close-knit group and would welcome outsiders.

Plus, they were raising money to buy fabric for more Quilts of Valor Foundation donations. Through her attorney Aurora had made several anonymous donations already, but she was afraid someone would find out. She liked to keep her private business private.

"I heard you play scales," Jake pointed out. "If you can play scales you can play country."

"That's not necessarily true."

Darn that Lucia. She and her mother had nabbed Aurora the minute they entered the school lobby and wouldn't let her sit anywhere else but with them, Sam, Winter and Jake. As if they were already a little family.

"You can improvise," he assured her. "We'll just do it for fun after dinner."

"I didn't know you played the violin," Lucia said, removing a buttered roll from Tony's plate. "You can eat that after you finish your ham and broccoli," she told the boy.

"I don't anymore," Aurora insisted, trying to sound casual about it. "Doesn't everyone have an instrument they used to play?"

"The flute," Lucia said. "In fifth and sixth grade. I was awful."

"I tried Jake's guitar," Sam confessed. "But he got mad."

"You broke a string," his brother pointed out. "You were hammering away at it with a fork."

"Because you wouldn't let me use your picks."

"I'm gonna play drums," Davey announced. "Next year I get to be in the band."

"The world needs more drummers," Jake said, and Aurora couldn't tell if he was being sarcastic or not. He looked at her and smiled. "Come on, we'll play a few songs for the kids, sit around the living room, drink coffee, eat cookies and make some music."

"I also made banana cream pie," Lucia said.

"With my recipe," her mother added. "You're gonna love it."

"I have no doubt," Aurora said. Cream pies were a weakness of hers, and she wouldn't put it past Lucia to use that in her obvious attempt to play matchmaker. She was still remembering how he'd defended her, how he'd come to the rescue and told Jim Doughtery to back off.

She didn't remember anyone ever doing that

for her before. She hadn't been able to resist the urge to kiss his cheek, which seemed excessive now that she'd had time to think about it. The rest of the building had been dismantled, the boards either thrown in the trash or stacked neatly in the space between the Dahl and the now-cleared cement slab that had supported Chili Dawg.

Due to Winter's excitement about the music planned, Aurora let herself be talked into stopping at her apartment to get her violin before joining the rest of the Swallows, Sam, Winter and Jake in Lucia's living room, but she had no intention of playing it. Maybe she would have to squeak out a few scales, but she could say something about her strings being old or her bow being dirty. She wasn't sure how to refuse outright without sounding ridiculous.

Aurora had to take deep breaths as she set her case on top of the dining room table and opened it. No one but Jake had heard her play in four years. No one but Jake had seen her violin, her precious beautiful violin.

Winter stood next to her. "Wow," she said. "It's really pretty."

"Thank you." She lifted it and attached the

shoulder rest, then plucked the strings. The E string was a little flat, so she adjusted it.

"Dad said it's really old."

"Yes." She removed the bow from its holder and held it so her fingers wouldn't touch the horsehair. The oil on her fingertips could create a dead spot and she had had the bow rehaired only six months ago. She felt another flutter of panic.

Surely she could put the violin away now and say that it was broken. She could sit on the couch and eat pie and let Tony hug her with sticky banana cream hands. That would be good, she decided. She would like to hear Jake sing. And later, if he offered to walk her home, she would refuse and slip away without worrying that he would kiss her and she would like him even more than she already did.

"Good," she heard him say. "You're all set. Tuned up?"

She nodded, frozen.

"What's wrong?" He put his large hand on her shoulder. "You've gone white. Are you sick?"

"Nerves," she managed to admit. "The last time I played it didn't go well." The last time she played she'd had to leave the stage in disgrace and had fainted before she reached the privacy of the curtains. Sean had alternated between fury and shame, having witnessed too many of her panic attacks to worry that she was actually ill. *"It's in your head,"* he'd scold. *"Why isn't your therapist doing anything about this? Isn't there medication you can take?"*

"You don't have to play," Jake said, looking stricken. "I forced you into something you didn't want to do. I'm sorry."

Aurora took a deep breath and attempted to smile. She wasn't going to be judged; no one had paid for a concert. Her heart no longer grieved to the point of pain whenever she attempted to find solace in her music. "It's okay," she said, hoping it would be. "What do you want to play?"

He hesitated. "Are you sure?"

"I'll give it a try."

Jake gave her an approving nod, lessening her nerves a bit.

"Can you play by ear or do you need sheet music?"

"You go ahead and start and I'll try to fill in," she said. She didn't want to chance the sheet music turning into dancing black dots on the pages. She would improvise. She'd tried doing that while he was jamming last week and it had been surprisingly challenging and fun at the same time. She had been forced to listen to the music, instead of worrying about the perfection of sheet music.

"What's the difference between a violin and a fiddle?" Winter asked.

"Attitude," Aurora replied. She posed as a classical violin player would, then relaxed and touched the bow to the strings to tease a riff of slurred scales from the instrument.

"I can't believe you never told us you could play," Lucia said.

"I like to be mysterious," she replied, smiling at the truth of what she'd said. She sat in one of the dining-room chairs and made sure that when she played she wouldn't stab anyone with the bow.

"You must have other secrets, too," Jake teased, sitting in the chair beside hers and lifting his guitar to his lap. "I wrote a song about secrets once."

"Nice segue," she murmured. "So, go ahead and play your song. I'll try to keep up."

He strummed the opening chords, nodded to her and began to sing. She recognized the song from the other night. It was a simple melody, in the key of G, with a simple chord progression and a key change to A in the verse after the bridge. She set her bow on the strings and echoed the simple melody, finding her rhythm quickly. She didn't notice Lucia's expression of delight or Sam's surprise. She attempted harmony on the second verse, relieved to see Jake's approving nod. He played an intricate solo before the bridge.

"Your turn," he said, indicating he wanted her to play by herself. She shook her head. She was content to play backup. She'd never been in the background before, and her nerves melted away as the children clapped at the end of the song.

A CLUE. SHE had a *clue*. As soon as her father and Aurora finished playing—and they played for an hour—Winter dashed off to Davey's bedroom for some privacy and a chance to email Robbie. It was almost four in the morning in London, so she didn't expect to hear from him for hours.

Violinist, she wrote. World-class, Jake said. She attached a picture of the violin, only because Jake had made such a big deal about it being really old. Maybe it was a Stradivarius, though when she'd asked Aurora that, the woman shook her head and said absolutely not. That it was better than a Strad.

What was better than a Strad? She typed that question into the search engine of her iPad and found the answer.

"What are you doing?" Davey stood in the doorway and studied her with great interest. "Playing Candy Crush?"

"No." She rolled her eyes. "I'm researching."

"Why?"

"Because," she said, dismissing the question with a wave of her hand. "Just because."

"You want pie? Cookies? Chocolate milk?"

She looked back up at him. "Duh."

"Then you'd better hurry up," her oldest cousin said. "Tony's waiting for seconds."

Winter shut off the iPad and hurried downstairs. Research could wait, but she knew she was on the trail of something Big.

AURORA DIDN'T PROTEST when Jake said he'd walk her home. She should have, she knew. She was in dangerous territory here, having spent a comfortable evening in Lucia's living room, playing music with Jake.

He'd kept the songs easy, using the keys of D

and G so that she would have no trouble playing along with him. She'd never been one to improvise, having been taught to play the notes—the exact notes—as the composer had written them. She'd memorized more work than she could remember.

But it had been fun adding riffs and piecing together harmonies to Jake's singing of old country classics and his own, newer, compositions. The violin had sung, and she'd had to ease up on the bow to keep the violin from overpowering Jake's voice. Twice, when she was playing along with only the guitar, she'd unleashed some of the violin's powerful sound. She'd stopped herself from standing up and letting it fill the room, but she'd seen from their little audience's faces that they were surprised and impressed by what she could do with her violin.

Or, as Jake called it, her *fiddle*.

He walked her, and her fiddle, home. Winter hurried off to Iris's house, to research a paper on Western myths for Robbie, her friend from England. She barely remembered to say good night.

"She likes it here," Jake said. "She talked

Sam into taking them to the ranch Monday to ride again."

"Owen is a very patient man."

"Do you know him well? Sam said he used to live in Washington but came back to take over the ranch."

"He was going to sell it." Their shoulders bumped as they negotiated the sidewalk curb. Jake had the fiddle case slung over his shoulder, the way Aurora had carried her instrument many times, despite her parents' objections. "And then he changed his mind."

"Men do that."

"Yes. I've heard." She waited a beat, but he didn't comment. "You've changed your mind about touring this summer, I hear."

"I found a replacement."

"For the star and lead singer?"

He chuckled. "There's always a new star and a new lead singer. We're a dime a dozen. This particular kid just had a hit record—his third—and has sold more copies than my last two combined. He's happy about the tour, because he never expected to move this fast."

"You don't mind?"

"No." He glanced over toward her. "You don't believe me?"

"Not really," she admitted, but couldn't help teasing him a little. "Musicians have big egos."

"That's true, but I have a lot to make up for." He cleared his throat. "I need to make sure Winter is okay before I start thinking about going back on the road. If I go back on the road. It was my life for a long time and I do love it. I'm not sure what I should do."

They walked around to the back of the Dahl, where Aurora unlocked the door. Jake followed her inside and up the stairs as if he'd been doing it for weeks.

She flipped on the light in the hall and walked through to the living area.

"So," he said, setting the violin case carefully on the coffee table. "What's next for the expansion?"

"There will be a vote soon, and I'll have my permit. Mike relented, and Owen is back in town, so I have the majority. Loralee told Meg who told Lucia who told me that Jerry was going to call a meeting Monday morning."

"That's quite a communications system you have here."

"I've learned not to underestimate it," she said, watching him gaze around the room.

"You've built a life here."

"I have."

"And you're no ordinary violinist, are you?"

She ignored the question. "Thank you for walking me home."

"I guess that's my cue to leave," he said, but he took two steps toward the hall and turned around. "You're not as tough or as cold as you think you are," he said.

She'd already started to follow him, to go downstairs and lock the dead bolts after he left. So she was closer to him than was comfortable, close enough to touch.

He set those large hands on her shoulders and looked down into her face. "I look at you and I see a woman who has a lot of walls up."

"So?" She lifted her chin. "I like my walls."

He bent to kiss her, and despite her common sense and self-preservation instincts, she kissed him back. His hands moved to the back of her neck, his fingers tangling in her hair. She ran her fingers up his chest, underneath his down vest, to feel his heart beating rapidly under her touch.

He tasted of cream and coffee, and his lips were cool from the chilly night air. And she realized she was melting into him as naturally as if she'd been kissing him for years.

"No," he murmured against her mouth when he at long last lifted his lips from hers. "You don't like your walls at all."

He left her then, and she trailed silently behind to lock the door when he disappeared into the night.

Jake was right. She hated what she'd become. But she thought, with some sadness, that it was too late to change. She couldn't give her heart again, and cspccially not to a man whose talent was well beyond what could be contained in Willing, Montana.

She could fall in love with him, just a little, but it would still hurt to see him leave.

CHAPTER TEN

"I KNOW WHO she is." Winter brought her iPad to Jake. "Robbie spent three hours this morning looking up violinists."

"What are you talking about?" Jake was deep into Iris's breakfast, which this morning was a sausage-and-egg casserole topped with cheddar cheese. This was the best one so far. He'd told Iris she didn't have to cook, that they'd be happy to eat at Meg's, but Iris insisted. She said she had a reputation to uphold and there were going to be more people coming in soon. She needed to keep her skills up or she'd get lazy, she said, which was fine with Jake. He'd miss the ornate dining room and Iris's hints about singing in the local band. Iris was convinced that Jake and the Wild Judiths were going to set the county on fire with new songs and a star stage presence.

"Aurora is not Aurora Jones. She's Aurora Vandergren Joneston Linden-March."

Jake looked up from appreciating his excellent breakfast. "Winter, what are you talking about?"

"Aurora was famous." She handed him the iPad. "Look."

An official concert poster showed Aurora, not smiling, posing with her violin. She wore a long, fitted red dress and silver shoes. Her hair was loose and halfway down her back. She looked stunning and very young.

"Where did you get this?"

"I told you, Robbie searched online. He loves research. The really old violin was another clue." She took the iPad back and swept her fingers across the screen until she found what she was looking for. "Here," she said, handing it back to him. "The Pietro Guarneri of Mantua."

He looked at a photograph of a violin. In the caption it said it was owned by Aurora Linden-March and had been purchased for her when she was a child. The music world had been shocked, but the child had grown into an impressive soloist.

He was stunned. The woman who played a Guarneri, the woman who gave concerts in

Europe, the woman who played scales above a bar in Montana…this was the same woman?

"It's bloody amazing," his daughter said.

"Watch your language."

"Bloody is not swearing in Montana," she countered. "No one knows it's swearing."

"I know it's swearing," he said, continuing to read the article. "So cut it out."

She sighed, something long and dramatic, but Jake paid no attention as he continued to read.

"The Pietro Guarneri is believed to remain in the possession of the Linden-March family. Hans Linden-March and his wife, Martine Vandergren Linden-March, were killed when their plane collided with another in Frankfurt, May 2008. Aurora Linden-March has not performed publicly since 2009."

So Aurora was a world-class violinist, who'd left the stage and moved to Willing.

He'd been right to call her mysterious. He'd sensed the walls she'd erected around herself, but he hadn't known the extent of them. She'd said she no longer played, and yet she practiced her scales on that priceless violin. If she no longer cared about music, she would have sold that violin years ago.

She'd lost her parents, so she'd left the stage. The grief must have been debilitating.

"Her parents died," Winter pointed out. "And she came to Willing. Just like me. An orphan."

He looked across the table at his fair-haired daughter with the blue eyes and serious expression. "You are not an orphan."

She shrugged. "I was, after Mummy died. I didn't *know* I had a father until Mummy's solicitor explained it to me."

"But you do," he said. "You do have a father."

Winter didn't answer immediately. And when she finally spoke, Jake's heart contracted painfully.

"I know you mean well," she said, looking down at her plate with her unfinished casserole growing cold. "But I think you should get on with your life."

"Get on with my life?" He wanted to reach across the table and pull her into his arms, but he resisted. She merely tolerated his occasional hugs and stiffened when he threw an arm around her thin shoulders. She didn't know him, didn't think of him as a father. She called him Jake and rolled her eyes when he spoke.

"I can stay here," she said, looking at him with such an intense longing that he blinked.

"I can live with Aurora. She doesn't have anyone, either, so we'll have each other."

"You also have Lucia and Sam," he pointed out. *And you have me,* he wanted to roar. But instead he lifted his coffee cup. "You'd better get dressed," he said. "We're going to look at places to rent today."

"How long are we going to stay? Can I go to school here? Can we buy a ranch? Do I get my own horse? We can keep it at the Triple M."

"One question at a time, and the answer is that I'm not sure," Jake admitted. "It's almost May. Let's spend the summer here and see how it goes."

"See how it goes," she repeated, looking as if she wanted to scream at him, but her Lady Pettigrew training restrained her. "What does that mean?"

"It means," he said, taking a sip of cold coffee, "there's a lot to consider before moving here permanently." He had a profession he loved, a condo in Nashville and now a daughter who didn't fit in either one. But was the answer here in this small town? He thought it might be, but now that he had a child he couldn't afford to make any more wrong decisions.

He had to do everything—*everything*—right from now on.

Winter picked up her fork, and he looked down at the iPad, wondering if he actually was looking at a photo of Aurora's beloved violin. No wonder she'd treated it as if it were solid gold. "And, Winter?"

"Yes?"

"Keep this information private," he said. "This is nobody's business but Aurora's."

"I can't tell her I found her on Google?"

"Absolutely not. This is her business and it stays her business. Got it?"

Winter hesitated, but she nodded. "Got it, Jake."

Someday, he thought, she'd call him Dad. But he wasn't going to hold his breath waiting for it to happen.

"THE SHOW MUST go on," Jerry muttered to no one in particular. Aurora, busy wiping already clean tables placed strategically around the barroom, paid no attention to him. She'd grown tired of his moping, and as much as his previously cheerful personality had annoyed her, she found herself missing it.

"Yes, you've said that about twenty times

this afternoon," she said, barely restraining the urge to throw a damp towel at him as he sat in the corner. He was supposed to be folding the programs.

"You should be nicer to me," he grumbled. "I called a meeting, I got the vote, you have your permit to build your girlie bar—"

"Please don't call it a girlie bar."

He sighed. "All right."

Aurora wished she'd invested in new chairs. These had started to look pretty worn, though an antiques dealer might say they had a nice patina. "I'm thinking of calling it Dollies."

He groaned. "Dollies? Really?"

She winced. "It was Janet Ferguson's idea. The quilters came up with suggestions when they were here last week, and that was the favorite. I'm afraid that no matter what I call it, Dollies is going to stick." She wished she'd taken pictures of the women with their sewing machines set up on the pine tables, with cutting mats on the covered pool tables and the grizzly holding a decorative basket of scraps like Red Riding Hood heading to grandmother's house. She'd set up appetizers on the bar, along with a margarita machine that served mango, lime and peach flavors. Everyone said it was the best workshop ever.

Four of the quilters asked her about Jake Hove. Wasn't he handsome? Had she heard him sing? Was she going out with him? Was he really staying in town? Janet had even brought one of his CDs, so they'd listened to his songs of love in the country while they stitched red, white and blue star blocks.

Yes, yes, no, she didn't know. Those had been her answers, which had satisfied no one.

"Tracy was going to do a reunion show." Jerry wandered over to the window and looked out at the street. "She changed her mind."

"We don't need her," Aurora assured him, joining him at the window. Every parking space on the street was taken, and tourists had been wandering around all day. Aurora had kept the Dahl closed all week and would finally reopen at five o'clock, three hours before the first episode of *Willing to Wed* aired. The official watch party would begin at seven o'clock, and the donations collected at the door would go toward the fund to purchase new uniforms for the school band. After the show, there would be a dance, with the Wild Judiths and Jake providing live music.

Willing was about to turn Monday nights into New Year's Eve, Valentine's Day and Mardi Gras, all at once.

"Easy for you to say." He pointed to the tall man across the street. "Look, there's your new boyfriend."

"He's not my boyfriend," Aurora insisted, but she did feel a flutter in her belly as he crossed the street and headed toward the Dahl. It was a beautiful afternoon, windy but sunny. He looked pleased with himself and amused by the number of people sharing the sidewalk. She hadn't seen him in a week, which had surprised and disappointed her. He had walked her home from Lucia's, kissed her with great enthusiasm and then…nothing.

"I'm going to ask him to perform at the finale party at the park," the mayor said. "Do you think he'll still be here in eight weeks?"

"He's looking for a place to rent for the summer." Only the summer. Winter might love horseback riding and baking with Lucia, but Aurora wondered how she'd manage in a rural school come August. Aurora thought Willing was a great place to raise children, but Winter had grown up in a completely different environment. As had Jake. The child might be able to adapt, but Aurora doubted the father could. She couldn't imagine what he'd find to do here in this town. Could someone spend all of his time writing songs? Jamming with amateur musicians? Attending ham dinners and watching reality television?

"Looks like he's coming over here." Jerry showed no signs of leaving. He was supposed to be here to help, but he hadn't done much of that. Aurora assumed he was lonely.

Well, that *was* the reason for most of her business. Except Jerry had never seemed like the kind of man to waste time.

Sure enough, there was a knock on the front door. And when she opened it, her handsome visitor grinned at her.

"Not working with Sam today?"

He looked as if he'd just stepped out of the shower. "We quit early." He stepped inside. "Sam's helping Lucia pack up all the food. Hey, Jerry." He wasn't quite as warm to the mayor, but he returned Jerry's nod politely.

"Hey," Jerry said.

Jake turned back to Aurora. "I stopped in to see if there was anything I could do to help."

"I think I'm all set. We're opening in ten

minutes," she said, ignoring the urge to step closer to him. "Does everything look okay?"

"It looks good. Are you glad to be open again?"

"I am. And the construction on the addition starts tomorrow. Only one week behind schedule." She couldn't help smiling, despite the fact that Jerry was watching them intently.

"I heard you're looking for a place to rent," the mayor said. "I have a house out of town for sale, if you're interested. It has potential. There are two new garages. In case you're looking for space for a recording studio."

"I'm set, thanks," Jake announced, leaning against the bar. "Mike Breen rented me an apartment in his building. It's small, but Winter and I will be comfortable. I was just there to sign the lease."

"So you're staying," she said.

His eyes, sparkling with humor, met hers. "Why do you look so surprised? I've learned my daughter is very persuasive." He grew serious again. "I think the kid deserves to stay in one place this summer."

"She must be happy."

"She told me she'd stay with you if I had to leave. She had it all figured out."

Aurora tried not to look too pleased. "Really?"

"She thinks it would be cool, she said, to live with someone who..." He paused.

"Who what?"

"Runs a bar. And Lucia told her that you don't cook and you have a freezer full of frozen dinners you buy from Mrs. Swallow."

She would have preferred that particular character flaw to remain private, but then again, not much that went on in this town was kept quiet. "Has Winter grown tired of kitchen duty?"

"She complains, but she likes it when Lucia teaches her how to bake." He smiled, but he looked uncertain. "I haven't seen much of you this week. You wouldn't jam with us Wednesday or Friday. Why not?"

"I've been busy," she said, which was true. The Wild Judiths had gathered at the community center a couple of nights ago to entertain the tourists and locals in an "authentic" Montana jam session, but although Jake had urged her to go with him, she'd refused. It was one thing to play in Lucia's living room, another to play in front of people she only knew from the Dahl.

She was afraid of having a panic attack.

"What?" He was looking at her strangely. "What's wrong?"

"Nothing." She banished the memory of not being able to breathe, of the pounding of her heart and the feeling that she was going to die. "I'm not used to playing with a lot of people."

"Then you'd better stick to playing with me," he said, his voice soft enough that Jerry couldn't hear him. "We could work on some of the old Texas swing numbers, the Bob Wills material."

Well, that was tempting. "I don't know...."

"Just the two of us. We'll go over a couple of my songs, and then there's the standard blue-grass, plus some Merle."

"Merle?"

"Haggard. All in the key of D. Can you work up some breaks?"

He meant solos, she knew. Once she'd learned the melodies, the songs were easy enough to play. She'd been lucky to have been able to play by ear once she really listened to the music. The riffs were simple but could easily be expanded into something tricky and challenging.

She didn't quite want to admit that she liked the challenge.

"I'm not going to play in public," she insisted. "I know what you're trying to do."

"I'm trying to put together a decent band," he admitted. "And we need a fiddle player."

"Put an ad in the paper."

"No way. Not when there's one right here in town. With her own rehearsal studio." He waved to the corner where the sound equipment was set up. "See? You're a natural."

"Forget it."

"You're having fun," he said, leaning closer. "I think music is in your blood."

Not anymore, she wanted to say. But instead she settled for an enigmatic smile and a shake of her head.

It would take more than the charm of Jake Hove to get her back on a stage.

IT WAS NOTHING less than a triumph, Jerry realized.

It was all his dreams come true.

Except that the woman of his dreams, the woman who had made those same dreams come true, couldn't be bothered to share it with him. She was in Victoria, in the arms of her Canadian lover, the muscled athlete who no doubt would play a future role in enhancing Tracy's career.

"Tell me," the seductive little redheaded reporter perched on the bar stool next to him purred. "How did you come up with this idea? It's totally brilliant, you know. Totally brilliant."

Jerry couldn't ignore her. He wondered absently if her red hair was one shade lighter than his or was it two shades lighter? On her it was attractive. On him? A subject of ridicule. His mother was the only person on the planet who thought it was attractive. Even Tracy had suggested lowlights.

"Your hair," he said, feeling the affects of his second zip code. "Do we match?"

She batted pale brown eyes at him. "We might. It's hard to tell in this dim lighting."

"The show is about to start," someone announced. He thought it might be Loralee, whose voice carried across time zones.

Aurora's five flat-screen televisions flickered to life around the bar. A round of applause and cheers erupted, but the only thing on was the *Jeopardy* game board, and three contestants battling it out over the two remaining Double Jeopardy categories.

A few long minutes later, the *Willing to Wed* promo filled the television screen. The graphic began with a vintage map of Montana; the camera zoomed in on the center. And a photo of a town appeared, and then the camera sped down the middle of Main Street. The music was Western, something like those old *Bonanza* shows. Jerry's heart started pumping so hard he thought he'd lose his balance and fall off the stool.

There he was, waving at the camera. The crowd in the bar cheered and booed, but it was good-natured heckling and he didn't take it personally. Who could?

And then it began, with the introduction of the Willing men stepping out of "Wanted" posters and twelve nervous and excited women climbing off a bus as the men greeted them.

The romance—and the salvation of a dying town—had begun.

Jerry blinked back tears.

AURORA, LUCIA AND Meg remained speechless for eight minutes after the ninety-minute premiere of *Willing to Wed* ended.

Aurora didn't mean to time it, but she looked at her watch when Meg finally spoke and she realized that the three of them had stood silently on the working side of the counter while the rest of their friends, neighbors, strangers, tourists and loved ones celebrated.

"We looked good," Meg breathed. "Except I need to start doing sit-ups again."

"The camera adds ten pounds," Aurora pointed out. "And you looked great. I, on the other hand, looked like a serious skeleton."

"I looked very short," Lucia managed, taking a sip of wine. She'd decided against sampling the zip code special earlier in the evening, claiming the caterer shouldn't get tipsy until after the event was over. "And did I hear Iris say she was going to start giving Zumba classes again?"

"She's going to have a full class," Meg said. "I hope I get pregnant soon so I don't have to take it."

Lucia brightened. "There's an idea."

"You might want to set a wedding date first." Aurora looked out at the happy crowd. The band members were carrying instruments in from the back and Jake was organizing the arrangement on the stage. Hip stood with cables in his hands listening to Jake's instructions.

Aurora felt a small pang of envy but quickly squelched it.

"Yeah," Meg said to her friend. "After bugging me about my wedding all winter, now it's your turn. When are you going to marry Fish Man?"

"When the bedroom is finished," Aurora told her. "That's what Sam said."

Lucia sighed. "I think we're going to have to get married, go off on a honeymoon and come back hoping the renovation is done. Otherwise it's going to take forever, and he'll be sleeping in the future kitchen classroom for months."

"No," Sam said, overhearing her. "I'm going to put Jake in charge and I'm going to get married." He put his arm around his fiancée. "The show has inspired me."

"Really?" Aurora thought the concept was a little frightening. The women, though nice enough, had seemed like aliens landing on a planet in a galaxy far, far away. The Willing bachelors had stepped up and put themselves out there to impress the ladies. She thought they would be television stars now. There was no doubt that women around the country would want to meet them.

"Yeah," Sam said. "I never, ever want to be a bachelor again."

"No kidding," Owen agreed, setting a tray of empty beer glasses on the counter.

"Poor Les," Meg said, watching the young man wander aimlessly around the room. Shelly hadn't come to the party tonight, choosing to stay home with her baby and go to bed early. Loralee was in the corner lining up dance partners. "His heart wasn't into being on the show."

"I can't wait to hear the band," Lucia said, leaning her head on Sam's shoulder. "I just want to dance a little while."

The boys were home with her mother-in-law, Aurora knew. And Winter was with them. Mama Maria had promised cream puffs and root beer floats, something all four children could not resist.

"Look at Jerry," Meg said, motioning toward the table in the back. "He's giving another interview, but this reporter looks a lot cuter than the others."

"They'll have lovely red-haired babies," Meg added. "If he gets over his broken heart."

"You have babies on the brain." Aurora refilled her wineglass. "Maybe you and Owen should head back to the ranch early."

"And miss the debut of Jake Hove and the *Willing to Wed* band? Are you kidding?"

Aurora felt the same way. She watched Jake give calm directions to the excited band members. He looked pleased to be up there on the stage. This was his world, after all, even if it was only a small stage in a very small town.

She realized she loved looking at him. She loved hearing him play his guitar. And his voice was rough and sweet and altogether seductive.

She was afraid that she was very, very close to being totally infatuated. Could she be any more ridiculous?

"So, when do I get a horse?"

Jake pulled up in back of the huge ranch house and shut off his truck. "Man, am I tired of that question!"

"I can pay for it myself," Winter insisted. "I can contact my solicitor and—"

"Your mother's money can go to fund your education," Jake repeated for, oh, maybe the seven billionth time. "I think I've said that before."

He was annoyed by a lot of things right now. In the almost three weeks since the show began, he'd moved into an apartment on First Street that overlooked a freshly painted real estate office and a yard of carved wooden animals. Hip Porterman was not only an EMT and a musician, but an artist, too.

Jake was especially fond of the elk, the largest carving. The bull stood about seven feet high and had a rack that would make a hunter weep. Hip said he'd probably never sell "Herman," owing to the size of the sculpture and the size of the price tag. But Hip didn't seem to care about the money. Or how many critters sat in his yard waiting for buyers.

As he'd told the other members of the band last night, he was doing an amazing business in Montana-shaped napkin rings.

"I want to buy Icicle," Jake's daughter said, ignoring his statement about education and money. "She's learning to go faster and we've bonded. And her nose is so soft."

Maybe these riding lessons weren't such a good idea, after all.

Owen had invited the Swallow boys and Winter out to the ranch to celebrate the last day of school. Classes had been released early, and Meg and Lucia had planned a party for the kids after they rode. Even Sam, intent upon finishing his new home as quickly as possible, had looked forward to stopping work early to go out to the ranch. They'd left a plumber, an electrician and detailed plans back at the house. The bedroom bridge was coming along nicely, and Sam had smiled twice today.

Boo, the black dog with the big bark, ran up to greet them. Winter jumped out of the truck and, with Boo trotting merrily at her heels, headed for the barn without so much as a good-bye. Jake took a few minutes to admire the Montana ranch and the impressive amount of open space that surrounded the property. The outbuildings appeared well cared for, though Owen had described the condition of the place after his great-uncle died as a run-down mess, a place that a real estate agent had suggested he bulldoze.

The rancher had had his work cut out for him, but it looked as if that work was paying off.

He'd been busy with the apartment, with helping Sam, who had grown increasingly con-sumed with finishing his house, completing a master bedroom and getting married as soon as possible.

His brother had grown very tired of being

alone. He wanted his wife. He wanted a wedding.

So Jake had given him twelve-hour days. Together, with the crew from Lewistown, they had made remarkable progress. Winter was content to be with Lucia or Meg or Aurora or even Mrs. Swallow. He and Sam, having spent so little time together in almost twenty years, found they were more alike than they knew. Both of them appreciated a job well done and were driven to complete tasks no matter how long it took. They formed an easy friendship, and the rare times they referred to their parents they did so with less bitterness, and with a determination to look toward the future. That, they had decided, was how they'd coped all these years. They both loved early mornings, good coffee—and lots of it—and little conversation before ten a.m. Jake was more outgoing, but Sam's sense of humor kept his older brother laughing, especially over the Swallow boys' antics.

He'd wanted to spend more time with Aurora, but his days and free time seemed to disappear. Besides, Aurora had been avoiding him, despite letting the band jam in the bar on Sundays, when she was closed. He assumed she was tired of hearing him ask her to play music with him. Just as he was tired of hearing about buying a damn horse.

Aurora pulled up behind him in her red SUV. She opened the door, then leaned back in to retrieve a bag of groceries.

"Hey," he said, hurrying over, "let me help."

"Thanks." She dumped it into his arms. "It's for the party. My contribution."

He looked in the bag and saw containers of cut-up fruit and bottles of lemonade. "Healthy."

"Lucia's instructions," she replied, getting her large purse out of the passenger seat. "I'd suggested beer and potato chips."

He laughed. "I owe you an apology."

"For what?"

"Bothering you about playing in the band." She started walking toward the back of the house, where the door to the summer kitchen was propped open. "Winter wants a horse," he added abruptly.

"There's a connection there?"

"Yeah. I'm pretty tired of hearing about that horse."

They walked in silence to the back of the house, until Jake spoke again.

"Look," he said. "I'm attracted to you. Really attracted to you."

He moved to block her from going inside. "Aurora, will you go out with me?"

"When?"

"Tomorrow night. We'll go to Lewistown for dinner. Or Billings, even."

She took her time thinking it over and then after a long moment he heard her say, "All right."

Jake stared down at her. She was totally composed, her silver hair pulled back in a ponytail that made her look younger. She wore jeans and old boots, but her T-shirt was bright blue under a denim shirt and her earrings were shaped like guitars. "You're actually going to go out with me?"

"You actually asked?" She smiled. "I thought you only wanted me for my fiddle."

"Well," he said, "I haven't given up the dream for that particular life highlight."

"As long as you don't ask me to play Orange Blossom Special or The Devil Went Down to Georgia." She groaned. "They're such clichés."

"A man can dream." He dropped a daring kiss on her lips before she could protest. "I've missed you."

"I've missed you, too."

"Have you been avoiding me?"

She looked surprised. "I've been busy."

He stepped aside to let her enter. He could hear Meg and Lucia talking, heard Sam's deep laughter and the clanking of dishes. Outside in the barn, horses whinnied and children laughed in excited, high voices.

He could get used to this, he told himself. There was more to life than playing music and touring the world. There was this, he realized. At least for now. But could it be enough?

Right now, at this moment, he didn't know why not.

CHAPTER ELEVEN

"LORALEE'S KNEE is acting up," Meg said, tossing salad in a bright red bowl. "And I don't know what to do about the café. Al doesn't want to work longer hours and Shelly is already working as much as she can with the baby."

Aurora sat next to Jake at the kitchen table and listened. Jake's knee rested against hers under the table, which made her want to giggle.

And she had never giggled in her entire life.

"Can you hire a manager?" asked Sam, who sipped iced tea and looked at home in the informal, old-fashioned kitchen.

"I'm not sure I can afford to," she said. "I'd hate to give up the restaurant, but it's getting hard running back and forth between the ranch and town. There's so much we want to do out here, and yet the café is the only place in town to get a meal. I can't close it."

"And when the babies come…" Lucia finished arranging sugar cookies on a platter and set it in the middle of the table. "Go ahead and help yourselves. You're all old enough not to spoil your dinner."

"That's why I love her," Sam told Jake, reaching for a cookie. "Did I tell you that she made me fall in love with her by bribing me with food?"

"Don't believe a word of it," Lucia said, pretending to move the cookies out of his reach. "That was Davey bribing him, not me. I played hard to get."

Aurora took a cookie. "Yes, you certainly did."

Sam turned to Jake. "Watch out for the women in this town," he said, his mouth full. "They're dangerous. In many ways. They lure you with cookies and bacon and pancakes and pie."

Aurora held up her hands in surrender. "Don't look at me! I can't cook."

"But you play the violin," Jake murmured. "And that's better than food."

"You play the violin?" Meg stopped what she was doing to stare at her friend. "I didn't know that. Did you play when you were a kid? Do you still play? Isn't it really hard?"

"Yes, yes and yes," Aurora replied, laughing again. "And it's just a hobby and I'm not very good."

"Right, not very good," Jake said, rolling his eyes. "I want her to play with the Judiths, but she's too shy."

"Shy?" Meg spoke the word as if she'd never heard it before.

"You're really good," Lucia protested, then turned to Meg. "Jake played for us and he talked Aurora into bringing her violin and playing, too."

"Where was I?"

"Out here on the ranch, with your new husband."

"Mom!"

A commotion at the back door put a halt to any more revelations, which Aurora appreciated…until she heard the intensity of the Swallow boys' voices.

Owen had followed the boys into the kitchen. "Jake?" He had his arms around Winter's waist. The girl was pale but silent. Her large eyes searched for Jake, and the second her eyes fixed on him she let out a low moan.

And that's when Aurora saw the strange, sickening, bent angle of Winter's left arm.

"Jake, I'm sorry," Owen said, his voice low.

"She just slipped off the horse and must have landed right on her arm."

"Icicle sort of stopped and I fell off." Winter's voice quavered, though she lifted her chin and attempted to look brave.

Jake was on his feet in microseconds, kneeling in front of his trembling daughter. "Oh, honey," was all he could say.

"I'll get a blanket," Meg offered.

"I'll drive," Aurora heard herself say. "You and Winter sit in the back. I can get you to town in record time."

"That's true," Lucia said, her eyes filling with tears. The boys gathered around her and Sam for reassurance. "No one drives faster than Aurora. We'll stop at the house and get your things and then we'll meet you at the hospital."

"Hospital?" Winter's eyes grew larger. "Hospital?"

"I think your arm is broken," Aurora said gently, taking the blanket from Meg. "You've had a riding accident. Now you really are a Montana girl."

Winter dared a smile. "I'm right-handed. That's good. I can still email."

"And use a fork."

"I'll carry you," Jake said, but Winter backed up.

"No, you can't touch my arm."

Davey peered at the broken area. "Does it hurt?"

"Not yet," she said, but she winced and looked away.

"You need pillows," Meg realized, running out of the kitchen again. "I'll meet you at the car!"

Aurora had never been so thankful for her oversize and comfortable SUV in her life. With Jake and Winter settled in the backseat, she drove as fast as she safely could manage. It was still a long drive, and by the time they reached the clinic in Lewistown, Winter had begun to weep large, silent tears. The shock was abating and the pain had begun to set in.

"I'm an awful father," Jake moaned, after Winter's arm had been encased in a cast. They were keeping her overnight to make sure she hadn't hit her head.

Owen and Sam had kept them company for an hour, but they'd sent them home. Owen felt terrible, promising to do whatever he could to make Winter feel better. Sam had sat wringing his hands and telling horrendous stories about near-death experiences in the Amazon.

Aurora had had to beg him to stop.

"I'm going to have nightmares," she'd told him. "Go home and tell Lucia that Winter is going to be fine."

"I've already called her. Three times." But Sam left, after patting his brother on the back. "Believe me," he said. "I feel your pain. We lost Davey in a snowstorm last year and it just about killed me."

"You *lost* Davey?" Jake looked as if he couldn't fathom such a thing.

"He was next door," his brother explained, turning pale at the memory. "With a dying woman. The one who... Don't ask."

"All right," he said.

Aurora once again ordered him to go home. She managed to get Owen to leave, too, once the gift shop closed. He'd bought two pink stuffed bears, a fistful of candy bars and three gossip magazines for Winter.

"Women are particularly fertile during times of high, emotional stress," she'd whispered so only he could hear. After all, how could one little lie hurt?

"Tea," she said, turning to the distraught father sitting next to her in the waiting area. "Or something stronger?"

He looked up. "What are you talking about?"

"Would you rather have a Coke or a cup of tea? You're in shock. You need sugar."

"Why did I let her ride a horse? Do you realize how big those animals are? I had a bad feeling about this. I should have listened to my gut. Maybe Merry knew what she was doing, after all. She wouldn't let Winter ride. Did you know that?"

"Your daughter is fine," she said, making sure her voice was confident. What did she know about children? "Kids fall off horses all the time."

"And you know this how?"

Obviously he needed more convincing.

Aurora shrugged. "I'm assuming," she admitted. "Given the fact that everyone in the radius of five hundred miles seems to own a horse or two. And the odds are high that people sometimes fall off them."

He lifted his head from his hands. "Aurora," he said, his voice low, "have you ever fallen off a horse?"

"Of course not! I wasn't allowed to do anything that would hurt my arms or shoulders or hands." She put her arm around him. "Look, Daddy, she's going to be fine. Two doctors, two nurses, the woman at the desk and the guy with the bloody face we sat next to in the waiting room have told you that."

There was silence for a long moment. And Aurora had a horrifying thought.

"She's never been musical, has she?" she asked. It was her left arm, the fingering hand. *The fingering hand.*

"No," he snapped. "I don't know." He leaned forward again and propped his head with his hands, his elbows on his knees. "I think she might be tone-deaf."

"Thank God." Aurora could breathe again.

"I've only been a father for a month and she's already in the hospital. She's already *broken.*"

"She's fixed up nicely," Aurora assured him, patting his back again. "Come on, let's go see if she's awake. Or, hopefully, sleeping like a little cowgirl angel."

Since Winter was, after all, sleeping peacefully, they ended up spending the night. Jake stretched out in a blocky vinyl chair in Winter's room and Aurora curled up on the love seat in the waiting room. They would need a ride home in the morning, she told herself, which was why she had to stay.

Besides, they needed her. And no one had needed her in a very long time.

"I WILL RIDE AGAIN," Winter told her father when she woke up the next morning. He was stretched out in a chair and drinking coffee from a foam cup. A half-eaten bagel sat on a napkin on the wide windowsill. She didn't like the grim look on his unshaven face or his frown when she said the word *ride*.

"That isn't something we need to talk about now," Jake said, running his hand through his hair. "But we will. Horses are dangerous. I didn't know how dangerous, but I should have guessed. I had a bad feeling from the start."

"You should take a shower or something," she said. Her arm ached, and so did her legs. Lots of stuff hurt, but her arm hurt more than anything else. "Aurora can help me get dressed."

"Lucia sent clean clothes."

"Cool." Her jeans probably smelled like horse manure. And she didn't want to smell that all the way home.

He stood and looked out the window. "You were safer at boarding school."

She stared at his back. "Are you kidding me?"

He turned. "What?"

"You're not sending me back," she declared, very close to tears. She blinked hard, willing them away, but the tears overflowed and ran down her cheeks. "I won't go!"

He was at her side in two steps.

"Sweetheart," he said, gathering her carefully against his chest as he sat down on the edge of the bed. "It's okay."

"No—" she sniffed "—it's not. You're going to send me back and I won't go, I just won't."

She felt his chest heave as he sighed. "No, you don't have to go. I admit, it did cross my mind, but you and me?" He drew away from her so she could see his face. "We've got to stick together."

"I—I know," Winter managed to tell him. "Because we don't have anyone else."

"That's not exactly true." But he hugged her against him again and she went willingly, her cheek resting against his plaid-shirted chest.

THE WILD JUDITHS played their Saturday-night gig at the Dahl without their star. He was tend-ing to his daughter in their apartment, thankfully furnished by Mike's sister before she and her husband moved to Spokane, Washington, last year. The sister had left behind everything she didn't want to bother to move, which was a good thing for Jake.

He had quickly invested in new mattresses and a television, thus declaring it to be home, before the accident. Lucia had contributed sheets and blankets until he could get his own, and Mama Marie filled the freezer compartment above the refrigerator with individual servings of lasagna and meatballs.

Aurora, overwhelmed with tourists and the almost constant questions from the contractor, wondered why she'd ever thought that attracting people to Willing was a good idea.

"The tourists are everywhere," she told Jake, who had stopped by to thank her for her help at the hospital as if he hadn't thanked her fifty times since Friday night.

"Your mayor must be ecstatic. Isn't this what the town wanted?"

"Yes. Business is booming everywhere. Iris sold out of T-shirts and is printing more maps. The Judiths are playing Mondays, Fridays and Saturdays. Karaoke nights are standing room only and Meg has hired Marie to cook three nights a week."

She would open at five o'clock for week five of *Willing to Wed,* which aired at eight. Tonight was the show filmed at the MacGregor barn and was sure to be a highlight, as most of the town had been there to participate. "I don't open until one o'clock on most days just because I'd have people in here taking pictures and posing with that bear all day long."

"I wouldn't mind a picture with him myself," Jake said, glancing over at the grizzly. For some reason it wasn't wearing a hat.

"How's your cowgirl?"

"Anxious to 'get on with her life,' she told me."

Aurora laughed. "And what does that mean?"

"She sent me out of the apartment so she could watch *Downton Abbey* in peace, without my asking questions. I guess *Downton* is less stressful than a hovering father."

Aurora agreed. She had brought the DVDs of seasons one and two to Winter, along with a bag of Al's special scones. The girl had been thrilled, but Aurora could tell she was in pain. But that was Saturday, and Aurora hoped the last couple of days had seen improvement.

"I'll stop in later to check on her," she said. "If that's okay."

"Sure, but what about the show?"

"Theo and Hip Porterman are helping out tonight. They'll be here any minute."

"Ah, I see." He hesitated. "I came to ask a favor. A big one."

"How big?"

"Huge." He grinned.

"If this has anything to do with the band—" Not that she would admit she'd been practicing, because she wouldn't. Just because she liked playing his songs, and had been curious about the difficulty of "Orange Blossom," didn't mean she was going to bounce up onstage with her violin and make a complete fool of herself.

"It doesn't," he promised. "I need help making Winter a blue bedroom."

She immediately relaxed, letting out a sigh of relief. "I can do that."

"Good. She said you would be the right person to ask."

"I am. I am a world-class shopper. And I can do it all online and have it here in two or three days."

"You're bragging."

"You got that right."

"And," he said, smiling at her with those hazel eyes, "after you're done decorating, we'll play a few tunes."

THE PARTICULAR RIFF she'd chosen worked.

She could tell by the look on his face as she spun the notes faster and faster in triplets, then brought the tempo down to join with the melody. Jake nodded and picked it up, singing the third verse to one of his old songs.

"Wow," Winter said when it was done. "I wish I could clap for you."

"We have to do that onstage," Jake said, his eyes shining. "We just have to. It's too good."

"I'm doing this for fun, remember?"

He didn't look as if he believed her. "That's what I call fun," Jake insisted. "Man, I wish we could record this."

Aurora played for another hour, catching on to a new song that Jake wanted to rehearse. And she teased him with the opening to "Orange Blossom." She'd learned it, just to see if she could.

Piece of cake, compared to the Chaconne. Bach's Partita No. 2 in D Minor was a killer, fourteen minutes of the most intense music ever written for the violin.

Later that morning, after Jake walked her home, kissed her and hurried back to his daughter, Aurora carefully removed her violin from its case and tried the Chaconne. Just the beginning. Just to see if she could still do it.

She couldn't.

Which didn't seem to matter anymore. The night she was to perform it, the night she collapsed onstage, had not been the worst night of her life. The miscarriage at nineteen weeks of pregnancy had been much worse. And the death of her parents the month before? The loneliest time she'd ever known.

Sean's leaving her had seemed to be inevitable and not the crushing, shocking blow of death she'd had to absorb before that. She'd been relieved, perhaps. Because she no longer had to live up to his expectations for her. She no longer had to carry on each day as if she wasn't eaten alive with grief. As if she wasn't strong enough or smart enough to put the grief aside and continue to play. She'd been expected to carry on. And she'd failed.

But that had been five years ago. And she hadn't died. She'd bought a bar. And met a man, who had a child.

She was in love with both of them, the father and the daughter.

Jake had no idea who she was or what experiences brought her to this point in her life. She was a prickly, outspoken and independent person who feared no one.

But he liked her. He liked her very much.

And that was good enough. For now. She would create a fancy blue bedroom fit for a Lady Mary. She would accompany Jake in his country songs. She would smile for the tourists and promote the show and welcome one and all to her town. The construction was on schedule, and the weather was holding.

The party atmosphere in Willing continued. And the tourists kept coming.

"I'M NOT SURE how much more of this I can take," Jake complained. He and Sam surveyed the interior of his house. Most of it was finished. Lucia had to decide between stainless steel and marble for the counters, but Jake thought she was leaning toward stainless. There had been endless discussions.

He wiped his sweating brow with his sleeve.

"We're almost finished," Sam assured him. "And I can do the rest by myself, don't worry.

The bedroom is finished, and that was the most—"

"Not this," Jake clarified. "Aurora."

"Ah." Sam perched on a sawhorse. "You're spending a lot of time together."

"As much as she'll let me, which isn't a lot." He grimaced. "Winter spends more time with her than I do. And I hate to say this." He paused. "I'm jealous. Of my own daughter."

Sam snorted. "You'd better stop fooling around and get serious about the woman, then. All this father-and-daughter dating isn't working."

"No, it's not working."

"So, take the lady out on a date. Without Winter."

"The lady works constantly. That damn TV show has taken over her life."

"And you're playing music three nights a week," Sam reminded him. "Mondays, Fridays and Saturdays."

"Yep." He loved it, and the guys were improving to the point where he didn't have to direct them so much. They'd all stepped up their game, and the crowd appreciated the effort. They were drawing more people every night they played. Jake got a big kick out of it.

"Do you miss being on the road? On the big stages?"

"Sometimes. Not as much as you'd think." Jake took a sip from his bottle of water. Lucia was always bringing over food and drinks. Meatball sandwiches and chocolate chip cookies were his favorites so far. "I'd like to spend time with Aurora without either my daughter or the whole town around."

"Something's gotta give," his brother declared. "If you're really interested."

They stood there staring out the window at Janet Street for a long minute. Theo drove by and waved.

"Is this serious?" Sam asked. "Or just something to do while you're in town?"

"I don't do serious."

Sam glared at him. "Then stay away from the Dahl."

Jake cleared his throat. "I, uh, might be changing that," he said. "I like that woman. I, uh, really like that woman."

Sam shook his head. "You and Aurora, who'd have thought? But I don't know, it could be a match made in heaven." He eyed his older brother. "Just say the word and Winter can stay here. You know, while you take Aurora some-where nice and decide how serious you are."

"Thanks."

"She might not be serious about you at all," Sam declared cheerfully. "I'd be afraid if I were you. You could end up like roadkill, bloody and flattened like a pancake right there on Main Street."

"Yeah," Jake said. "I've thought that myself. She could hurt me."

"Yeah, she could. Real bad," Sam added. "But I have a feeling it's already too late."

"NOTHING WOULD HAVE prepared me for this," Lucia said. She motioned toward the crew of shirtless men parading around Aurora's con-struction site. Some were on scaffolding; oth-ers strode across the new roof erected above the addition. "They're *preening*."

"It goes on every day. You should see what happens on karaoke nights, when the Dahl is full. The construction guys end up staying in town to sing, and some of them are pretty good. Even when they can't sing they get a lot of ap-plause." She stood with Lucia on the sidewalk and watched the female tourists watch the con-struction workers. Friday mornings were no different from any other mornings now that the show had been on television for five weeks, with three to go. Curious women from all over the West had come to see if the men in Willing were available. Facebook fan clubs had been established. Pete had become an expert tweeter. Iris was leading tours, and Owen had had to put a gate on the ranch road to prevent strangers from driving right up to their house.

"I didn't know. Why didn't I know?"

"Between Sam, baking and kids, I'm surprised you ever get out of your house. Speaking of your house, how's the new bedroom coming along?"

She rolled her eyes. "Not as quickly as Sam would like, but it was his idea to wait for the house to be perfect before getting married."

"And he's regretting it?"

"I think he thought it would be finished by now. I've suggested a nice little ceremony at the county courthouse any morning, but so far he's not taking me up on it."

"How little a ceremony? Could your friends come?"

"You'd better," Lucia said. "I don't want a huge wedding like Meg had. Just the family.

You and Meg. And Mama. This won't be easy for Mama, so I'd like to keep it simple."

"No, but she's happy when you're happy." Marie's son had been killed when Lucia was pregnant with four-year-old Tony. She'd supported her widowed daughter-in-law with all of her heart, and she'd grown to love Sam Hove for taking over as a father to her beloved grandsons.

"What about you and Jake? You two have been dancing around each other for weeks and you both look a bit starry-eyed."

"We were supposed to go out," Aurora admitted, waving to Janet Ferguson who had stopped on the other side of the street. She looked as if she was giving directions to two elderly women and their poodle. "On an actual date."

"When?"

"The day after Winter broke her arm. Of course, that didn't happen. Which is probably for the best." Janet disappeared into the recently revived clothing store, where the window advertised a cowboy hat sale.

"She could have stayed with me any day, any night," Lucia said. "Why didn't you say something?"

"Jake wouldn't have left her," Aurora said. "He's been blaming himself for letting her ride."

"That's silly. It's not his fault. She loved it, and she couldn't have had a safer horse."

"And look what happened."

"But she was over here this morning and seemed fine. She's bouncing around with that cast as if it's not even on her arm."

"It's been two weeks," Aurora said. "He hasn't said anything about going out again, so I think he's changed his mind. I think I'm in the friend zone."

"Idiot." They both knew she was referring to Jake.

"No, I'm the idiot," Aurora admitted. "I shouldn't have fallen for him in the first place."

Lucia's eyebrows rose. "Fallen?"

She shrugged. "Well, maybe just a little." And then she pretended she didn't care. He'd turned out to be more than just a charismatic musician stopping in town to entertain his new daughter. The man loved his music, was devoted to a daughter he barely knew and committed to doing the right thing by her, even giving up what must have been a lucrative summer tour. He'd settled here, for the time being.

He'd been kind to the Wild Judiths and other amateur musicians in the area.

He'd completely charmed everyone in town, except for Hank Doughtery's brother, who'd deserved to be told to be quiet.

That memory made Aurora smile.

"I hope they're careful up there," Lucia said, squinting into the sun at the two men on the roof. "The women are distracting them."

"The whole town is feeling the effects of a matchmaking television show," Aurora said. "There's a strange vibe around here."

Lucia grinned at her. "Well, my friend, you would know."

HE STOOD ONSTAGE, played his guitar, sang his songs. He cued the band, kept track of the set list and nodded approvingly as more and more couples took to the dance floor.

Jake also kept an eye on the silver-haired owner with the blue T-shirt and skinny black jeans. She moved in and out of the crowd with ease, and yet spent most of her time behind the bar with Theo Porterman, a jack-of-all-trades here in town and a neighbor of Sam's. Theo, Jake noticed, kept a careful eye on the customers, the alcohol and the cash register. Aurora needed the help, what with the crowd in the bar on a Friday night.

He had it bad. She'd been there for him when Winter got hurt, she'd stayed and comforted his daughter, she'd created the blue bedroom of Winter's dreams in the modest little apartment above the newspaper office.

And she was an international star, a world-class violinist, an heiress and the owner of one of the finest musical instruments ever created.

Jake Hove was out of his league, all right.

At the end of the song, Jake removed his guitar and told Hip to take over.

"I'm gonna dance with my lady," he said, which made two of the Wild Judiths within hearing distance laugh.

"See if she'll sit in on a couple of tunes," one of the guys said. "We could do some old-fashioned Western swing and get the crowd goin'."

"I'll try," he said. "Play a waltz, will you?"

"Sure," the keyboard player said, hitting the opening chords to "Tennessee Waltz." "Good luck getting her attention."

He needed more than luck. He needed a crowbar to get through the crowd to the bar, and then he needed a bullhorn to call Aurora's name.

He didn't have either, so by the time he reached her and asked her to dance, the intro was over and Bob Carmichael was singing the first verse.

"Dance?" she repeated, looking harried.

"Dance," he said, pointing to the dance floor. "With me."

He might have sworn he saw her blush, but it was hot in the room and she'd been working nonstop since he got here. She said something to Theo, placed three bottles of beer on a tray and stepped around the end of the bar into his waiting arms.

"At last," he said, steering her into the crowd of dancers. "Have you been avoiding me?"

"No," she said simply. "I've been waiting for you."

He looked down into those calm blue eyes. She looked serious and formidable and altogether adorable, in her prickly Aurora way. "I'm sorry."

She didn't say anything, but she was in his arms and they were waltzing and he was so pleased with himself he wanted to break into song.

"I really am," he repeated. "Very sorry. I

missed our date. And I've been acting like Super Dad ever since."

"Understandable."

"I might not be as crazed now," he said. "Though I'm putting a stop to future riding lessons."

"O-kay," she drawled. "Good luck with that."

"Will you go out with me tomorrow night? A fancy dinner in Lewistown? We'll get dressed up and hold hands under the table."

"It's Saturday. I can't."

"Sunday, then." He willed her to look at him instead of the other dancers. "Come on, sweetheart. Say yes."

Her cheeks reddened even deeper, but in a pretty way.

"You're killing me," he muttered, holding her closer to him. "You're going to make me beg, aren't you?"

"Begging can be attractive in a man," she whispered against his ear.

"I will get down on one knee, if that's what it takes." But he couldn't help laughing as he spun her around the room.

"Desperation is also kind of appealing," Aurora said. "I like that in a man, too."

"Then I must be looking pretty good to you

tonight." He let his lips touch her ear lobe and felt her shiver.

"Possibly," she conceded, her body warm against his.

"Dinner? Sunday?"

"Mmm."

"I'll take that as a yes," he said, smiling down at her again.

"People are staring," she whispered. "Get that look off your face."

"What look?"

Aurora sighed.

"The I-want-to-kiss-you look?" he asked. He dropped his mouth to her cheek and paused.

"Stop teasing," she said, but he heard the laughter in her voice. "You know this will never work."

"This?"

"You're such a flirt." She sighed, but she made it sound like a compliment, so Jake didn't protest.

"What won't work?"

She laughed again. He wondered if she had been drinking her own wine tonight. "I've decided," she said, "not to encourage you."

"Too late," he said, tucking her closer against his body as they crossed the dance floor. "I'll pick you up Sunday at five o'clock."

CHAPTER TWELVE

"YOU'RE WEARING that dress," Jake said when Aurora opened her apartment door to greet him.

"This dress?" She looked down at the purple-and-yellow floral dress she'd worn for Meg's wedding. Tonight she wore cream heeled sandals instead of boots. She'd treated herself to a pedicure at Patsy's salon and had her toes painted a delicate shade of pink. She had, she admitted to herself, primped all day. And she'd loved every minute of it. She smiled to herself. His reaction had been worth the effort.

"I like that dress," he said. "It's the one you were wearing when we first met, when you thought I was going to rob the bar."

"I'm a suspicious person." Aurora sniffed. "And you acted odd, you know. Not knowing where your brother was and having a daughter who called you Jake."

He surprised her with a quick kiss on her

mouth. And then said, looking down with a frown, "I feel like I should have brought candy and flowers."

"Why?"

"To woo you properly."

She could feel herself blushing, something she only did when she was around him. "Wooing? That's an old-fashioned term."

"You have me flustered," he confessed. "I changed my shirt three times."

She eyed the one he had chosen. It was an ivory oxford shirt, with a button-down collar, and meticulously ironed. Tucked into dark brown slacks, it was a totally acceptable shirt. "There's nothing wrong with it."

"Thank God," he said, exaggerating his relief. "This seems so official."

"Official?" She locked the door and led him downstairs, where they left from the back door of the bar. "What do you mean?"

He didn't answer her until they stepped out into the small parking lot behind the building. He helped her into his truck and went around to the driver's side. He didn't answer her question until they were headed south on the road to Lewistown.

"It's an official date. I need to impress you,"

he said. "I could have taken you to Meg's. Marie Swallow is cooking an Italian feast."

"Really?" Just the thought made her mouth water. Marie made an eggplant parmigiana that rivaled anything she'd eaten in Rome or Milan, but Aurora had only tasted it once. "I didn't know she was cooking at Meg's."

"I understand it's going to be a Saturday-night tradition, to give the newlyweds more time together. Lucia told me that Marie is thinking about opening her own restaurant." He slowed the truck. "Would you rather go to the café instead of Lewistown?"

"No," she assured him. "We'd never have a private moment without someone coming over to the table."

"That's what I thought, too," Jake said. "I wanted to talk, just you and me."

"I'd like that. What exactly do you plan to talk about?" She smiled, surprised at how serious he looked. "Do you have an agenda?"

"Yeah," he said, stepping on the gas. "We're going to start with the story of our lives and go from there."

"Really?" Aurora wondered if it was too late to change her mind about going out for dinner. Over the last years she'd turned being private into an art form. Just the thought of revealing an ex-husband and a broken career was enough to make her wish for a microwaved dinner in front of the television set. "That might take a while."

"Sweetheart," he murmured, turning at the flashing red light on the corner of Main Street. "I hope it takes all night."

To stall, she asked him about his childhood and he shared the disappointments, the frustrations and the music that saved him from going crazy.

"I've been avoiding family life ever since," he confessed. It was a beautiful sun-filled evening, and the wheat fields stretched endlessly on both sides of the road. Aurora had slipped on sunglasses. "Marrying Winter's mother was crazy, but it seemed like a good idea at the time. I'm not sure why."

"And she never told you she was pregnant?"

"No. Merry was used to getting what she wanted. And what she wanted was to go back to England and marry someone who was very, very rich. Which she did, eventually."

"And he didn't adopt Winter?"

"No. He knew she wasn't his and, from what

Winter said, was nice enough but not at all interested in her."

"How sad."

"But that means I have her now," Jake said. "And I don't know what I'd do without her."

"She's a funny child. I like her."

"And she likes you. She thinks you're very glamorous and interesting."

Aurora laughed. "Most people around here have other ideas."

"They know how important you are to the town," he said. "Don't underestimate yourself. And wait until they hear you play the fiddle."

She groaned. "Please, you're not going to make me do that, are you?"

"Oh, yeah, I am." He glanced her way and grinned. "Every band needs a fiddler, and the Wild Judiths are no exception. We've got a big gig for the night of the finale, and you're going to be onstage with us."

She winced. "I don't know about that, Jake."

"I do. It's going to be an event they'll never forget."

They talked of other things for the rest of the drive. Sam's addition, Aurora's exhibitionist construction crew, Meg's plans for the ranch and Jerry's broken heart. Jake thought he was smitten with a reporter at the moment, but Aurora wasn't convinced.

"He's not himself," she said. "He won't argue with me, no matter how much I try to annoy him."

"And he likes to argue with you?"

"He loves it. Gives him a little spring in his step, you know?"

It wasn't until much later, in their quiet corner table at the Stockman Steak House, that their conversation grew serious. The waitress had cleared their plates, coffee had been ordered, dessert refused and wineglasses refilled. He took her hand across the table.

"Tell me this is not just me feeling this way," he said.

Her heart lurched and her fingers tightened around his. "It's not just you," she replied. "But it's a little frightening."

"I know." He smiled at her. "I'm more terrified than I've ever been in my life. I keep thinking you're going to push me away."

"You don't do well with rejection?"

He shook his head. "Not this kind."

"Neither do I."

"You were married once before."

"Yes." She took a deep breath. "I suppose this is the time to explain?"

"Yep." He squeezed her hand. "You can't remain a mystery forever."

She smiled at that. "Okay. A lot happened to me, all at once. My parents were killed, in a plane crash. They were in a private plane and, well, it was bad. I was five months pregnant at the time and I lost the baby."

"Oh, Aurora," Jake whispered. "I'm sorry."

"I started having panic attacks." She left out the part about the concerts, the collapses onstage, Sean's frustration and her inability to leave her house. That was a bit too much drama for an official first date. "And my life—and my marriage—fell apart. My husband was my manager and the fallout was, well, cataclysmic. It was a mutual decision to end the marriage," she added. A long moment passed before Jake said anything else. She could tell he didn't want to pry, and yet he wanted to know what brought her here, to Montana, at this point in her life. And she didn't blame him for being curious.

"So," he said, still holding her hand. "How did you end up in Willing?"

"I wanted to die," she confessed. "So I packed up the things that mattered to me, bought a car and started driving. I wasn't a very good driver—it wasn't something I did very often—so it took me a while, but I eventually drove into Willing." She frowned, trying to remember. "I was in Billings, right off the interstate, and I took a wrong turn. It took me hours to catch on that I was going the wrong way."

"And by then you were in Willing?"

"Yes. And, miraculously, I wasn't dead." She smiled at the incredulous man in the white shirt. "So I bought the Dahl."

He studied her, his expression serious and even sad. He looked as if he wanted to take her in his arms and make everything okay, but of course he couldn't. "You went from a world-class musician to buying a bar. On a whim."

"I wanted to be far away from where I'd been," she explained. "Does that make sense?"

"I suppose." He took a deep breath. "And you were happy."

"Maybe not happy," she admitted carefully. "But content. Content enough with what I had, I think."

"And now?" He looked as though he wanted to lean across the table and kiss her. But the expanse was large and there was a low votive candle and a bud vase between them. "Could you be happy now?"

"I don't want to be made a fool of, Jake."

"I'm not fooling around." His eyes darkened. "I'm serious about this, Aurora."

"I'm really too old to have boyfriends," she said, lifting her chin.

"And I'm too old to be one," he growled. "And if we don't get out of this restaurant soon, I'm going to have to come across that table and kiss you in front of forty people eating steak and potatoes."

"That's the most romantic thing anyone has ever said to me." She reached for her purse. "Let's go."

HE LIKED HER attitude. And he was relieved she'd finally told him why she'd run away to Montana. She'd lost her family, an unborn child and a husband who sounded like a man who hadn't been sympathetic. Reading between the lines, Jake guessed that Aurora had been on her own long before her marriage ended.

But no longer.

Jake settled the bill with a minimum of fuss and escorted his gorgeous date out of the restaurant, where in the shadows of the overhang and the privacy of an isolated corner of the building, he took her in his arms and kissed her.

Finally, he thought as her arms went around his neck and her head tilted to allow him closer. *Finally*.

"YOU HAVE COMPANY," Sam announced, when Jake stopped in to check on Winter. If she was awake, he'd take her home. If not, he'd pick her up in the morning. Winter liked bossing around the little boys and helping Lucia in the kitchen, but Jake wondered if her arm ached after a long evening of playing with the Swallow kids.

"Company?" He was still beaming from his evening with Aurora. They'd kissed. And talked. He'd driven her home and then, upstairs in her apartment, they'd played a few songs together. She'd perfected a stunning solo break for his third hit song and she'd worked up an arrangement for "Midnight on the Water." They would bring the house down during the finale party, he'd assured her. And she hadn't protested.

"Your band arrived tonight. They're on their way to a festival in Billings. I think they were in Canada a few days ago." Sam leaned against the counter in Lucia's quiet kitchen.

"My band?" Jake couldn't quite comprehend what his brother was talking about. "My band? From Nashville?"

"Yeah. Nice group of guys. They're camping in the backyard." Sam chuckled. "They seemed glad to get out of those vans. And the truck with the sound equipment is parked out front. Didn't you notice it?"

"Not really." Jake hadn't noticed anything but the lights on in the living room, meaning Sam and Lucia were still up. He wanted to tell Sam—well—he wasn't sure what he wanted to tell Sam.

"Winter's asleep on the couch. You should just leave her there, because she's wrapped up in a quilt and snoring. That is one funny kid. She's teaching Davey how to speak with a British accent and he goes around calling himself Lord Grantham." He frowned. "Or is it Lord Wrentham?"

"Grantham," Jake replied, going to the window to peer outside. He saw two tents but no one was around. The guys had always appreciated any excuse to camp. This particular group of musicians loved roughing it whenever they could and traveled with camping gear, propane stoves and sleeping bags. John, the drummer, never tired of telling them he'd been an Eagle Scout.

"Your lead singer went ahead with his girlfriend, but the guys here wanted to stop and say hello."

"Should I go out there?"

"Nah. They were wiped out. Lucia fed them and the bass guitar player took a shower."

"I owe Lucia for this."

"She enjoyed herself. They entertained us with stories about life on the road." Sam pushed himself away from the counter. "Go home and come back in the morning. I'll send them to Meg's for breakfast."

"Call me when they get up?"

"Sure." Sam smiled. "How's Aurora?"

"Beautiful," Jake declared. "Absolutely beautiful."

"THE THING IS," Manny said, stabbing his pancake with a fork. "We need you. Just for a couple of nights. That's all. It's a three-day show and all the money goes to help Paula. We figured you'd want to know."

"You figured right." Paula Davis had hired

him when no one else would. She'd given him his first break, backed his first album and made sure he had enough to eat. She mothered a lot of struggling musicians, but she also had a gift for spotting talent.

And now she had cancer. Insurance wasn't covering all the expenses, she was in danger of losing her Austin club and she needed help. Musicians were uniting in south Austin to raise money by doing what they did best: play music. It was to be a weekend event, with local restaurants donating food and distilleries donating beer. And it was going to start in six days.

"Then you'll come?"

"Of course."

THE PARTY AT the Dahl that Monday night would go down in history.

"People are going to be talking about this for years," Jerry said, sounding humbled as he looked around the barroom.

Aurora didn't disagree. Jake's friends and the Wild Judiths had combined into one large band, taking turns cramming themselves and their instruments on the tiny stage.

"The show was pretty good tonight, too," Jerry noted. "You can see how Mike and Cora are falling for each other. And you can't tell if Pete is heartbroken or not."

"They sure created a lot more drama than I remember," Aurora said, watching Jake help break down the equipment. The bar was officially closed for the night, though Jerry showed no signs of following the rest of the customers out the front door. "I didn't know that the girls were crying so much."

"Just ask Iris," Jerry muttered. "She started wearing earplugs because she couldn't take the whining."

"Wow. I missed that, thank goodness."

"Yeah. You saw them at night, all happy and dressed up and ready to party." He sighed into his glass of scotch. "But there was a dark side."

"There usually is." She turned on the faucet, rinsed the cloth in hot water and squeezed the excess water out of it before wiping down another section of the bar.

"I hear your boyfriend is leaving us."

"Yes."

"Going to Texas. Austin. Live Music Capital of the World." He sighed again. "They've got it all down there. A river. Good weather. Music venues. Tex-Mex. A university. Bats."

"Bats?" she asked as Jake turned and smiled

at her, holding up two fingers, telling her he'd be with her in two minutes.

"Big tourist attraction. I wish we had something like that."

"You wish we had bats?"

"Yeah. Thousands—or millions, maybe—come flying out from under a bridge every sunset. Tourists love it."

Aurora shuddered. "I can't imagine." She waited for a moment, wondering if he was through talking about the wildlife in Texas, before she refilled his drink.

"On the house," she said.

"Thanks." He lifted his glass. "Cheers."

"What about you? Are you going to be okay?"

"You mean about Tracy?"

"Yes."

"I'll survive. The pain is easing. And I still think she'll come to her senses and realize what a stud she could have had." He took a sip of his drink. "Wow. The good stuff."

"Special occasion." She smiled as Jake headed toward her from across the room.

"Good luck with that one," Jerry muttered as he swiveled on his stool to see who she was smiling at like a lovesick fool. "You know, if we can get him to stay, we could turn Willing into the Live Music Capital of Montana."

"He's staying," she assured the mayor. "He's staying."

"I WANT TO GO," Winter said, watching her father toss his clothes into a duffel bag. His guitar case stood by the door, and a bag of music sat next to it on the floor.

"Not this time. Another time. We'll go down for the SXSW Festival one of these days."

It was annoying how he could put his foot down and say no to her, just like that. She didn't like being left behind. She didn't like it one bit. They'd been together since Seattle, since she got off the plane and trudged to the baggage claim, where Jake had stood holding a sign so she'd recognize her own father.

"I can't believe you're leaving," she yelped. "It is so not fair!"

"I told you," he said, using his irritating Calm Father Voice. "It's a fund-raiser for an old friend who has cancer. I need to be there."

"You can take me with you."

"I can't. There will be too many late nights and too much going on. I don't know where I'm staying and I won't have anyone to look after you. You can't go with me, not this time." He stopped packing and wrapped her in his arms. "I'm sorry, sweetheart."

"Yeah," she sniffed. "Me, too. At least I have Aurora."

"And Lucia, Sam and the boys. And Meg, Owen and everyone at the café," he reminded her. "And Mama Marie."

"But I get to stay with Aurora," she reminded him. She liked staying with Lucia and Sam, but the cousins? She couldn't picture living with those three noisy little boys for a week.

"Yes." He kissed the top of her head. "Remember what I said."

"Respect her privacy."

"That's right."

"Don't worry, Dad," she promised. "I won't do anything to mess up what you've got going."

"You just called me 'Dad.'"

"It's okay," she assured him, pulling away from the hug. "You're starting to act like one."

"Which is a good thing?" His smile was movie-star handsome.

"Most of the time," she conceded. "Except about riding horses."

"We'll talk about that when your bones heal,"

Jake said, turning back to his packing. "In the meantime, stay away from Icicle."

She looked down at the cast on her arm. "It's not like I have a choice."

"I love you, kid."

Winter couldn't look at him. She felt her throat tighten and she wanted to cry. She sort of loved him, too, though she wasn't going to get all soppy and tell him that.

"You're going to miss karaoke night," she reminded him, following her father down the stairs. "How can you miss karaoke night?"

"I'M NOT SURE if I should act like a mother or an aunt or a much older friend," Aurora told Meg. She'd taken Winter to the café for breakfast, and after filling up on pancakes and eggs, she'd joined Loralee and Shelly to play with the baby in the far corner of the room. Little Laura never failed to attract attention whenever she made an appearance at the restaurant.

"Whatever you're doing seems to be working." Meg took a sip from her coffee and winced. "This tastes funny. Does your coffee taste funny?"

"I'm drinking tea."

She pushed the mug away from her. "When does Jake come home?"

"Today's the last day of the concert. He's supposed to fly back to Billings Monday or Tuesday." She watched Winter laugh along with Shelly while the baby made faces at them. "I like that child."

"You seem to have a family now," her friend said. "Is this turning out to be serious?"

"It feels that way," Aurora offered. "When we're *together* it feels that way. And he left me his daughter. That's saying a lot."

"I've seen the way Jake looks at you." Meg eased herself out of the booth. "He's a man in love. I'm happy for both of you. And now I have to go throw up."

Aurora watched Meg scurry across the room to the narrow hall behind the counter that held the cash register and the gum. Either Meg had the stomach flu, food poisoning or was pregnant.

Aurora laid a hand on her own abdomen. She remembered feeling as if her body had been taken over by an alien force those first weeks of pregnancy. She'd settled into the calm, hungry stage at the end of the third month, her waist disappearing rapidly while her energy returned along with her appetite. Meg was in for an adventure, and she envied her so much it hurt.

Winter's yellow hair flew around her face as she rushed across the room.

"Shelly asked me to babysit," she said. "Loralee, Meg's mom, will be at the house." She paused. "Did you know they live in one of the cabins? I mean, how cool is that?"

"I did. And it is."

"Anyway, Loralee will be there but I'm going to be there, too, so Loralee can get ready to go out tonight. She has a date." Here Winter rolled her eyes. "Shelly said she has to work until two, but if I could stay, then maybe she could get her laundry done and take a shower."

"But you can't pick the baby up." Aurora looked at the cast. "You're not hurting, are you? Not doing too much?"

"No, it's cool. She'll be on the floor having tummy time and then she likes to lie on her back and play with the toys that dangle from this cage thing that hangs over her."

"That sounds good," Aurora said, unsuccessfully trying to picture what kind of baby toy Winter was trying to describe. "Call me and let me know when you're heading home."

"Have you talked to Dad?"

"Not since yesterday morning. He sounded really busy."

Winter sighed. "Is he coming home soon?"

"He'll let us know," Aurora assured her. Winter surprised her with a quick hug before returning to the baby and Loralee. Meg was still in the bathroom, and Aurora decided to go home and practice the violin. After all, she had a gig in eight days, and she'd promised to show up at the band jam this afternoon. The guys were taking over the Dahl, and everyone was determined to come up with a set list that would guarantee a standing ovation at the finale party.

Aurora had a few surprises planned herself. Jake Hove had better get ready.

"I'M NOT SURE," Jake hedged after his daughter asked him when he was coming home. Aurora listened to the conversation from the speaker phone, Winter tucked against her on the chaise longue.

"But when?"

"I have business here," he said, sounding mysterious. Or at least, that's what Aurora sensed.

"I miss you," Winter whined.

"I miss you, too," he said. "Let me talk to Aurora?"

She handed over the phone and flounced off. Aurora turned off the speaker and held the phone to her ear. "What's going on?"

"A little business," he said, his voice low and soothing. "I'll tell you all about it when I get back."

"All right, but—"

"Hip said practice went really well Sunday. And that you played."

"You talked to Hip?"

"The guys were impressed. You've been practicing."

"You'll never make a bluegrass fiddler out of me." She laughed. "But I do like those country-rock riffs."

"Look, I have to go, but I'll call again tomorrow."

"But the fund-raiser—your friend—"

"It's all good," he assured her. "Tim and Faith showed up, and Willie. Trisha Yearwood put on a huge lunch for everyone."

"I've seen her cooking show." She would have loved to have lunch with Trisha Yearwood, even if she had never heard her sing. "She seems really nice."

"They auctioned off one of Taylor Swift's guitars, and Garth was there to emcee the whole thing. We sang together Sunday morning. Did some gospel, then—oh—wait a sec." She heard him talk to someone else, something about buying a guitar. Then his voice came back on the line. "Sorry about that."

"You're having a good time," she said, her heart growing heavy.

This town wouldn't hold him, not for long. He sounded so happy, in the middle of the world where he'd made a living for so many years. Aurora looked over at Winter, who was typing furiously on her iPad.

"Yeah," Jake said. "Lots of excitement here. We might make this an annual event. We raised a lot—"

And then he was gone, the connection cut.

"Wow," she said, to no one in particular, but Winter looked up.

"Yeah," the girl answered. "He's in 'big star' mode again, don't you think?"

"It must be fun," she said, hoping Winter wouldn't be too hurt by her father's delayed return. He certainly hadn't sounded upset about staying in Austin for a while longer. Today was Tuesday, and she'd thought he'd be flying home. But now that she thought about it, she realized he hadn't said exactly when he'd return.

"It's fun *here*," Winter insisted. "With *us*."

Yes, Aurora thought. But maybe not fun enough.

"ARE WE GOING NOW?"

"Yes, we are." Aurora picked up her violin case, her violin secured inside it. Jerry had organized the huge Monday-night finale party in the park. There would be hot dogs and hamburgers on grills brought from the Triple M, who used to host large parties back in the nineteen fifties when Owen's grandfather was entertaining the county. Owen had hauled in twenty of his new picnic tables for the event.

And the Wild Judiths were going to perform. With a fiddler.

And without Jake Hove.

Because, Aurora thought for the hundredth time, Jake Hove wasn't coming back. She hadn't heard from him in three days, though he and Winter texted every morning. Had he regretted their romance? Found the bright lights of Austin more appealing than Willing? Been swept up with the glamour of his famous friends' lifestyles? Forgotten that tonight was the big night they'd been rehearsing for? They had *special songs* to do together, and he'd forgotten. Or no longer cared.

Was he already regretting living in Willing? Was he regretting getting involved with someone who wasn't part of his musician's lifestyle? The thought hurt. She was also nauseous. And having trouble breathing.

"We don't want to be late." Winter picked up the basket of cookies she'd helped bake with Lucia. She also grabbed a grocery sack filled with bags of potato chips.

"No, we don't want to be late," Aurora said, wishing she could be sick in private. She slowed her breathing and prayed for rain. Rain would stop the concert. She couldn't possibly perform in the rain, not even under a tarp. The Pietro couldn't take the dampness.

"I'm so glad it's sunny!" This was from Winter, who wore one of Aurora's designer T-shirts and a pair of denim shorts.

"Bring your hoodie, just in case," Aurora told her. "The weather can change in an instant."

Please let it change in an instant.

The construction crew was still working when she and Winter left out the front door.

They'd been joining the new construction to the old building and, along with entertaining the female tourists by waving and posing for photos, had been at the site since seven. Tomorrow they would knock a hole in the wall of the Dahl and begin the process of joining the two spaces.

"I wish Jake was here," Winter said, scrambling to keep up with Aurora as they walked down the sidewalk. "He was supposed to sing."

He was supposed to do a lot of things, like keep in touch.

Return.

Live happily ever after with Aurora Jones.

Aurora kept silent, gripping the handle of the violin case, as they made their way to the park.

"Wow," Jerry said, coming toward them. He wore a bright blue *Willing to Wed* T-shirt and khaki slacks. The sunglasses were pure Hollywood, as was the gelled hair, his red curls slicked back from his freckled forehead. "I heard rumors that you could play the fiddle," he said, eyeing the case. "I find that frightening."

"I imagine you find talent of *any* kind intimidating," she retorted. "Considering."

"Very funny, Aurora. Along with my people

skills, of which you have none, I have talents you will never know about."

"To that I say—thank God."

He turned to Winter. "We'll miss your father tonight, but I hear he's busy in Texas."

"Yes," the girl said with a sigh. "He's singing with Garth Brooks."

Jerry's eyebrows rose and he glanced meaningfully at Aurora's violin case. "How can you compete with Garth?"

"I can't even begin to try," she drawled. She eyed Jerry's hair. "I see you've gone all Hollywood on us."

He grinned. "Some of the crew came back into town for the party. And some of the ladies, too."

"I know. Everyone was in the Dahl Saturday night."

"Yeah, but more came in yesterday." His face clouded. "But not Tracy."

"She wasn't worthy of you," Aurora assured him seriously. "I mean that."

She had the uncomfortable sensation of actually having something in common with the man: rejection.

Mike, with his beaming fiancée in tow, hur-

ried up. "We're gonna be famous after tonight,
I think."

"Maybe you'll have one of those televised
weddings," Aurora said, greeting Cora. "I'm
sorry I haven't been in your shop yet. I hear
you opened this weekend."

"Thanks. And stop in anytime." She glanced
at Aurora's boots. "I have some very cool vintage Tony Lamas you might like. Size nine?"

"Yes. How did you—"

"Is Jake back yet?" Mike interrupted.

"Not yet," Jake's daughter piped up. "He's
real busy in Austin right now with Blake Shel-
ton and Garth Brooks and Trisha Yearwood."
Aurora noted that Winter's accent had gone
from British to drawling Montanan.

"Wow." Mike looked impressed. "Well, have
him get in touch. He only rented the apartment
on a week-to-week basis, and I've got three different people who want to rent it with a year
lease. I need to know what his plans are."

"Of course," Aurora said, hiding her surprise. Week to week? She'd thought he'd rented
for the year, or at least the entire summer. She
didn't want to believe that he was just enjoying a temporary fling with the local bar owner,

whispering secrets and words of love while taking advantage of free child care.

No, she didn't want to believe that. She really didn't.

But then again, maybe she had no choice but to face the truth?

"Just because he's not here doesn't mean he's not coming back," Meg insisted. Lucia stood next to her and nodded.

"Of course he's coming back," her other friend said. "His daughter is here."

"He seems so distant on the phone," Aurora tried to explain. She held a burger in one hand and a Diet Coke in the other. "Like he barely knows me. As if he's gone home. I don't know how to explain it."

"I'll ask Sam," Lucia said. "When he gets back."

"I didn't know he was gone," Meg said. "Is he filming somewhere awful again?"

"No." Lucia laughed. "He's meeting with a publisher in New York about a series of children's books. Educational, nonfiction books about the strange fish he's seen in the Amazon and around the world."

"That sounds like something Sam would be

really good at." Aurora looked over at Winter, who despite her broken arm was leading the Swallow boys around the small park. She'd taken photos of herself with the statue of the bull and sent them to her friend in London before eating two hamburgers, a hot dog and half a bag of potato chips. She'd declared she loved America and then polished off three of her own cookies before bossing around Lucia's children.

"Winter has adapted quite well," Meg said.

"She's a strong child."

"And she's lucky to have you," Aurora's friend declared. "Jake did a good thing by coming here."

"My future brother-in-law has excellent taste." Lucia gave Aurora a quick hug. "Don't give up on him just yet."

Lucia hurried off to supervise her children, leaving Meg and Aurora watching the Wild Judiths assemble the sound equipment on the makeshift stage.

"So, you're going to play tonight?"

Aurora gulped. "Jake and I had some songs worked out."

"But you'll play, anyway," Meg said. "I hope. Lucia says you're wonderful."

"I used to be," she confided, wondering why

she was keeping her past a secret now. "I was a soloist. A child prodigy. A star."

"I'm not surprised. You do still have that star quality." Meg helped herself to another cookie. She looked down at Aurora's boots. "I mean, the crystals on the fancy cowboy boots are impressive."

"I always liked to look good onstage," Aurora admitted. "I wore a diamond cuff bracelet that looked great under the lights. How are you feeling these days?"

Meg blushed. "I'm a little sick to my stomach and I'm no longer drinking coffee, but that's our secret, right? At least for a few more weeks until I see my doctor and know that everything is okay? I don't want Owen getting his hopes up before—"

"I won't say a word."

"Thanks. And to heck with Jake Hove," Meg said, waving her cookie toward the stage. "You don't need him to get up there and knock 'em dead. You can do that all by yourself!"

And that's exactly what she did. One hour and ten minutes later, with the finale due to begin in seventeen minutes on the large-screen televisions placed around the park, Aurora and her violin brought the house down, exactly as they'd planned. They played Jake's songs, with the lead guitarist and the drummer sharing the vocals. Aurora played every song they'd rehearsed, including the haunting "Midnight on the Water" with Hip's bass accompaniment that she loved so much.

Her version of "Orange Blossom Special," practiced for hours each day, was to have been a surprise for Jake. The Wild Judiths were prepared, having been sworn to secrecy at the last two band practices. The crowd whistled, stomped their feet in the grass, hollered their appreciation and applauded for long minutes while Aurora took several bows.

Carnegie Hall had nothing on the Willing Town Square.

Aurora took one last bow, her violin tucked under her arm, her bow dangling from her index finger. Her flowing yellow dress whipped around her knees as the wind began to pick up. She looked past the crowd and toward the bar and wished Jake had been there to see this.

And she saw smoke.

Smoke?

She couldn't quite believe what she was seeing. Shock took her voice, but she pointed, stricken, to the stream of black smoke pouring into the darkening sky.

"Fire," she heard the drummer announce.

"Fire!" echoed through the microphones and blasted from the huge speakers.

"Fire," Aurora croaked, then asked the question she was so afraid she already knew the answer to. "Where is the fire?"

CHAPTER THIRTEEN

"WINTER IS SAFE," Lucia assured Jake. "Aurora is safe. They were in the park when the fire started."

He stood on South Congress on the cracked sidewalk outside the Continental Club. The Monday night happy hour had just finished and he was about to get a slice of pizza and walk back to the Austin Motel.

"Jake? Can you hear me?"

He cleared his throat. *A fire. They both could have been killed.* "I hear you."

"Where are you? Why aren't you back?"

"How are they? Where were they?"

"At the party. In the park. Tonight was the finale of the show, remember?"

He didn't. He almost dropped the phone, recovering it before it slipped out of his fingers and onto the cement. Winter had been texting details, but he thought it was next week. *Next* week.

Lucia continued. "They think it was from the construction. Something about a blowtorch, smoldering old wood, I don't know. Half of the Dahl's second story is gone."

"Where are they now?" He had to call, had to hear their voices, had to reassure himself that they were all right.

"They're with Meg. I want them to stay with us tonight, but they might stay at your apartment. Although Winter doesn't want to sleep on the second floor of that old building, and I don't blame her."

"I'll be back as soon as I can," he promised. "I have some things to wrap up." He paused, but Lucia said nothing. "Can I talk to Sam?"

"He's in New York, remember?"

He hadn't remembered that, either.

"I'll get back," he said. "Soon."

"I hope so, Jake." And then Lucia hung up. Without saying goodbye in her normally sweet voice, he noted. He tried dialing Aurora, but the phone went straight to voicemail. Same with Winter's phone.

He wasn't used to having to account to anyone for his whereabouts, but he liked it, when he remembered. He loved listening to his daughter talk about what she was doing and how her cast itched. He loved the sound of Aurora's voice, though he wanted her so much he immediately grew tongue-tied when she spoke.

He couldn't see her face when she talked to him.

He hated that.

There was so much to tell her, and yet she had lost her home and her business. Or come close to losing it. She wouldn't want to hear about his. Not yet.

He needed to get back to Willing, but it was going to take a few more days. Jake huddled against the building to block the sound of traffic and dialed again.

AURORA SPENT MONDAY night in one of Meg's cabins, the one with the modern wall-hanging she had quilted and donated for the renovation last fall. She liked lying in bed, Winter curled up beside her, looking at the uneven rows of fabric stitched with black thread.

She'd lost all of her quilts. There were a few survivors that suffered from smoke damage; Aurora would keep them for now, but knew she'd have to get rid of them eventually. That smell was almost impossible to get rid of.

Winter had lost her iPad in the fire and her

cell phone in the park when she'd dropped it on the sidewalk in the rush to see where the fire was.

Aurora listened to Winter's gentle snores and tucked the soft sheet over the child's shoulders. Meg had gone to Jake's to get more clothes for the girl. Lucia had offered beds at her house, but Aurora yearned for someplace more quiet. Winter wouldn't leave Aurora and had been glued to her side since she left the stage. Loralee had sent the cabin's occupants to Iris, who lost two guests who said they couldn't possibly sleep with the smell of smoke in the air and had departed to the Super 8 in Lewistown. Shelly had remade the beds and cleaned the cabin for them, all the while weeping because Les had burned his hands while helping put out the fire.

Aurora supposed it would have been easier to just stay with Iris, but she would have had to talk to people there. The little cabin, with its tiny kitchen area and queen bed, gave her the privacy she needed to think things through.

Tomorrow she would meet with the crew and the sheriff and the county fire marshal. Half the roof of the Dahl was gone, as was the back end of her apartment. The new construction had fared better, but some of the framing would have to be redone, as did the new roof.

Everything was insured.

Everyone kept telling her that as if it made it all right.

It didn't, of course.

It took Jake three days to return on what would have been karaoke night.

He would go straight to Lucia's because, according to Sam, everyone would be gathered for dinner.

"We'll be glad to have you home," his brother had said into the phone last night. "Winter's doing okay, but Aurora is very quiet."

What did "very quiet" mean?

He thought that sounded ominous. Jake had been in only one long-term relationship, with Winter's mother, if you could call six months long-term. But he assumed Aurora was heartbroken to lose the top half of her bar.

"There's going to be a fund-raiser," Sam said. "She has plenty of insurance, but the quilt group wanted to do something more personal. To show community support."

"I'm there," Jake assured him. "I'll do whatever I can."

"Where the hell have you been?"

"I'll tell you all about it when I get there," Jake promised. He'd taken a flight out of Austin at two-ten, which put him into Billings a little after six o'clock. A couple of hours of driving and he'd be in Willing, hopefully while Aurora and Winter were still at Lucia's.

Winter greeted him as if he'd been gone for a year, uncharacteristically throwing her arms around him and screaming with joy.

Aurora, seated between Winter and Tony, didn't move. She stayed in her seat, a half-eaten piece of lemon meringue pie in front of her, a full cup of coffee next to her plate.

Jake realized that staying away for two weeks might not have been the best decision, no matter how important it was for the future. The little boys all greeted him with various degrees of excitement, as did Lucia and Sam.

He put his hand on Aurora's shoulder and squeezed gently. "Hey," he said. "I'm sorry."

She nodded.

"Thank you for taking care of Winter."

"You're welcome."

"We're staying at Meg's," Winter babbled. "Did I tell you that? The cabin's really cool. Like camping but not like camping, you know?

My phone is gone. So's my iPad, but Aurora said she'd buy me a new one. We're going to Lewistown tomorrow. Or we might order one online. We haven't decided."

"I'll take care of that," he promised. "Why aren't you staying at the apartment?"

"Winter was afraid it would burn down, too," Lucia explained.

Jake lifted the shopping bags. "I brought presents," he announced, and distributed four pairs of cowboy boots to the children. Winter's were aqua and tan, with feathered stitching.

"I love them," she said. "You know that's a riding heel, right?"

"Yes, but that doesn't mean you're riding again for a while."

She ignored him and tried them on.

Lucia laughed as Matty clomped past in his new boots. "That was really sweet of you, Jake. Have you had dinner? I can fix you a plate."

"I'd like that."

Tony bounced off his seat. "You can sit here, Uncle Jake. I'm gonna go play."

"Thanks."

He couldn't wait to get Aurora alone. He hadn't been able to talk to her since the fire and had had to settle for relaying messages through

Lucia. He wanted to put his arms around her and tell her it would be okay, but he'd seen the Dahl as he drove through town. It looked terrible, as if it had had part of its head blown off. It would take months to reconstruct, and that was if the building itself was sound enough to salvage.

"I saw the Dahl," he said, watching her take a careful sip of her coffee. "Can it be rebuilt?"

"I don't know yet."

"I hope so." She was pale. Very pale. He shot a worried look at Sam, who nodded as if to say yes, there's a problem. "Aurora? I'll help. We'll all help."

"Me, too." She attempted a smile, but it didn't reach her eyes. "I'm still trying to figure out what to do next."

"Jake?" Lucia called from the kitchen. "Come out here and tell me how much you want of this chicken."

He did as he was told.

"I'm worried about her," Lucia whispered. "I don't know if it's shock or depression or what, but she's too quiet."

"I don't blame her for being shocked. Or depressed." He ran his fingers through his hair. "I mean, have you seen that place? What if they'd been in there when the fire started? I'm having nightmares just thinking about it."

"She wasn't there, because she was at the finale party, performing with the Wild Judiths."

He brightened. "Really? She played in public?"

"She had intended to surprise you," Lucia said, handing him a plate fresh out of the microwave. "But you weren't there."

"I have a good excuse."

"You'd better, because that woman out there didn't think you were coming back." Lucia glared at him. "And I was beginning to worry myself. I thought you were happy here. Are you going back to Austin? Going back on the road? What's going on?"

"Wait a sec. I can explain." He watched her rummage through a drawer and then hand him a fork. "Thanks."

"Go eat."

"Okay."

"And talk to Aurora. She needs you."

"Right." He followed her into the dining area and sat down beside Aurora, who sipped her coffee and nibbled at her pie.

"How was Austin?" Sam asked, giving him a nod.

"Good. We raised a lot of money."

Winter stood next to his chair and leaned against him while he ate. "Do you want to stay in the cabins, too? I can ask Meg if she has room."

"Honey, we have a place. You have your own bedroom, right there on First Street."

"But it's on the second floor," she whispered. "It could be extremely dangerous."

"The fire was caused by the carelessness of the construction workers," Aurora said, sounding weary. "You're two blocks away from any construction. You need to be with your father now."

"But—"

"No buts," Aurora insisted. "You and I both know you'll be fine with your dad."

"Thanks for taking such good care of her," Jake said. "I didn't plan to be gone so long, but—"

"Two weeks," Winter reminded him. "You were gone for two weeks."

"I had business to—"

"It's okay," Aurora interrupted. "You don't have to explain anything." She stood and collected her dirty dishes. "Thanks again for dinner, Lucia. Can I help you clean up the kitchen?"

"Absolutely not," Lucia said. "It's Sam's night to clean up."

Winter laughed. "Cool." She turned to her dad. "So I'm not going home with Aurora?"

"No."

"Your things are in my car, honey," Aurora reminded her. "Why don't you go get them?"

"I'll do it," Jake said. "I'll walk you out."

Winter gave Aurora a hug. "I'm going to miss you."

"Me, too," she said, resting her cheek on the top of Winter's head for a moment. "I enjoyed your company very much."

Jake followed Aurora out the front door and down the steps to her car. She opened the back door and bent to retrieve Winter's bags.

"Aurora."

She stopped and turned around to look at him. "I can't do this now."

"Do what?"

"Deal with you."

"No problem." He gently tugged her against him and wrapped her in his arms. Her body was stiff, but he felt her relax against him as he held her. "I'll come by in the morning. I'll bring coffee."

"No."

"Okay. Lunch, then. Or dinner tomorrow night? Just the two of us? I want to help with the Dahl. And I have something—"

"No," she said, pulling away from him. "This isn't a good time for me. I'm not sure what I'm going to do and I don't think getting involved with someone is a good idea right now."

"I think we're already involved."

"I don't have time for you, Jake. I can't worry that you're going to leave me, or that you're going on tour for six months, that your life is really in Nashville or Texas or that you've met someone else, someone young and available for the night, wherever you are."

That stung. He drew back. "What are you talking about?"

"While you were gone partying with 'Garth' and playing with 'Trisha,' I was taking care of your daughter and practicing with your band. My house burned up and my business is probably gone, too. None of that is your fault, but maybe if I hadn't been distracted I would have kept a better eye on the construction guys. Maybe I would have been more on top of things, instead of learning 'Orange Blossom Special' and being a stepmom."

"I want to help—"

"You can go anywhere you want," she said, her voice shaking. "I'll keep Winter here with me, because I care about her and she cares about me. But I'm not going to feel alone, not the way I've felt the last few days. I've been really alone, Jake. Because I loved you." She opened the door to her car and got in. "I don't want to be in love with you. It's just not a good feeling. It's dangerous and I don't like it."

With that she slammed the door, started the engine and was gone, leaving Jake standing at the curb with his daughter's suitcases and blue satin pillows.

"CAN'T YOU DO something?"

"Like what?"

"Tell her you're sorry," Winter demanded. "Tell her you love her."

"She doesn't want to hear it."

"That's why you have to keep saying it."

They were eating lunch at Meg's, in the midst of a busy lunch hour with a BLT special, along with cups of creamy corn chowder. Jake had chatted with the old guys at the counter, commiserated with Shelly about the baby's sudden onset of sleepless nights and thanked Les for helping so much with the fire before taking a seat at a booth underneath a window facing the parking lot.

The burns were minor, the young man assured him. And Shelly was bandaging them for him every day.

"A win-win," Jake said.

Les tilted his hat toward him and winked. "You bet."

"You need a grand gesture," Winter explained, after Les had moved back to his seat at the counter. "The way they do in the movies."

"This isn't *Downton Abbey.*" Jake had grown weary of being badgered by an eleven-year-old child, a daughter who thought she knew a lot more than she did about love and relationships.

"Of course not." Winter sniffed. "That's not a movie, that's television, and that love story was much more subtle, with lots of smoldering looks. We do *not* need smoldering looks."

"I could give *you* one."

"Ha."

"Finish your lunch," he ordered. "I've got work to do."

"Like what?"

He ignored the question. A man was entitled to his secrets, even if there was no longer any reason to keep them. He'd intended to surprise Aurora with his new business, something that had made so much sense when he saw the sign on the program in Austin that he couldn't believe the perfection of the timing.

"Do you really want to live here?" he asked his daughter.

She looked up from her soup and gave him one of her serious, what-is-he-really-asking-me looks. "I've told you a million times."

"I do, too."

"So, fix it with Aurora."

"I intend to," Jake said, resolving to make it happen. "But it could take a while."

"We're not going anywhere," she said. "I have faith in you."

"Yeah?"

His daughter grinned. "Yeah," she drawled, imitating his accent.

Well, that made one of them.

FOR BETTER OR worse, she was famous again. Mike Breen had used research skills he didn't know existed and ferreted out the real story behind Aurora Jones. It hadn't helped when he'd overheard Hip discussing the Pietro and its glorious sound.

Even Mike, small-town reporter and a man distracted by love and fame, could put two and two together and sniff out the story behind the story. So when the newest edition of the paper came out, the Dahl's fire was the headline and number one story. Underneath that he'd described the great success of the prefinale party and the ratings of Monday night's show.

There were photos of the volunteer fire department putting out the fire. There was a grainy picture of Jerry, his arms around newly engaged Mike and Cora before the fire and before the music.

And then, Aurora noted, at the bottom of the front page, was a photo of "violin virtuoso" Aurora Vandergren's first appearance onstage in five years. Her hair covered her face, her bow was blurred, but the photo wasn't terrible. The article underneath detailed her childhood, marriage, parents' deaths and subsequent early retirement from the world stage. She sounded quite mysterious and extremely brilliant.

Intimidating, even.

The final sentence was the kicker: *Aurora Jones, as she is known in Willing, is the owner of the Dahl, the structure whose future is uncertain after the fire that destroyed its second story last Monday night.*

She reached for the phone and called Mike. "My future is not uncertain," she snapped.

"The Dahl's future," he replied. "That's what I meant, Aurora. The Dahl. Has it been declared safe to rebuild?"

"Yes," she lied. "Of course."

The truth was she had no idea. That was to be decided this morning, after the county inspector assessed the building. For now she huddled in the cabin, her sweet little cave of a cabin, and hid from a curious town. She hadn't replaced her cell phone, relying on Meg's generous offer to take messages for her at the café.

"Everyone asks for you," Meg had told her last night. "We're all worried about you."

"I need a few more days," she'd said. "Then I'll be fine."

"You've been hiding in here for almost a week, Aurora."

"I went to Lucia's Thursday, remember?"

"She thinks you're depressed." Meg held up her hands as if to ward off the protest. "Not that you don't have the right to be. It's just that we hate to see you like this. Is there anything we can do to help?"

Aurora had shaken her head. "No. Tomorrow I meet with the inspector. And the builder. And the insurance people."

"There are a lot of people who are rooting for you," Meg insisted. "Come on out and let us help you get through this."

"I will," Aurora said. Another lie. How could anyone help? Five years ago she'd lost her parents, her unborn baby, her husband and then her career. And she'd survived, because she was an heiress who could afford to buy a huge SUV and drive west and buy a business on a whim.

She'd built a new life for herself, and now that business had burned down.

It wasn't the end of the world. She'd experienced the end of the world years ago. This wasn't it.

What she hadn't expected was that this new pain, this new disappointing loss, would hurt so much. She'd dared to believe she'd found a man who would love her, who she could love back.

She'd believed she'd found a home and a place in the world.

A safe place.

With an interesting and talented man who understood her.

And a child who needed her.

She'd dared to believe she could be happy again, and look what had happened.

"You have to come out of here," Meg had said. "It's not healthy."

"Who says I'm healthy?" she'd grumbled. "I'm determined to feel sorry for myself, and I'm not going to be stopped."

"Lucia's coming to see you tomorrow morning. With Sam. And the boys," Meg warned. "That should scare you out into the sunshine."

"I won't be here."

"Good," her friend said with some satisfaction. "Then my job here is done."

So now she had to get dressed. She assumed all of her clothes were gone, as were all of her lovely boots. Her closet, in the middle of the back part of the upper section of the building, would have been either burned or damaged by water.

No problem.

She could replace everything. Eventually. And she still had her violin. Of all the things that mattered, she still had the Pietro, the gift from beloved parents.

Lucia had gone to Lewistown and bought her some jeans, T-shirts, makeup, toiletries and underwear. From her new shop, Cora had produced a nicely worn jean jacket, two pairs of Tony Lamas (one black, one blue and gray) and a neatly ironed, pale blue, nineteen fifties sundress. She chose to wear the sundress and the blue-gray boots but decided against the jacket once she opened the door and felt the warmth of the morning sun on her face.

She slung her purse over her shoulder, shut the door and trudged across the parking lot. She walked the two blocks down Main, to where it intersected with First and turned right. Where the Dahl and its addition stood at the ninety-degree angle.

The street was blocked off, picnic tables cutting off traffic and diverting them to South or North Second streets. She heard music, saw a crowd gathered in front of the Dahl. Aurora didn't want to look at the Dahl. The last time she'd seen it, on that awful night, she'd felt as if parts of her own body were burning. She'd been hurting and helpless and sick to her stomach as the volunteer fire department rushed to save her buildings and her business.

She hadn't had the courage to look at the result. When she visited Lucia's she'd gone round the other way, avoiding Main and First streets and any glimpse of the catastrophe.

Aurora stopped, unwilling to push through the crowd of people in order to find the men she was supposed to meet at the building site.

"Aurora!" Winter's yellow curls bounced around her face as she crossed to her. "You're here! Yay!"

"Honey, I have a meeting—"

Winter rolled her eyes. "Oh, I know that. But first you have to come with me." Winter took Aurora's hand and tugged her toward the street.

Aurora dug in her heels. "Where is the music coming from?"

"The Wild Judiths are playing over there, in front of Cora's."

"Why?"

"The mayor's planned something special." She tugged again. "Come on."

"I thought he was through with all that," she muttered, but she went along with the child. Her neighbors smiled at her, patted her on the back, waved and gave her the thumbs-up sign as she made her way around the edge of the crowd.

"There she is!"

Aurora saw Jerry, standing high above the crowd halfway up a ladder. He held a microphone and wore a yellow hard hat.

"Good morning, Aurora! We're going to make this right for you. Everyone here wants the Dahl back and wants you to know that we care." He cleared his throat. "Okay, folks," he announced. "We have our assignments, right? Everyone knows what they're going to be doing?" There were cheers and muted applause from the crowd. Now Aurora realized that a large number of men were gathered in front of the Dahl. The construction team that had been working on the addition were off to one side, but many men she recognized from the town and the surrounding county stood on the sidewalk and in the street also. Large Dumpsters sat next to the sidewalk, and a line of pickup trucks blocked the street.

A man she'd never met before stepped up to her, a sheaf of papers in his hand. He introduced himself as the insurance adjuster, gave her a brief explanation of the amount of money his company would be giving her for the renovation and asked her to sign. Aurora signed, gratefully. The building inspector was next, explaining there was no structural damage, that once the burned areas were removed the re-modeling could proceed.

"Yes?" Jerry shaded his eyes and looked over to Aurora. "We have a yes?"

The insurance man gave him a thumbs-up. The building inspector waved an okay. The crowd roared its approval. And the work began. At least sixty men began dismantling the burned sections of the Dahl, while others carried the pieces into the Dumpsters. The members of the Wild Judiths stowed their instruments and picked up hammers, crowbars and work gloves. Meanwhile, women began to arrive with bowls and casseroles and platters filled with food, which wcrc arranged on the picnic tables and protected from various groups of excited children.

"It's like the Amish," Winter said, leaning against her. "Like a barn raising."

Aurora was speechless. Sam and Jake were among those carrying new lumber from a delivery truck to an open area near the addition. Jake turned to her once and smiled, but she was too stunned to smile back. He was still here, obviously. And he was the kind of man who would help a neighbor in trouble.

After all, he'd gone to Austin to help an old friend.

Lucia sidled up to her. "Were you surprised?"

"I'm *still* surprised," she confessed. "Who did this?"

"Everyone. The quilters wanted to do a fund-raiser, with a potluck dinner and an auction. The men in town wanted to help with the cleanup after the fire but had to wait until the inspector gave the all-clear. Just about everybody who came into Meg's wanted to do something to help out somehow."

"I can't believe it." She worked very, very hard to keep tears from tipping out of her eyes.

"Then Jerry thought we should combine everything and make a big party out of it."

"That's typical." Aurora couldn't help laughing a little. "No one loves a community event more than our mayor."

Winter looked up at her. "Are you happy, Aurora?"

"Yes." She eyed her old building, looking better by the minute. "I am so happy I could cry."

"Me, too," the child said. "I want to live here forever."

Aurora sighed and put her arm around the girl's shoulders. "I know exactly how you feel."

JAKE DIDN'T HAVE a grand gesture for Aurora. At the end of the day he had a tired back and sore hands and a sunburned face. And a great feeling of satisfaction now that an almost miraculous transformation had taken place at the Dahl. A new roof covered the old building. Sam told him that Aurora would work with the contractor and an architect to redesign her apartment's bedroom, bathroom and storage. For now the upstairs was enclosed, which was nothing short of a miracle. He'd never seen so many men work so hard and accomplish so much in one day.

And the addition, affectionately and not surprisingly called the "Dollie" by the construction crew from Lewistown, had been cleaned and reframed. Its brick sides had sustained no lasting damage, so framing had gone quickly once the mess was hauled away.

He'd watched her serve food and pour lemonade. He'd watched her blush and stammer when her neighbors and friends hugged her and wished her well and donated fabric and quilting supplies into big plastic tubs set up in front of the community center.

Les had won the raffle quilt, which he'd presented to Shelly. The young man had whispered something in her ear that made her smile and give him a kiss. So there was progress, he noted, on another Willing romance. He'd heard Les had been suffering from unrequited love since last October, so he wished the young man luck.

And now it was his own turn. He'd sent Winter home with Lucia, who along with Sam had gathered children and empty casserole dishes and headed back to their house at dusk. Aurora, her silver hair streaming down her back, stood in the middle of a small group of women who were packing containers of food into boxes and loading them into SUVs. The streets had reopened and the day was over.

It was time.

"SWEETHEART." SHE FELT his hand on her shoulder before she turned around. She would have protested that "sweetheart" business, but her quilting friends were listening and exchanging amused glances.

"We'll get going," Janet said. "All of your

new quilting things will be stored right here in the community center until you have a place for them."

"Thank you." She hugged each one of the four women goodbye, which gave her a good excuse to move away from Jake's touch. To move away from Jake.

But Jake didn't budge. He was still there, on the sidewalk, when she turned around. He wore jeans and a dirty white T-shirt and held a pair of yellow gloves in one hand. He looked dirty and gorgeous, which was so unfair.

"Thank you," she said. "I know you and Sam worked all day on the building. I really appreciate it."

"I should have taken a shower and cleaned up," he said, frowning. "But I didn't want to miss talking to you."

"We don't have much to—"

"Yes," he said, taking her hand in his. "We do. Come on." He led her around the corner, to the empty storefront beside Cora's vintage clothing store. Both stores faced the Dahl, whose dark windows looked lonely.

"Jake—"

"Do you know what this is?" He gestured to the empty store.

"No." It looked as empty as it had as long as she'd lived here. Meg said it used to be a jewelry store.

"That is going to be one of the finest guitar stores in the West."

She stared at him. "You're going to sell guitars?"

"I hope so."

"This is a very small town," she reminded him. "I'm not sure how many—"

"Wait," he said nervously. "This isn't about guitars. This is about us."

"I—"

"Wait," he repeated, interrupting her protest. "Hear me out. Please." Aurora shut her mouth and waited, though she wanted to pull her hand from his and run down the street to the safety of the small cabin. She didn't want to believe he intended to stay. She didn't want to believe, period.

Jake took a deep breath. "When I was in Austin I heard of a guitar-making business that was for sale. I'd heard of them. They were a fine company, a small company. And just like that, things fell into place." He smiled wryly. "Remember you told me that when you came here you saw the Dahl for sale and you bought it on impulse?"

She nodded.

"Well, that's what happened in Austin. I bought it. I don't know anything about making guitars, but I know what a good one should sound like. I hired Hip, because he has the carving and the wood skills. And I'm bringing three of the former employees here, to Willing, to work in the shop. I've leased a building on the other side of the co-op and I've bought this store. We'll be shipping and selling guitars all over the country, if things go right."

Aurora couldn't think of a single thing to say.

"So," he said. "I'm staying. I can write songs here. I'm not going on the road, I'm not going to change my mind and go back to Nashville and I'm not going to suddenly run off with some young groupie, which, by the way, was pretty insulting."

"You were gone for two weeks. And you didn't say very much on the phone."

"I didn't want to spoil the whole guitar-building-business surprise."

"That was a bad move."

"Yeah." He winced. "I admit, I'm not used to answering to anyone. I'll do better in the future. I will follow you around and tell you every single thing that is on my mind from morning until night." He tugged her closer to him. "I know we're on a public street and anyone could drive by or walk over here any minute now, but could you please tell me you will at least *think* about marrying me?"

"*Marrying* you? Is that a proposal?"

"Is that so hard to imagine? Come on, sweetheart. I could sing you a song, serenade you outside the cabin tonight. I'm sure the folks eating at the café would be thrilled."

"I would be mortified." Though she wondered what song he would choose.

"Then say yes now," he urged. "I love you. I fell in love with you the moment I saw you in those yellow boots, when you thought I was going to rob you."

"That's ridiculous," Aurora said, but she wanted to laugh. She wanted to dance. She wanted to lean into him and melt into the warmth of his body. "I thought you were a kidnapper."

He kissed her, a long, slow, sweet kiss that left her gasping for air. "I'd prefer to be a husband," he said, whispering the words against her cheek.

She hesitated, scared to agree, and Jake moved back. She saw the hurt in his eyes and realized she didn't want to live without this man in her life. She didn't want to look out at the world from behind the safety of her bar or the windows of her apartment. She wanted to be part of Jake's family, part of Lucia's family. She wanted to be Winter's mother and Jake's wife. And the risk was worth it. *He* was worth it.

She wanted to stand onstage and bring the house down, with her man beside her.

"What's it gonna be, Aurora?"

"Us," she said, moving back into the circle of his arms. "It's going to be us."

EPILOGUE

JERRY WAS IN the middle of planning the Fourth of July parade when his phone beeped. Only four weeks away, he had a lot to do. The holiday was a reunion weekend for the school and for many local families; he expected an extra thousand people for the parade, especially with the expansion of the tourist industry.

The text was from Tracy.

Tracy.

His finger hesitated over the button. Should he read it? Did she want him back? Had he left something at her place? Was she lonely? Did she miss him? Had her new boyfriend dumped her on the side of the road and did she need a ride?

Good news, he read. Show renewed. We'll be in touch. Filming in August. No snow. Get more men.

Well, who did she think she was? Did she think it would be easy to find more bachelors?

Did she think he'd want to put the town through another round of filming? Did she think they would be interested in their little television show?

There was only one way to find out. He'd have to check with Meg, but she was out at the ranch suffering with all-day morning sickness. He'd have to go to the Dahl and ask Aurora. He looked at his watch. Karaoke wouldn't start for another hour and a half, but she and Jake would be playing at the happy hour tonight.

There had never been a happy hour at the Dahl until Jake Hove arrived in Aurora Jones' life. If that particular woman could end up happy, then there was hope for them all. Which made Willing the romantic town he'd envisioned from the very beginning.

Jerry, the parade forgotten, hurried out the door. Man, it was good to be mayor.

* * * * *

LARGER-PRINT BOOKS!

GET 2 FREE
LARGER-PRINT NOVELS
PLUS 2 FREE
MYSTERY GIFTS

Love Inspired

Larger-print novels are now available...

ReaderService.com

Manage your account online!

- Review your order history
- Manage your payments
- Update your address

> *We've designed*
> *the Harlequin® Reader Service*
> *website just for you.*

Enjoy all the features!

- Reader excerpts from any series
- Respond to mailings and
  special monthly offers
- Discover new series available to you
- Browse the Bonus Bucks catalog
- Share your feedback

Visit us at:
ReaderService.com

V